CW00520645

Naomi, Thank

Copyright

Produced by: Eve Alexander
Published: This Edition - First Edition August 2021

This novel is entirely a work of fiction. The names, characters and incidents portrayed in it are the work of the author's imagination. Any resemblance to actual persons, living or dead, events or localities is entirely coincidental.

Eve Alexander asserts the moral right to be identified as the author of this work.

Eve Alexander has no responsibility for the persistence or accuracy of URLs for external or third-party Internet Websites referred to in this publication and does not guarantee that any content on such Websites is, or will remain, accurate or appropriate.

Designations used by companies to distinguish their products are often claimed as trademarks. All brand names and product names used in this book and on its cover are trade names, service marks, trademarks and registered trademarks of their respective owners. The publishers and the book are not associated with any product or vendor mentioned in this book. None of the companies referenced within the book have endorsed the book.

Acknowledgements

11 types of dating men you meet on dating sites chapter 3 – rewritten from a blog by Leona's love quest on PS I love you website. https://psiloveyou.xyz/the-11-types-of-men-you-meet-on-dating-websites-16483876fd5c

Jar of Hearts lyrics excerpt taken from:-

Label

Atlantic

Songwriter(s)

Christina Perri Drew Lawrence Barrett Yeretsian

Producer(s)

Barrett Yeretsian

And who do you think you are?

Running around leaving scars

Collecting your jar of hearts

And tearing love apart

You're gonna catch a cold

From the ice inside your soul

Don't come back for me

Don't come back at all

Prologue

Gripping one arm he forces me through the hole and I stumble onto my hands and knees, his foot slams into the small of my back flattening me into the ground. Straddling me his face kissing my neck I can smell his breath and feel it hot on my skin, I squirm under him, struggling to make him think he is in control "You like that huh, you girls all same, get drunk and have no self respect, I have many girls like you in my car" he says in his thick Eastern European accent.

Reaching under me with his hands he pulls the fly buttons undone and drags the jeans down to my ankles. I pretend to resist pulling at the waist band, as he wrenches the fabric out one hand reaches under me as if to protect my vagina, the other sliding up under my top to reach the dagger between my breasts, my fingers wrap around the gripped handle and I pull it from it's sheath.

Chapter 1

This is me, well for today it is anyhow. I've built my persona to appeal to as many guys as possible as I want to draw them in. Not that you need words with most guys, pictures are what they tend to focus on.

Name: Lori

Age: 33

I'm looking to meet nice guys for dating and fun; maybe I'll find my knight in shining armour along the way. Up for cosy nights in on the sofa with dinner for two?

Not too obvious but the 'fun' bit gives just enough suggestion that I might be up for sex.

This particular app is supposed to be about meeting a 'partner'. It's not about hook ups or casual sex, hence the knight in shining armour bit. I need to make it appear like I'm looking for something long term so it fits with the apps style. It's not the only app I use, in fact I use most of them, but today I'm focusing on this one.

Let's see who is out there:

Name: Phil

Age: 39

Build: Average

Interests: Netflix, fishing, pub quizzes, sport

Tell us more about you:

My mates made me come on this, so I'll fill it out later LOL.

Who is your ideal partner?

I'm looking for a nice girl to spend nights out and nights in with.

Phil has just two pictures on his profile, in the first one he's holding up a fish, grinning proudly as if he's just landed Jaws and saved the town. Why do men think holding a fish is attractive? Maybe it's the hunter gatherer thing, "Me man, provide food."

I don't know about you, but all it says to me is; 'I'm perfectly able to do nothing for several hours then come home smelling of fish'.

I'll try not to judge Phil too harshly as this might be some women's idea of the perfect man, I can't imagine why though. His picture sparks a childhood memory for me, I recall a friends parents; Geoff was a fisherman, not the Captain Birdseye type, more the sit alongside a duck pond or a stinky canal all day type. Carol would go along with him and happily sit in a folding chair all day just doing her knitting and watching him fish. Would Geoff have sat and watched Carol knit all day? I don't think so. I'm not Carol.

The second picture looks like it was taken in a pub toilet mirror. Women are just as guilty of this as men, do you not have a mirror at home? Is a public toilet lighting the best you can find? All this really says to people is 'I'm sat in the pub, a bit pissed and I want to get laid…. I know I'll go on a dating app!' Perhaps they've been egged on by friends and it's a spur of the moment thing but unless it's the same night have you really not had a chance to find a better one?

A few pointers here for those of you who are new to dating apps or perhaps those that are having little success; take some decent photographs! It's not hard, we all have smart phones. Secondly, be yourself, why have five pictures of you with your friends so it's impossible to pick out which one is you?

Worse still, don't post the picture where you looked great on holiday back in 2004, nobody wants to know what they could have had. Keep it current and be proud of yourself, but also be realistic. Be bothered to put some words down, that actually explain a bit about you, yes many people do not read them, but the ones that do build up an impression of you from what you have written. If you write nothing it just looks like you can't be bothered or are not serious, or worse you think this whole thing is above you and the reader should be grateful you've even bothered to grace it with your presence, not a good first impression.

There are so many clichés on dating sites. The absolute favourite for women with kids is the line; 'I have x amount of children WHO ARE MY WORLD'. Yes we get it, you are a parent well done, thanks for stating the obvious. Apart from making a dubious decision to open your legs several years ago probably whilst drunk, what else have you achieved, tell us that instead.

Try to stay away from covering all the bases too, 'I like nights in and out' yawn. A lot of the dating sites have pre set questions, think about what you want to put, sure your life might be boring but pick out the good bits! Try to be original too, every third female profile contains the words "Just a girl, standing in front of a boy..." Which is from a well known romcom, it's not original ladies and the men are probably not going to recognise it anyway!

Whilst Phil's face looks pleasant enough and his dad body might actually be ok to fuck, he's too basic for what I'm looking for.

I swipe left.

The next one is Kevin

Name: Kevin 'Easy Going Guy' This is his tag line. Massive eye roll. It's like writing on a CV 'works well on own initiative or as part of a team'. So fucking what?! Has anyone every written 'Up tight prick who gets really jealous of everything' on their profile?

Age 36

Build Athletic (You didn't really need to fill this bit in did you Kevin? Seeing as five out of your eight pictures have your six pack and muscles on show)

'Hi I'm Kevin I'm hard working and enjoy the funny side of life well we all try' (FFS Kevin, is this the best you could do? I mean it's fun at least but so generic)

Good job (ask me) solvent with a grate network of friends, looking to meet someone to share the good times with. A little better Kevin but poor spelling looks bad.

I'm easy to talk to, ladies don't just say the simple 'hi there' be adventurous, live a little, confedence is key, I hope to chat soon I won't bite J

Oh dear Kevin you were doing so well (He wasn't) Judgy much? Kevin probably doesn't realise he's being so obviously misogynistic how dare he demand a certain type of behaviour, he's already 'negging' In one form it's where you point out negative things about someone in a backhanded way, he's already decided that there is a certain way the responder should reply and thus attempted to put himself in control.

I swipe right. Kevin is just what I am looking for. He thinks he is friendly but he's cocky and dripping with arrogance, he also thinks he's clever but judging (yes it's my turn to judge!) by his grammar and spelling, he's not that smart. He also assumes that if he flashes a six-pack he'll have girls falling over him.

Saying that he does have a good body though.....

He has a decent number of pictures, there are eight of them in total. Kevin on his bike, Kevin on a paddle board, Kevin with a puppy – nice touch this one if not a little obvious, but who doesn't love a puppy??

My Message reads:

"Hi Kevin how are you? I'm Lori pleased to meet you, great body BTW, you must work out a lot!"

The idea is to appeal to his vanity and feed his ego about the area he clearly wants me to focus on.

I await his reply. It takes him just four minutes, Kevin is keen, very keen.

"Hi Lori that's an unusual name, I like it. Thanks for messaging I like your pictures too"

Ah yes let's talk about my pictures. Picture one, is full length with a plain background, now in the interest of full disclosure I must confess this was taken in a hotel toilet mirror but only because the wall behind me was plain! I'm wearing a black calf length dress with a thigh high split, my leg of course showing all the way down to the high heel, I'm pointing my toe to accentuate the leg muscles. My tanned skin, push up bra and cleavage on display make the picture overtly sexual without revealing too much. I have long blonde hair in this picture and the mobile phone I used to take the mirror selfie is covering half my face. Strategic.

The sunglasses are also strategic. The light reflection is bright, you can tell I'm pretty but you can't really pick out too much detail. I know this goes against what I said earlier but men are far less selective than women and a flash of thigh normally is enough to get a positive swipe.

Pictures two and three; A group of friends, a girl who could be me, but isn't, she's pretty, caught in mid laugh so her face is distorted, the back ground is a bar with dark lighting and lots of movement so the quality is not great. The thing is it looks like so many other profiles, so it's easily believable.

Picture four. The obligatory protective face mask shot. Good old Covid-19.

Picture five. If my first picture hasn't already done the job, this is the one that seals the deal. A Lacy corset, my body turned to display the top of my thigh and the side of my boob, very suggestive but nothing pornographic actually on display, also no face apart from the bottom of my jaw line. People are so fickle, just the merest suggestion of sex and they are hooked in.

13

"Aww thanks Kevin that's really kind of you" – I try to sound submissive, and be pleased by the compliment.

"No problem babe, what do you do?" – Standard question but at least he's trying to get the conversation going.

"I work as a dental receptionist, it's fun, what about you" It's a classic job for a 'girl' Kevin will like this, it gives him an opportunity to potentially have a higher status and thus more power in a relationship the question also turns it back to him.

"I work in security" Keeping it brief Kevin, Christ do you want to get laid? Typical gym bunny nonchalance, he thinks he's playing it cool and I'll do all the chasing as his six pack makes him a catch. Fine Kevin I'll play along.

"Oh that sounds interesting, I can't even keep my car keys safe"

"Lol I'll help you look, they're usually down the back of the sofa, although you look like you're good looking... oh sorry I meant good AT looking lol"

Good boy Kevin, this is exactly the sort of cheesy clumsy chat I expected and stop lolling all the fucking time you cretin.

"Well I'm blushing, thank you. You look pretty hot yourself, how often do you work out?" He'll love to tell me how fit he is. I continue with; "I go to the gym sometimes but I'm never quite sure what I should be doing" This is the come on; if he's a player he'll be straight in here.

"I work out four times a week, I love going to the gym I could help you, although whatever you are doing seems to be working! Maybe I could show you?"

He's a quick mover, no messing about for Kevin, I'm going to plant the going out seed, make it easy for him, he is so cocky he won't be fazed.

"I'd like that Kevin, that sounds exciting! We should go for a drink first though, get to know each other"

"Sure that's a great idea, Fancy meeting this week?"

"That would be great! It's always nice to meet face to face especially now this lock down is over, we have to get out as much as we can!"

Of course I knew he would ask this question and I'm ready to do my research into where would be best to meet him, I want a smaller area outside of town, so when he suggests a location I can pitch for a local country pub, less likely to have cameras you see. Sure we could meet anywhere now with the advantage of face masks keeping it discreet but if I meet him at a country pub, he'll most likely have to drive and then he'll be perfectly positioned to drive me back to his. I need to work out where he lives, I also need a lot more information on Kevin before I meet him.

I'm currently in Manchester searching within a 20 mile radius. Public places used to be a no no, too many camera's but with Covid-19 it's been an absolute dream, you can walk into a place dressed like a wild-west bandit or a 70's bank robber and nobody bats an eyelid. I reckon the members of Slipknot could walk into a newsagent in full masks, ask for a quarter of sherbet lemons and not raise so much as an eyebrow.

"It might be easier to chat off this app, shall we use Whatsapp?"

Getting him off the Internet and onto a burner phone keeps me moving. I'll need to keep the same number for Kevin for a while but that's OK. The phone isn't registered to me and I'll ditch it when I'm done. I use a Tor server, which keeps my IP address secret, I constantly move locations and change devices frequently too.

It used to be hard work to make sure I had enough tech, but now with the pandemic I can walk into any electronics shop and buy a tablet or a laptop or whatever all whilst wearing a very handy disguise, second hand tech is still very capable and the smaller phone repair shops ask few, if any questions. Once you know what you are doing it's easy to move profiles and set up new ones, all you need is a little time and know how.

Coffee shops are a great invention, you head in for a takeaway coffee, connect to their WI-FI whilst you wait and then you can sit outside in a car and still use the connection even after they are closed, if you pick the small independent ones they probably won't even have it set up to collect details. Not that this matters, fake email accounts are easy to set up anyway and I have hundreds I can use.

Getting him onto Whatsapp also means I can ask questions a lot quicker and build up a picture of him, I'm only here for a week and shorter if possible. Today is Tuesday, ideally I need to meet Kevin by Friday. If he is not right for what I need, then I still have time to connect with someone else.

I only ever stay in one place for a maximum of a week., that's my rule, move quick stay out of trouble. Working for myself means I can work from anywhere and makes my life a lot easier, I doubt an employer would let me have this much time off or be anywhere at any time although perhaps that has changed too with the pandemic.

Kevin replies, "Great what's your number?"

"07700 900736, text me x"

We switch to Whatsapp and so begins the conversation, I need to know where Kevin lives and with whom? Of course I'm not going to ask him for his address, I'll find that myself later, but I can get some quick information simply by chatting to him and flirting.

"So where do you live Kevin?"

"I live in Leigh North West Manchester"

Google is a wonderful thing. Within two minutes I've zoomed in on a map and checked out the history of the town on Wikipedia

"Ha-ha Kevin that's not Manchester that's practically Liverpool!"

"Ouch that hurts, I'm a born and bread Lancastrian and proud to be a Manc I'll have you know"

"I'm only joking precious, I'm not that far away from you I'm actually in Bolton!"

I'm not in Bolton obviously, but Google maps tell me its eight miles or twenty five minutes away, convincing enough to be able to meet nearby and far enough that he hopefully won't be too familiar with specifics.

"Ah not too far, that makes you about as Mancunian as me!" Replies Kevin

"Ha-ha I guess it does, except I'm not from Manchester originally, it makes it easier to meet up though I guess as we are not that far from each other?"

"Definitely does, where are you from?"

"Near London" I tell him. Not a lie, depending on how you are measuring it, I mean New Zealand is near Australia right?

I also want to know what turns Kevin on. That bit is easy, I'll throw out a few flirtatious comments and Kevin will take the bait, he'll reply with something slightly more risqué and the game continues.

"So what else are you into Kevin apart from getting hot and sweaty in the gym?"

"It's not just the gym I like getting sweaty in..."

We continue like this for a while, I laugh at his jokes, he laps up my flirting. We chat for a few hours backwards and forwards and by the end of this evening, I know the following information;

Kevin has a sister Andrea, always useful to have family member names for password hacking.

He went to university in Leeds but didn't finish his course.

Kevin's favourite position is girl on top, no doubt so they can still see his six pack.

He likes stockings.

His favourite food is 'A curry'.

His 'Ask me' Job is in security. Vague again and after some probing it turns out he works for G4S in a detention centre for 'illegal immigrants' as he so deftly puts it.

I'm fucking incensed although not surprised, we are all citizens of the same planet you absolute knob head! It's only circumstance that we're in any different position to each other. I guarantee that he'll make some sort of racist comment without even realising it on our date.

We arrange to meet at the Yew Tree Inn near Rivington. A lovely pub set in the rolling hills of the West Pennine moors It's perfect for what I need, located out in the countryside so he'll have to drive but well known and big enough to have people in it so we're not the only customers and popular enough to be open again.

I do my research; Kevin lives alone in a rented flat at the suburban edges of a small town called Leigh which whilst in Greater Manchester is closer to Lancashire in it's attitudes and idea's than the big city. He works shifts at the detention centre and drives a second hand BMW, the car features only slightly less often than his six pack on his Instagram feed. It is taxed and insured and the MOT runs out in a few months. Thankfully he doesn't have any fish pictures but I wouldn't be surprised. His parents live a few miles away.

Now I bet you're thinking you need loads of computer knowledge and to be like Lisbeth Salander to find all this out right? Wrong! I found all this out on a laptop sat outside a closed coffee shop using nothing more than websites openly available on the internet and social media apps. Once you have a surname you can do a Google search which often throws up a surprisingly large amount of information. A bit of time digging around on Facebook for a deep dive into lots of personal stuff, things like; which pubs they use, who their friends are, ex-lovers and such. If they have a Linked-in profile you have their employment details. Even Instagram can be useful, you'll be amazed at what pictures people post, for example in Kevin's case a picture of him outside his flat tagged with a GPS map location standing alongside his car with the registration plate in the picture! Once you have this sort of stuff, then the electoral register and HMRC websites give you more facts. The more you find the deeper you go, putting it all together into a bigger picture. Combine this with seemingly innocent questions whilst chatting and you can really have a lot to go on , in a very short time.

Kevin is a typical British white male; unknowingly misogynistic complete with a sense of entitlement that he wouldn't ever admit to having or understand what that actually means. The lack of any real hardship in his life means he has no concept of what sort of conditions those 'illegal immigrants' have come from.

It's not Kevin's fault per se' more a reflection of what is wrong with western society as a whole.

21

He's from a working / middle class background but in a western country you still live like a king compared to someone from an oppressive regime in a drought and famine ridden third-world country. He just exists in his own bubble without a concern for what else happens in the world or any of the consequences of his actions.

I have my charm offensive ready. He likes cars and football. I know a lot about the first and nothing about the second but I can pretend to be interested enough in a few attractive players to make him think I'm the sort of girl who will hang out in the pub with him on a Saturday match day. I imagine Kevin's dream girl is pretty, with big tits, she isn't too bright or too mouthy and will think Kevin is big and strong and tough as he works in security. I can play that role.

The journey goes off without any dramas, I ride the bike to the next village and park it in the pub car park where it'll be easy to collect in a day or two. I already have the taxi booked to get me to my date with Kevin. I spend the taxi ride pretending to talk on the phone so there is no need to chitchat, the driver seems disinterested, probably nearing the end of his shift,and he listens to the local radio station. I get him to let me out on the quiet village road outside the Bay Horse telling him I'm going hiking.

It's a nice pub and hotel with a pretty pond over the road. It's just a 500 metre walk to where I want to get to, over the bridge that crosses the

M61 on a B road that is lined on each side by dry stone walls and fields, it's already really quiet out with barely any traffic but dressed like this I'm invisible anyway. Plain coloured walking trousers, a vest top, sturdy walking boots, a reasonable sized backpack and a peaked baseball cap pulled down over my blonde weave which is pulled back into a ponytail. Nobody will even remember I was here, just another countryside walker.

I head off the road and into the fields as soon as I'm over the motorway, skirting the edge of the left hand field, the grazing cows paying me little attention. This track leads right up to the edge of the pub but there is less cover than I would like so I head inland a little. I came by yesterday to check things out so I know that the farmer takes the cows for milking around 6pm. It's 5.15pm now and I need to get into cover before then. I'm meeting Kevin at seven so I'll have plenty of time to lay low. Still as it's the middle of July I do not have the luxury of the cover of darkness and I want to be long off the radar of any passers-by before I meet him.

Making my way to the edge of the field directly behind the pub I keep moving until I am a few hundred metres back, there is a drainage channel which is dry from the long summer we have had the pleasure of enjoying, thanks to Covid it's mostly been spent indoors. A few trees and bushes provide enough cover and once I have the camouflage tarp out of my backpack and over the ditch I'm completely hidden from the casual eye, the cover gives me the time I need to change and pack my walking clothes into the backpack.

I have a folding military shovel in there, my clothes and makeup, a wig and a handbag. I dig a hole in the ditch to bury all the things I don't need, taking a small squirty bottle from the backpack I place all the items into a black bin bag and spray them in bleach, this should destroy the DNA and also put any animals that fancy digging them up off the scent. The clothes from the journey also go in along with the boots and finally the rucksack itself. I cover it all back with the loose earth pulling the weeds and plants back over the disturbed ground.

I load up the few remaining items I need into the handbag; my makeup bag, purse and a pepper spray, it's unsafe these days, a girl needs to be careful! The final few bits and some shoe covers. I've wriggled into a pair of tight jeans to show off my curves, and a low cut top that offers plenty of cleavage under my waist length leather jacket, a pair of gray Converse pumps finish off the look, casual but sexy.

By the time Kevin arrives I've positioned myself fifty metres away on the edge of the field behind the small dry stone perimeter wall, it is still bright in the summer evening light and the August sun beats down on my neck, I don't really need the binoculars in my hand to watch him arrive.

He pulls up in a metallic blue BMW 3 series. According to the Daily Mail, a publication that's always striving for journalistic integrity, men who drive blue BMWs "are more likely to be aggressive than motorists in any other car." No surprise there then. A different car and colour to the one I saw on Instagram though, this is way more flash. His music is a little too loud, this guy is a living, walking, talking cliché. I watch as he checks himself out in the mirror before getting out. Teeth, check, hair, check, extra button undone on the shirt, check.

He opens the car door and steps out admiring himself one last time in the reflection of the window. It's a warm evening and he has on a short sleeved shirt with no jacket, chosen no doubt, to show of his muscular arms. He's even rolled them up a bit, they do look good though and he's better looking in real life with his nice jeans and brown leather brogues. I thought he'd be a bit more chavvy but he actually looks well turned out.

He marches across the car park, turning to lock his car with the remote gazing back at it as it beeps in acknowledgment of his request, admiring his wanker wagon lovingly. Actually it's not a bad car, just a shit colour.

I wait until he enters the pub, slip off the shoe covers and taking a lighter from my bag I hold the flame to the thin blue plastic, it shrivels quickly becoming a hard black lump which I grind into the dirt with my foot, my phone vibrates in my pocket.

Table 16 see you soon, x

I reply, "Perfect my cab is just coming into the village, I'll have a gin and tonic. Decent gin not the house rubbish" Time to be a bit of a princess, make him work a little.

"Lol, is Bombay Sapphire OK?" He replies.

"Absolutely"

I wait two more minutes, another car approaches with a couple in it, they park and walk to the door, the man pauses and runs back to the car for his face mask. As he heads back towards the pub door I do a quick three sixty scan of the area, nobody else is about and there are no other cars approaching. With hands on the top of the wall, I scramble over, landing assuredly with both feet, I get to the pub entrance just as the staff member is greeting the couple.

"Are you together?" he asks looking at me. I have my phone out already pretending to scan the QR Code.

"No I'm meeting a friend, table sixteen" the reply muffled through the face mask and I avoid direct eye contact as I take a squirt from the hand sanitiser dispenser. The waiter points to the corner of the right hand bar then continues to talk to the newly arrived couple, he won't even remember me it in two minutes.

Kevin stands as I approach the table, his mask is under his chin already, "Hey great to meet you, you must be Lori" He leans in for a peck on the cheek, which is awkward in these socially distanced times. I keep my mask on. He sits back down.

"And you must be Kevin"

We've been seated in a sort of booth with banquette seating along each side of the table, I couldn't have chosen it better myself. There is no site line across the pub, you'll only see us if you are walking past and look directly into the booth.

I take off my jacket, shaking my arm out as I do, making sure my cleavage is facing Kevin, so he gets an eye full. I smooth down my blonde wig and slide into the booth.

"You look nice, I've ordered, your drink it's just coming, did you find it all-right?" He babbles, the first date nerves getting the better of him momentarily.

"Thanks, so do you"He actually does and he smells good too "I took a cab, I figured it was easier, I was going to drive but I didn't want to get lost" Play the hapless female card a little, I'd already told him I was getting a taxi but lets underline the fact.

"It's a decent distance from Bolton that must have cost you a fortune!" he replies

"it's only twenty five minutes, it was fifteen quid so not that bad, this weather is amazing though, the cab was hot!"

"Well let me buy the drinks then, I insist"

I was planning on it Kevin, the feeling of control you'll get from this will play to your ego, You think it will also make seduction easier as I'll feel like I owe you. Psychologically this can actually be a common thing for women, being vulnerable to men, we will often do things that we might not be fully committed to in order to avoid confrontation or even worse the threat of violence.

Men take the lead and we let them, they pay, perform like peacocks and we say yes to them simply because we feel obliged to do so, like we have been conditioned into it by our childhoods, don't upset anyone, be grateful, make sure you show that gratitude, don't cause a fuss.

I stare intently at Kevin. I take off my mask for the first time and he takes my face in, red lipstick the obvious choice for this type of guy. Teeth and tits that's what he is drawn too. I smile at him, making sure I flutter my eyelashes, flashing my blue eyes at him, well they are blue today anyway.

"You look gorgeous" he says, "you look familiar, probably the dating site photos I guess"

My body language is carefully crafted to draw him in and make him feel at ease. I use subtle signs that he will pick up on subconsciously that say I am available to him. I mirror his body, I touch my wrists, play with my hair, laugh at his jokes and hold his gaze.

After a few minutes of small talk, the conversation is broken by the arrival of the waitress with the drinks, a bottle of lager for Kevin and the G and T for me.

"I thought you would be a pint man, being so tough and all that" I rib him.

"Yeah I normally am, but I'm driving, so thought I'd stick to bottles" More conscientious than I thought. He starts to pick at the label nervously.

"Apparently that's a sign of sexual frustration, picking the label on bottles" I smirk suggestively at him, and so the flirting begins and the conversation continues. Kevin has been doing his dating homework, he asks me lots of questions but I deftly keep the conversation on him, where did he go to school? Where did he grow up? Tell me about your job? What was your last girlfriend like? Do you get a lot of attention from girls in

29

the gym? You must do, you're so fit! What type of girls do you like?

After an hour Kevin is how I expected, he tries to appear pleasant and to not be cocky but he is definitely aware of his looks and he can't help but let slip those controlling comments that we all recognise. The ones that he thinks say 'I will look after you' but actually mean, 'I'll try to control you and get you to do as I say' I'm certain he is a dick.

The flirting develops into innuendo and I push the agenda, Kevin looks to be having a great time.

Three bottles of beer later for him and two large gins for me (trying to get me drunk Kevin?) and the last orders bell rings, these new ten o'clock curfew times are doing wonders for my liver and my beauty sleep.

"Well, I've had a lovely time, but I guess I better call a taxi" I say.

"Don't be daft I could give you a lift" Kevin offers, 'yes you could' I think to myself, my plan starting to take effect.

I reply with "No I couldn't ask you to do that, it's well out of your way, you have come much further than me too." I act coy not wanting to seem to eager.

"It's not out of my way, it's on my way!" It's not really anywhere near where he lives but with the flirting he thinks he's on to a sure thing and doesn't want give up that easily. I want him to feel like he has put lots of effort in, that way he will feel he deserves a reward.

"Well if you're sure, that's really kind of you"

"My pleasure" He winks at me which would normally piss me off, but he is kind of hot.

We get into his car, it's freshly cleaned and smells strongly of Magic Tree vanilla, he's pulled out all the stops to make sure he makes a good impression, clearly he figured he might get the chance to get me in here and has prepared accordingly.

"What kind of music do you like?" Kevin asks.

"All sorts, put the radio on maybe, so we can still chat?"

He flicks through the stations stopping on a local radio station WISH FM. The evening DJ is playing a cheesy love songs selection, he leaves it on this.

We begin the drive, through the country lanes and I start the conversation picking a topic I know he'll like….. himself.

"You look good driving this car, it's way bigger than mine, it seems really powerful, is it hard to drive?" If he only knew I was lying, this is nothing special, a 3 series with the M-sport package giving it a little extra oomph but not a full M-series. I've driven cars with 5 times the power of this but It'll stroke his ego.

"Yeah I got it recently, it's a cool car right?, I love the colour too, great stereo although I sometimes get the buttons mixed up and end up blasting the stereo instead of turning it down."

When he turned up in a different car to the one I expected, I did a quick search on my phone, turns out it's actually his mums car! I'll play along and let him pretend it's his if he thinks that's what impresses me.

What do you drive?" Kevin asks.

"MX5" I offer another lie.

"Hairdressers car" He laughs "Actually good cars though, rear wheel drive, proper drivers car that, I'm impressed" I figured this or an Audi TT would appeal to him, girly but still enough petrol head credentials to be cool.

Switching the conversation back to him I ask "So how did you get into working in security?"

"I was applying for loads of jobs and not getting any, mates were always saying how it was immigrants taking our jobs, when I saw the detention centre job I thought, what better way to prevent that from happening than actually being there. Some of them are OK, I feel sorry for them but we're already full so they can't come over here and take our jobs or benefits"

I nod as I pretend to agree with him, even though my own view-point is polar opposite to him, I change the subject.

"This lock down has been a bitch huh?" Great to be finally allowed back out again although it's pretty weird isn't it? It's so boring now the pubs close early, Friday night at ten and we're going home already, pity as I fancy another drink" I offer suggestively.

"Can't you have one when you get back to yours?"

"I don't have any booze left at mine, maybe I could stop and get some somewhere?" waving another carrot for Kevin.

"Well I know it's a bit forward but there's plenty at mine if you fancy it?" He's gone for it, the bait has been laid and Kevin has stuffed it into his face with gusto.

"I don't know, is that not going to make you think less of me on a first date, coming back to your place? I can get a cab later though, if you don't mind me coming back?" Still playing carefully, I still don't want to appear too eager.

"Of course not, I think you're lovely, and like you say it's only early, shame to end such a nice evening so soon, if it gets too late you can take my bed and I'll take the sofa, I can run you back in the morning"

"Crafty Kevin are you trying to seduce me?" I look at him with a face that says I hope you are.

He smiles "I might be"

We pull up to his flat. I recognise it from my Google Earth searches, the route out to the East Lancashire Road, memorised in my head. A small three story block of bland modern flats, probably built in the eighties or nineties by one of the large home builders with a notorious reputation for low quality work. He unlocks the front door and we enter a well-lit communal hallway, we take the stairs to the first floor and I admire his arse as we climb.

His flat smells fresh and his security guard uniform dangles from a coat hanger on a door in the hallway to the left, I assume this must be the bedroom. To the right opposite I can see a tiled wall and a pull cord light, obviously the bathroom.

He takes his shoes off and I follow suit, kicking off my pumps into a pile of shoes by the door without undoing the laces. I follow him straight ahead into the lounge, which has a kitchen off to one side through a separate door. It's passably decorated with modern furniture and some generic art work, a large TV dominates one corner of the room, it's cleaner than I expected and I wonder if he has cleaned it especially in case I came back, probably, or more likely his mum still does it for him.

Kevin points to an I-pad sat on a dock "Put some music on if you like and I'll get some drinks, Is Rum and Coke OK? I've got Kraken?"

"Now you're talking" I pick a playlist on Spotify, choosing a Northern Soul list, my own in joke and a little nod to the fact that we are less than eight miles from Wigan Pier. Band of Gold by Freda Payne wafts out of the speakers.

He comes back into the room, nodding approvingly at the music choice. Carrying the drinks and sits down on the brown leather sofa next to me, handing me the drink. "Cheers" We clink glasses, the rum and coke tastes sweet but strong, I take a mouthful then place the glass on the side table next to me.

"Kevin can I use your bathroom please?"

"Of course it's just by the front door"

I excuse myself, I walk towards the bathroom but pop my head quickly into the bedroom, the bed is made and neat with what looks like clean bedding, my earlier assumption about the cleaning repeated in here too, he has clearly made an effort in case he got lucky tonight. It's a tidy room, a chest of drawers with aftershaves on the top, nothing about Adams flat is unique though, it's like it has all been put together from a catalogue, rather than having any ideas or taste of his own, instead it seems to be constructed from things he thinks are acceptable.

I slip back out and into the bathroom, looking at myself in the mirror I check my make up, gripping the side of the sink as my hands tremble, giving myself a minute to regain my composure and to calm the Adrenalin. If I am going to change my mind, now is the time to do it, the point of no return. I stare at my reflection, gazing deeply into my own eyes and whisper "you can do this, remember why" As I leave the room I turn my smile back on.

Walking back into the living room Kevin is still sat on the sofa, he looks up at me and returns my smile, so I sit down next to him but closer this time, pretending to be a bit tipsy and falling into him with a bump, giggling "whoops, clumsy" I say as I turn my head to look at him, close now to his face.

Our eyes meet and that moment that passes between two people where they consent to kiss without speaking occurs. Kevin leans in a fraction, I lean in to meet him and our lips interlock, gently at first finding each others rhythm, then deeper more passionate our tongues exploring each other.

I run my hand over his chest, he really is well defined, his hands are around my shoulders pulling me to him. Our hands moving as we touch each others bodies, exploring through the layers of clothes at first. The angle of the sofa makes it awkward to get items untucked but Kevin manages to slide a hand under my top, his hand touches my left breast through the fabric of my bra, finding the nipple easily as it stands proud against the lace. His other hand works around to the back, expertly unhooking it between finger and thumb, the three clasps coming apart surprisingly easy. Both hands slide up my sides lifting the bra and my top up and I raise my hands to allow him to pull them over my head, my blonde weave staying firmly in place.

He looks admiringly at my ample breasts, cupping them, one in each hand. "Gorgeous' he mumbles. Planting a kiss on one nipple, he then flicks it with his tongue and sucks on it. I close my eyes, leaning my head back. He follows the same suit with the other one. This time biting a little. I suck air in through my teeth as he does but don't let out any sound of pain, my eyes narrow in pleasure and I bite my lip.

Pushing him back on the sofa I straddle him, my boobs level with his face, he cups them again, I pull up his chin towards me and kiss him, placing a hand on his chest to keep him where he is, I lean back and pull up his t-shirt over his head revealing his toned body, the pictures did not lie I'm going to enjoy this.

I pinch his nipple hard, he winces "ouch ah"

"Two can play that game" I smirk. I lean in and kiss first his neck then his chest, working my way down his body my legs find their way to the floor until I'm on my knees. He holds my gaze as I look at him suggestively, then slowly down to his crotch, I unbuckle his belt, his designer boxer shorts protrude over the waist band of his jeans and as I unbutton the fly, I am greeted by his cock straining hard against the fabric, Kevin's muscles are not the only big thing about him.

Pulling the top of his shorts forward the tip of his dick pokes out, I glance up at him to see him watching me intently, I lean in flicking the tip with my tongue and I hear him let out a small sound of pleasure, reaching in I grip his cock, taking his length in my hand and I pull the shorts down further exposing his manhood, I lick the length of it letting my tongue drag from bottom to the tip, flicking it over the end as I reach it, taking the head in my mouth as Kevin lets out a more audible moan.

I repeat, licking down to the base this time and back up, once again taking the head in my mouth and sucking, my hand glides up and down his shaft as I do so.

I can feel and see his dick twitching, I don't want him to get too excited, not yet, not until, I've had my fun. I stand up, topless and pull at his hand. "Bedroom" I command.

He stands holding my hand with one of his and steps out of his jeans, kicking them off on to the armchair, grinning as he does, "you are so fit" He tells me as he leads me to the bedroom.

Standing at the foot of his bed, he kisses me, I put my hands firmly on his shoulders, pushing him downwards, he gets the message, turning me around so my back is to the bed he lowers me onto it. As I lay sitting up, he unbuttons my jeans and pulls, I lift myself up on my elbows to help him. He pulls off my jeans and throws them to the side.

Kneeling between my legs, he kisses my left thigh, dragging his tongue up and letting it continue over the fabric of my panties and across the line of my vulva, it feels good and I tell him so. He pulls my knickers to the side with two fingers, holding them there whilst his tongue begins to explore me, parting my lips, seeking out my wetness, moving up to locate the delicate hood of my clitoris. He pauses flicking lightly with his tongue.

Kevin is good, better than I had hoped, I feel the pleasure creeping up my body like a rising heat, and I can feel how wet I am between my legs. He pushes a finger inside me and licks slightly harder at my clit as he does so, I let out a moan "Kevin that is so good"

His finger slides in and out of me "Pull it upward as you slide it out" I tell him, guiding him towards my g-spot. He does as I ask, his tongue working faster now, moving it around and applying pressure. It's good but it's not going to get me close enough to an orgasm so I push his head down a little, moving my hand on to my clit myself and starting to rub in small rhythmic circles.

"Push another finger in me" He obliges, sliding it alongside the other. This feels good, I feel myself stretching to accommodate. I want to cum first before I give him what he wants. "Faster I tell him, matching the speed of his fingers with mine on my clit.

I feel it building, almost reaching the point of orgasm "faster, don't stop, I'm going to cum" His fingers move deftly, pulling upwards as I told him, he's a quick learner. "Yes, Yes!" A shudder washes over my body and my pussy spasms around his fingers. I tremble a little and clamp my legs to his head as my clitoris becomes hyper sensitive.

He stops and looks up at me grinning, his mouth and chin shiny with my juices in the low light. I wait a few seconds for the pleasure to subside, panting despite him doing most of the work, then I pull at his hand, encouraging him to stand and as he does I use his momentum to push myself up. I turn him around pulling his boxers down, taking in the full size of him. It's impressive. I push him down onto the bed pull his pants over his feet and his socks off as I do.

I kiss up his legs, regaining control, as I reach his balls I lick at them playfully and then once again run my tongue along his length, his cock is hard, pressed against his belly. It bounces involuntarily as I flick it with my tongue. I clamber on to the bed, straddling him.

"Condoms ?" I Ask

"Bedside drawer" I lean over him sliding open the drawer to pick out one of the foil squares. Tearing the corner with my teeth then squeezing the air out of the teat to roll it down his thick shaft, it doesn't quite reach the bottom but it'll do the job. "You are a big boy Kevin" I tell him and I mean it. He looks pleased with himself his chest swelling as I deliver the first honest compliment of the evening.

Admiring his strong thighs and his taught belly I hover my pussy over him, sliding myself up and along his body with my own weight pressing down on him. As my pussy lips becomes level with the tip of his penis I reach my hand down and angle it up into me, lowering myself slowly on to it, pausing to allow myself to adjust to the size. I pause a second time then lower again, taking the whole of him into me, my vagina expands to take it although it feels momentarily too big to fit inside me, the sense of fullness is delicious. I look down at him, gazing up at me. His hands reach to play with my tits but I gently push them back down, "lay back, it's your turn"

Gradually I grow accustomed to the size and I begin to ride him, rocking gently back and forward, the size still taking my breath away at full depth. Keeping it deep in me is creating a different kind of orgasm to the last one, stronger, less surface level and more intense, I want to time this just right. Intently I watch his face, feeling him as he begins to thrust upwards in time with the motion of my hips, his breathing is rhythmic his hands above his head on the pillow. Placing my hands on his muscular chest propping myself with my arms to lift my body weight up and down on him rocking my hips just a little keeping him mostly deep into me pushing at my deepest point.

"That feels amazing, that's sooo good" Kevin murmurs, looking from my tits to my eyes then down to watch himself sliding into me.

"Tell me when you're going to cum, I want you to cum for me"

"Keep going, this feels great, I'm nearly there"

I lean further forward onto him, my chest pressing against his, our bodies' slick with sweat from the summer heat. My hips rocking faster encouraging him onward, his arms hold me, hugging me to him.

I slide my hand down the edge of the bed carefully and retract the object I placed there earlier between the bed base and the mattress, I push myself up, releasing his grip until I am sitting straight upright, I quicken the pace again my hips doing all the work, grinding our pelvises together, used to his size now, I rock on him faster, harder, I feel his hips push towards me and his buttocks tighten, his breathing is shallow and he starts to mutter "I'm going to cum soon Lori, I'm nearly there"

My own orgasm is tantalisingly close, "I'm going to cum too" I tell him.

"Yes, yes cum with me" His hands on my hips pulling me onto him, his body goes rigid pushing his hips up as he says "now Lori, now!"

I take the blade and in one movement cut across his throat making sure it goes in deep enough to sever the windpipe, the Fairburn Sykes dagger doing its job perfectly. The orgasm wracks my body as his blood pumps out of the open wound, his eyes open in surprise and his hands immediately clutch his throat in a futile attempt to stop the flow, a gurgling sound emanating from deep in his chest. I lower my weight onto him as his body thrashes around. It takes longer than you might think to die from having your throat cut, I feel the warm pulses of blood hitting my own neck as the final life ebbs from his body prolonging my orgasm as it does.

When the moving stops and the pleasure finally subsides, I climb off the blood soaked bed and catch sight of myself in the mirror, my sun kissed skin now the colour of crimson. I take a minute to compose myself, still getting used to the site of my handy work and controlling the Adrenalin coursing through my body before I begin the next part of my ritual.

Chapter 2

Female killers are usually a product of men, either working alongside one to commit crime or forced into it in some way, perhaps to protect a son or husband or as the ultimate revenge for some mistreatment by a man. To quote some statistics only 14.5% of women choose to kill a stranger with over 80% of women seeming to know or have a connection to their victim. Women rarely kill for sexual gratification and it's often financially motivated.

Fortunately I do not have the financial problem and whilst I sometimes fuck my victims I don't do it just for the sex. Seduction and sex are easy ways to control people and to gain their trust. The act itself is not my primary motivator but if the mood is right then I don't see why I can't enjoy myself. If I'm brutally honest, and I'm often brutal and always honest, it has definitely started to turn me on. The power of taking a life is like nothing else.

I have to-date, killed 5 people. The first two were from a time before, both of those were unplanned but became the catalyst for something bigger. Those two are not on the media radar and I don't expect or want them ever to be. The other three however they should have absolutely no doubt about, I made sure of it by leaving them my calling card.

All the memorable serial killers have a handle, usually given to them by the press, it's what makes attention grabbing headlines. Names like The Zodiac or The Ripper or less flattering ones like the Doodler or the Giggler. some of the women have such pathetic names; the grinning Granny or Jolly Jane I needed to make sure I got a good one.

Whilst I was dreaming up my name I got an idea from a song called *Jar of Hearts by Christina Perri*. It's not really my sort of thing but I like the fact that in the lyrics she recognises that the guy is a prick and refuses to take him back. You go girl! The chorus has the following lines:

And who do you think you are?

Running around leaving scars

Collecting your jar of hearts

And tearing love apart

You're gonna catch a cold

From the ice inside your soul

Don't come back for me

Don't come back at all

I mean if that isn't just perfectly sinister in the right context what is?! Each time I kill, I leave a line from the song in a nice and obvious place, blood can make such a pretty medium to work with, Kevin got;

'Collecting your jar of hearts'

The British press can be a witty and creative bunch when it comes to headlines but you need to make sure you get noticed, wanting to underline my point I cut out part of my victim's hearts and leave a Queen of Hearts playing card. I mean that gives them only one obvious choice right?

Before you judge me too harshly, Kevin was not quite as innocent as he may have seemed. According to my research he has, sorry had, two children by two separate mothers, neither of which he bothered to see or mention to me at any point. Granted it may not be his fault that he can't see them but the fact that he chose to pay the grand total of fuck all child maintenance makes me doubtful. The fact that one of the women had an anti-molestation order against him also highlights the type of guy Kevin was.

My first two victims as the Queen of Hearts or should I say murder three and four didn't make it much beyond the local press, it's surprisingly hard to get yourself in the news for killing people these days, with mass random stabbings, people driving into groups of others, suicide bombers,

US elections and Trumps antics in general, not to mention the distractions from the COVID-19 pandemic, there is hardly any bandwidth left for little old me, I was just getting started with the first two so I'm actually grateful that my story hasn't been picked up immediately, I'm about ready for them to take notice now though.

It does no harm to help the process along a little either, so I sent a package to the Independent newspaper, directly to the award-winning journalist Elizabeth Banrigh. I thought in today's digital society a nice personal letter rather than an email might get her attention, especially with the pictures and the vial of blood.

Banrigh initially made the press whilst at university, then rose to fame, or perhaps notoriety, when working as an investigative journalist she exposed a celebrity paedophile in a honey trap, setting him up in dramatic fashion. More recently however, she has faced a backlash from some of her colleagues and women's rights groups for posing as a victim of domestic violence to infiltrate a hostel and once again exposing the perpetrators.

Alongside her sensational expose's she also writes a regular column called 'Banrigh Writes' I need attention and someone in her position will relish the chance to regain public favour by exposing a serial killer. Of course she'll try to trap me wanting the scoop but I'm prepared for that.

My letter read like this:

Dear Elizabeth

Big fan, love your work. I am writing to you as I know you'll appreciate what I am doing. As you often say yourself, the time has come to make a stand, the patriarchy has been oppressing women for too long. Well that's exactly what I am doing, taking a stand against those that think they can just walk all over other people.

I'll write again soon, in the meantime enjoy the enclosed pictures and just to show you I am who I say I am, here's a little gift that the police might find interesting.

Q.O.H

I enclose a Queen of Hearts playing card. Printed photographs showing the words I have written from each murder scene and some extra special close ups from all three. The vial of blood contains DNA from all three victims. I know that most of the pictures won't make the paper but at least she'll know I'm serious.

A high percentage of murders are committed by people who are known to the victim, seemingly random acts of violence are hard to trace especially if there is no DNA records of the perpetrator, this is why serial killers can take so long to catch, the police have nothing to go on until the killer strikes again and hopefully makes a mistake. If they work across a large geographical area it makes catching them harder still as you need police forces to join together and share resources. It is usually the need to kill that finally gets killers caught as they chase the buzz leaving less and less time between each victim and eventually making mistakes. Of course the police and computers are far more sophisticated than they once were and as soon as similarities pop up in crimes, somebody somewhere is notified. Whilst my progress may have not yet reached the papers, it will definitely be on the police radar by now.

Forgive me! I haven't told you about my other victims yet. Why don't we work backwards from Kevin? The one previous to him just three weeks before was a chap called Shaun, a 47 year old Scottish man living in Brighton.

Brighton is close to the town I grew up in and a place I know pretty well, I didn't choose it because it was familiar but it did make it easier in some ways. It was the same sort of thing, I picked up Shaun on a dating site, this time it was Tinder not Bumble. Tinder tends to be much faster moving with the implication that it's a quick way to meet for casual sex or 'Netflix and chill' as the euphemism goes, not everyone on there is looking for that but it's definitely one of the livelier and more direct websites.

Even with the quick nature of the app it can still take time to build up to something, so starting chats early in the week tends to mean I can drag it out to the weekend. In order to get him interested, I send him some suggestive pictures, ones I've taken from the internet of course, I'm not going to send him actual pictures of myself, I make sure they all have no heads, telling him I don't want my body plastering all over the internet for all to see thank you very much.

Shaun worked for American Express, some sort of call centre manager, quite a bit older but obviously happy to sleep with younger women as his profile was set so that my age range would show up in searches, just how young I wonder? I fished around with the app, setting up another profile and pretending I was 18, Shaun still came up in my search, so no lower age filter then. Dirty boy.

This was the profile that hooked him in:

Name: Dina

Age 30

Not looking for Mr Right but maybe you could be Mr Right now? Looking for more than just Netflix & chill. Mind connection is important but I'm not going to demand your babies. FWB not ONS.

It's highly flirtatious and obvious but still requiring some work on their part. Basically it says meet up to my mental requirements and you'll get laid. This will put off a surprising number of guys. Maybe their ego isn't strong enough to live up to the expectation or perhaps they are scared off by a forthright female.

I've chosen to be a redhead for this profile, same situation as before keep the pictures vague but sexy, I always use new photos for every profile, there are sophisticated bits of software out there that can match similar images and facial recognition so it's important not to get lazy to avoid getting caught. I use one of myself by the old West Pier, an iconic Brighton image, my face is far enough away to be difficult to tell much about me but a perfectly reasonable looking picture, the type of shot you would find on any local profile.

His Profile reads:

Name: Shaun

Age: 47 (bit old to be messing around with 18 year olds aren't we Shaun?)

Looking for mates and dates, hang outs and see what happens. Not looking for anything serious but open to it if the right girl comes along.

Leaving it open nicely there, you couldn't be accused of not being honest right? But then you leave it open to interpretation, I'm sure you've got zero intention of any girl becoming the right one but you'll make them feel like there is a chance by leaving it hanging. I know your type, you'll be charming, the perfect date, you'll be giving me all the signals that things are going great and we have a connection. You'll probably be great in bed, and then once it's happened, you'll ghost me or send me a vague message about not wanting anything serious. Not this time Shaun.

I do some research into Shaun, being a player might not seem like grounds for murder but I prefer to think as him not as a victim but as a casualty of the war on patriarchy. It takes me a while but then I find an IP address to a website he runs. It provides some very interesting material.

It's a double edged sword, being in an area you already know, it's more familiar and easier to plan escapes but it's also easy to let familiarity cloud your judgement, I don't let that happen. Shaun suggests we meet on Friday night and lists off a number of bars in the city centre that we could meet at, safety in numbers you might think but the cameras in a busy city like Brighton will also be in full swing, meaning much more chance of my face appearing all over the news, even with face masks.

We're texting back and forwards during the day, him from his desk at home, me from mine, or at least that's what I lead him to think. I'm actually staying in the Hotel Pelirocco's Paradise room in

Regency Square, a flamboyant boutique hotel designed for the classic dirty weekend and it makes no bones about it. Well I'm here for a dirty weekend, just not in their hotel. You might think it's a bit of an over the top place to stay but people are so enraptured by the décor and getting up to their own things that they barely notice the other guests, it's so centrally located that I can pick up 14 different free Wi-Fi accounts from my room.

"I live in Hove and I'm working Friday until a little late could we meet somewhere more local?"

I know from my research he lives just around the corner in the 'Poets' area of Hove so he'll be able to walk to the venue I have selected. Brighton is so easy to get around, I can walk from where I am, keeping to the seafront most of the way until I'm in the more suburban area and away from CCTV. No need for a motorbike on this one, although I have one parked near to Shaun's, you know, just in case. You can't be too careful, there are some dangerous people out there.

"I'm in Hove too! Poets Corner do you know it?" Shaun asks.

"I do! How about the Ancient Mariner? I've been in there a few times, it's not a bad pub, we can sit outside" I checked it out the day before, recently built screened off outside area's perfect for staying relatively unnoticed two entrances, plus it's only five minutes' walk from Shaun's place on

Clarendon Road. It'll be nice and easy to get him home with minimal opportunities to be noticed, the pub has strict Covid protocols in place so I booked a table in advance.

"That's perfect it's only around the corner from me, shall I book a table?" Shaun asks

"It's OK, I'm online now, I can do it. Shall we meet there at 7.45?"

"Brilliant Dina, I'm already looking forward to it" ....I wouldn't if I were you Shaun.

Just as Shaun is leaving his apartment building I run towards the door pretending to be a fellow resident in a rush. A baseball cap pulled down and a bandana covering the lower part of my face, I'm dressed in a large bulky coat with my bag in my hand. I say thanks and nod appreciatively waving a set of keys as if by way of acknowledgment that I live there too. As he holds the door open for me I enter the building, our bodies almost touching as I brush past him, I turn and watch him leave.

He lives on the fifth floor of Conway Court, a building that in another town might be considered undesirable, a sixties built ex-council block that's five or six stories high. In this city where space is at a premium and expensive, it's become a nicely maintained residential block where the flats are mostly now privately owned.

There are two lifts in the well-kept foyer that has a couple of plants and artworks of iconic Brighton landmarks on the walls, but I prefer to take the stairs when I can. I head up to the fifth floor, looking from the landing window I can see the small figure of Shaun reaching the end of the road heading towards the pub.

Checking nobody is around, I slide the piece of plastic, cut from a Coke bottle down the side of the crack between the door and it's frame, manoeuvering the plastic until it is next to the lock. I wiggle and drag the plastic so it pushes between the lock and the frame, leaning on to it with my shoulder, the door pops open with no damage to the lock. It's a slightly risky approach, especially if someone from a neighbouring flat comes out but I'm practised at it and I'm quick. The credit card scene in movies doesn't really work, however with the right kind of lock.

Thirty seconds later and I'm inside Shaun's flat, I close the door quietly behind me. There are a couple of flakes of paint on the floor, where the plastic has grazed the paintwork but nothing that will be instantly noticeable, I pick them up anyway.

His flat is cool and I like his style, a 1950's sideboard sits along one wall adorned with eclectic objects, the walls are covered with arty prints and posters from old psychedelic music gigs and Jimi Hendrix stares down from one and Marc Bolan from another. As they are both dead, perhaps he needs a blood motif to pull it all together?

A pile of photography and travel books adorn the coffee table and there is a big leather egg chair in one corner of the living room that contrasts with the vintage looking sofa, probably an Ercol.

First things first I need to get changed, I put on a figure hugging 1940's style green and red silk dress in an oriental print, I roll on my stockings pulling them up and clipping them into the suspender belt, aware that the clips are visible through the fabric of the dress, that's OK I want them to be. Overt sexuality works but so does subtle hints, the shape of a body through clothes, the edge of a lace bra poking through, an inkling of what is underneath all act as tools of seduction. I put my red hair up creating a messy bun at the back with two silver chopsticks securing it, touch up the make up and a squirt of expensive perfume and I'm ready. I stuff my backpack behind the sofa, I'll need it later when I return with Shaun.

Brighton is a vibrant city and its residents take their fashion and image seriously, if you haven't had the pleasure of a visit, think individuality rather than haute couture. You can walk along the street in a top hat and a monocle with a Shetland pony on a lead and nobody will bat an eyelid. I've checked out Shaun's Instagram. He's all smart suits and vintage brogues so I think he'll go for my look, the hairstyle change from my photos will distract his attention from comparing my Tinder pictures too closely.

I head into the bedroom, opening and closing drawers, in the bedside table I find the usual stuff, receipts, ear plugs as well as condoms and lube. In the bottom of the wardrobe there is a box containing a vibrator and some handcuffs, They might come in handy later if you're lucky. An old acquaintance of mine used to say 'no plan survives contact with the enemy' what he meant was plan but stay adaptable.

That's what I do with regards to my kills, I have a plan and they are definitely going to die, it's just not always completely clear exactly how or when. I dig further into the box, there are at least twenty pairs of women's underwear in here individually packed in plastic bags, there is a name written on each of them in Sharpie, Amber, Jane, Tina, Stephie the list goes on, mail order perhaps or trophies from his conquests? "Well then, who's a naughty boy Shaun?" I say out loud to nobody.

I dig further in the box and find a whole pile of memory sticks, I wonder what's on these? There is a MacBook on Shaun's bed, password protected of course. Scanning the room, I look for inspiration, he has a Celtic football shirt hanging on the wall. I try 'Celtic' and then a few variations of the same word with numbers but no luck.

Next I try the obligatory 'Password' and 'Password123' but no success. I look around the room for more clues, Scotland? Nope. I'm about to give up when I look at the shirt again, standing up from the bed I turn it around, it's hanger stuck into the picture rail around the top of the room.

The shirt is emblazoned with the name LARSSON and the number 7. I tap that into the keyboard, the desktop loads up! Slotting the first of Shaun's memory sticks in, I enter the finder and browse the files. The stick is full of video clips, I click on one, the picture starts on the room I am in, the bed empty, I fast forward a little, two people enter the room, Shaun and a girl, I skip forward again and they are naked on the bed fucking, I notice Shaun occasionally glancing at the camera. I click on the next video, it's the same girl and the same time but from a different angle, the third video the same. I scan through the stick, there are a number of girls on here all being secretly filmed.

This confirms what the website showed me earlier, he runs a page called Voyuervision.uk it's a paid for site offering 'Amateur real life voyeuristic videos of unwitting girls'. In the videos on the site his face is blurred out but not those of the girls.

The second stick is from a different location and features a different guy and several other women, no doubt a contact of Shaun's that provides material for his site. As I scan through the sticks I find a variety of material, some clearly showing women in toilets unaware that they are being filmed.

I put everything back in the box and lock the laptop, checking myself one last time in the mirror and double checking everything is as I found it I leave the bedroom. A quick look through the spy-hole confirms the landing is clear so I head out, face mask on. My gloves and the plastic that I opened the door with goes down the rubbish chute, already wiped for prints. I take the lift, no chance of risking the stairs in these heels.

I'm nervous as I approach the corner, sure I've done this before but it's the unknown that causes fear, the fear in turn causes Adrenalin to flow and sparks the flight or fight instinct something bad is about to happen and your body knows it, it's learning how to control that Adrenalin that makes things work. I haven't always been a killer and I'm not a stone cold one. My emotions still work and I still feel things the same as you, it's just that I've just trained myself to suppress them. I'm highly aware that I'm playing god, I take a moment and a few deep breaths to compose myself. "Stick to the plan" I say under my breath.

I scan the outside seating of the pub as I walk up to it, spotting Shaun immediately, I take a squirt of alcohol gel from the dispenser positioned in front of the door like some sort of robot sentry. I make a show of waving as one of the staff looks up and gesticulate towards Shaun with his large glass of red wine in hand and an opened bottle on the table. She nods in acknowledgment and I weave around the dispenser making my way to him.

"Are you Shaun?".

"Hiyah, wow, you look stunning, Yes indeed I am, pleased to meet ya," He says in his soft Scottish accent. He stands, pulling out a chair for me "There you go hen, let me get your jaykit" He helps me out of my coat and hangs it on the back of my chair.

"Thank you it's far too warm for a jacket, with this lock down I'm sure I have no idea what to wear anymore! I like your waistcoat by the way" Shaun is in a three piece suit, his jacket on the back of his chair and his sleeves rolled up revealing strong hairy forearms.

"Ah you are too kind hen, I got a wee bottle of Malbec, there's a glass here for you if you like, or would you prefer something else?"

"Red is fine, thank you" He pours the wine, his hand seems to tremble a little as he does.

"Sorry I'm a wee bit nervous, you look fantastic, sorry I said that already"

"It's fine Shaun, how's your day been?"

We chat about his accent and he tells me he relocated from Scotland ten years ago, it's a classic Northerner moves South for work story. My earlier assumptions were correct, he's utterly charming, but I detect a whiff of condescension as he replies to my questions, he's most definitely an expert in mansplaining too. He also keeps calling me hen, which if we are talking about animals, is getting my goat. Apart from that he is affable, attentive and no doubt well practiced in the dating game. I imagine his shaky hand and apparent nervousness is all part of his act too or perhaps judging by his alcohol consumption early signs of addiction? He quickly slips into a relaxed well-polished patter, his arms spread wide on the back of the bench in a pose of confidence that betrays his pretence.

He's good looking and handsome, in a rugged weathered sort of way. Nice suit, clean finger nails, his beard trimmed and shaped in contrast to his closely shaven head; a man embracing the baldness rather than trying to cover it up. His accent keeps making me think of Ewan McGregor although his look is wilder than that with a lot more facial hair, for all of his patriarchal ways I definitely want to fuck this one before I kill him.

Shaun, drinks most of the bottle and suggests a second one, just as last orders is called.

"Ah pish, these bloody closing times! Dina, would ya like to get a wee bottle to take away and we could go for a walk on the seafront and sit on the beach?"

"Sounds lovely Shaun but it's getting a bit chilly now and it's a decent walk to the seafront from here. Why don't we just go back to yours?"

Shaun leans back and grins like a man who has just found a tenner in his washed jeans pocket. "Right enough then, you dinnae haf to ask me twice" His accent increasingly Scottish with the booze, clearly happy that he can skip forward in his plan to bed me by a few hours.

He holds my hand as we walk to his. Stopping in a door way he pulls me too him and kisses me, a good move in my book, if the signals are right boys then it's OK to take the lead, however make sure the signals are definitely right!

"Sorry I've been dying to do that all night"

Shaun smiles, giving me his best come to bed eyes. It's not the only time you'll be dying tonight Shaun.

"Don't apologise, do it again"

He pulls me too him, we kiss again, his hand on my arse as he does so. I grab his dick through his suit, average but pretty hard.

"Nice and hard huh? I took a Viagra twenty minutes ago, you know just in case like"

Probably too much information but I appreciate the effort, even though it was very fucking presumptuous on your part Shaun.

"let's get home and see what we can do with it then shall we?"

I kiss him again biting his lip as I pull away I raise an eye brow and smirk suggestively, making my intention clear.

"Aii right enough hen" He beams.

I noticed a security camera on my way down in the lift earlier, keen to avoid getting caught on it for more than a second or two, I push him up against the back mirrored wall kissing him hard, staying there for the whole five floors keen to avoid the camera.

As the doors open I jump up into his arms giggling, forcing him to carry me out of the lift and allowing me to hide my face behind him. "Woah steady girl, let's get the door open" he laughs fumbling with his keys as he opens the lock and swings the door wide, placing me back on my feet and turning on the hallway light.

"You carried me over the threshold, does that mean we are married now?" I tease.

He laughs "Aii if you sez so gorgeous, shall I open the wine to celebrate?"

He clearly loves a drink but I'm keen to get on with things.

"Fuck the wine Shaun"

I tug at his belt. He pulls his jacket off, dropping it on the hallway floor, his hands reach for mine and he takes over and undoes the fly and belt himself. I turn around lift up the dress and peel my knickers down until they are around my ankles. I put my hands on the front door and look over my shoulder.

"Fuck me, hard" I demand.

He lifts up my dress exposing my arse, my legs and buttocks taught in the high heels. He pushes himself against me, facing resistance for a second and then his dick slides in.

"Yes, that's it" I tell him.

His hands are on my hips pulling me on to him, my face pressed against the front door. His trousers and underwear still around his ankles as he drives into me, he kisses my neck and I hear him panting as he does, smelling the wine on his breath. I slide down the door a little and reach one hand between my legs touching his balls and he begins to moan, I love the feeling of being pounded from behind, the power of someone else's weight driving into you but Shaun is not going to last long like this.

"Wait, lets go on the sofa" I suggest

He reaches down and pulls up his trousers holding on to the waist band.

"The bedroom is just here hen" He points to the room off to the left. But I ignore him, thinking to myself 'I know where the bedroom is and all of your camera's Shaun, I'd prefer to keep this one off the record thanks'. I kick off the knickers from around my ankles and head into the living room , he follows me in and looks at me as if waiting for directions, I scan the room as if it's the first time I have seen it.

"Lie back with your head on the armrest" He positions himself on the length of the sofa, his head on the arm looking back and up at me smiling eagerly. I lift up my dress standing above him at the end of the sofa and position my pussy over his face. "Lick me" I demand.

He obliges and I manoeuvre my hips so that I am working his tongue against myself, rising and lowering to increase or decrease the pressure.

"Shaun I want to watch you touch yourself" He wiggles his trousers down again and takes his dick with one hand beginning to stroke his cock, the Viagra has clearly taken effect and he stands proud and hard.

I watch him as he does and I get aroused by the sight of it. It's incredibly personal, seeing someone do something that's usually reserved for when they're alone, it's interesting seeing people like that, vulnerable, exposing their most intimate act, I like it when they get lost, and I get to see something truthful.

Some women claim not to like looking at dicks, and I accept that unsolicited pics via a dating app may not be an immediate turn on but for me there is something about the look of them, the shape, texture and size combination, the power and the strength that makes you feel the irresistible desire to touch it, certainly when it's a dick you want anyway.

He licks enthusiastically perhaps knowing that the sight of him touching himself is having an effect on me, I certainly feel wetter and I move my hips in response to him.

I use my hand to work my clit, pushing myself harder on his face, trying to bury his tongue inside me. denying myself the desire to be filled by his cock again is turning me on more, I want to cum and I tell him so "Keep going, I'm nearly there" He makes a muffled affirmative sound and pushes his tongue harder into me, moving his head from side to side as much as my thighs and weight upon him will allow.

The orgasm comes quickly, almost out of nowhere, as it starts to take over I put all of my weight onto his face, moaning;

"Yes, yes, that's it Shaun, make me cum"

It's an orgasm from my clit, shallower and less earth shattering, they type of orgasm I give myself when masturbating.

Even though he probably can't breath he keeps going, good boy Shaun, ten out of ten for effort and enthusiasm. As my body starts to convulse and tremble, I pull the silver chopsticks from my hair, the light momentarily flashes off their sharpened points and I thrust them down hard, one in each hand, my thumb pressed over the ends to drive them home. Taking my aim carefully to force one into each of the soft fleshy parts at side of his neck, piercing his trachea. His body lurches as if an electric current has been driven through it, his back arching.

I step back looking down, his horrified eyes stare back up at me, I pull the chopsticks out and he gurgles, a jet of blood arcs out from the left hand side where I have pierced the carotid artery, good shot I think to myself, the spurts from the narrow holes in his neck covering a surprising distance, some of it hits the ceiling and sprays on to the walls and furniture. As he tries to sit up I drive the chopsticks into his eyes. He drops back onto the sofa, most likely already dead his brain speared by the vicious metal points but just to be sure I snake my arm around his neck above the holes made by the chopsticks and I squeeze my forearm across his wind-pipe until Shaun's body stops convulsing.

I step back to take in the scene, blood splatters the walls in various arcs, the heart is a powerful pup and when blood is released through a small hole the distance covered is impressive, arcs of red stain the white walls and run down the glass of the framed pictures. The body of this large man looks less threatening in death, the skin taking on a blueish tinge as the blood leaves his body. His face is covered in two red streaks where the blood and eye matter has dribbled from the sockets.

I get my bag from behind the sofa, it's time to get to get out of here but I have work to do first. I put on medical gloves, there is no point touching anything else. Thanks to all the blood and the chopsticks it's pretty easy to write on the white wall above the sofa, clambering over his body I take a few pictures down and then using the pool of blood that has gathered in Shaun's neck I write the words:

'Runnin round leaving scars'

Next the messy bit, watching the movies you might think it's easy to open somebody up but the sternum is seriously thick bone and the ribs are tough. There's an old joke that the easiest way to a mans heart is through his chest with a bread knife, I don't like to carry too many tools, preferring to adapt on the go, I try to use whatever is at hand. The bread knife in Shaun's kitchen drawer looks to be a good one. I rip open the buttons on his shirt and then using both hands, I plunge it into his belly just below the rib cage.

Using a sawing motion I cut through the skin opening him up along the bottom of the ribs until there is a hole big enough to push my hands in. It's not too difficult to find the heart from here, just under the sternum. I grip it with both hands and pull, using the weight of Shaun's lifeless body against my strength, his heart tears forwards with a sucking noise still connected via veins and sinew.

Several strokes with the bread knife and the superior vena cava, pulmonary artery and aorta tubes are all severed, keyhole surgery this is not. I plop most of the heart into a jam jar, squashing it in as I screw on the lid. I remove the lid from the other full jar that I brought with me and start to work the contents around his body smearing some into the body cavity, I got this idea from a Dean R Koontz book I read when I was a teenager, funny what you remember from childhood.

The jar is filled with entrails from my previous victim and a load of bodily material I managed to obtain from a hospital, it's surprising how far you can wander unchallenged with a white coat and a stethoscope, I just found the right bin and helped myself, I must admit I nearly puked. There is less of an urge to vomit this time, I must admit I'm already getting used to it and find the internal workings of the body fascinating.

The confusing mixture of DNA makes it very difficult for the police to work out what belongs to who. I'm careful about what I touch and where my bodily fluids go but this gives me excellent insurance. It's also a pretty awesome motif for a serial killer don't you think?

I position Shaun so he is sitting up on the sofa, he limp cock shriveled against his leg, the trousers still gathered around his ankles. His upper body covered in blood, already it starts to congeal in his chest hair. His intestines, grey and purple in colour hanging out of the gash across his belly. I push the chopsticks deeper into the eye sockets just for the visual effect, or in Shaun's case perhaps the lack of visual effects, they make a sucking sound as I do that makes me say 'fucking disgusting' out loud in a Scottish accent, I can bare most things but I'm not a monster!

Leaving the Queen of Hearts card in Shaun's hand I collect my bag, working backwards out of the room, careful to wash anything I may have touched with a bleach wipe and spreading more of the jar contents on the living room door handle as I close it behind me.

In the bedroom I daub the password in blood onto the top of the laptop, that should help the police along.

I head into the shower, I'm not concerned about my DNA in here, Shaun had plenty of bleach in his bathroom, I'll wash the shower down with that and then spread more mixture around before I leave. I just want to make sure I'm clean.

I pack my dress, stockings, wig and shoes into a zip top plastic bag, pouring in the bleach and some water, ensuring it coats everything, watching as it leaches the colour from the fabric and hair. I put the bag in my backpack, next to the jars.I wash, the water runs red for a while, then fades to pink as a I lather up the soap, the smell the same scent I could detect on Shaun's body not more than ten minutes ago.

As I walk back to my hotel along the seafront from Hove, I take a brief detour on to the beach, even with the reduced opening hours Brighton is still a busy place especially in the summer heat, there are a few people about but nobody pays me any attention. I walk to the waters edge, stooping to pick up a handful of pebbles, I discreetly drop them into the plastic bag, piercing a couple of holes in it to make sure it sinks before I throw it into the sea. It might wash up tomorrow but even if it does, by then it'll just be a bag of bleached rags,if it makes it to the police they will have nothing to find.

As I stare out over the water my emotions are mixed, the ever present fear of getting caught mixes with remorse at having taken a life, sure he was a scumbag but there is still part of me that deep down battles with it. Each time it becomes a little easier to suppress but I also move further away from the person I once was, hardened by every experience. Instead I focus on the plan and allow a smile to play across my lips satisfied that things are going as predicted.

My first official murder as the Queen of Hearts was perhaps the hardest, actually planning to kill was not something I had done before. It was the beginning of March 2020 just before the first lock down started and everything went pandemic crazy. I was scared yes, but still calm, I had a well-structured plan, as long as I could keep my Adrenalin under control I would be fine.

His Plenty of Fish name was 'Jakemeoff' Could this guy be any more obvious or anymore crass? I'd set my profile to say I was a single mother of one, I'm not sure why, being the first one I guess I was trying to make my profile as unlike me as possible.

His first message was this:- 'Hi I've matched you even though your a single mother, I normally never date single mums. Lots of baggage and they are like an anchor to a guy. You look quite tasty tho so am prepared to meet up for drinks and we can have a good time. Message me to arrange our date.' The spelling and grammar all his own, he closely follows the first message with a picture of his erect penis. What a guy!

He was exactly what I was looking for in the first one, I wanted what is commonly referred to as a fuck boy. Anytime I have seen a message like this I wondered if it ever works, I can only assume it must, perhaps it's about numbers? If you send a dick picture out a hundred times and get one response does that count as a success? From experience I know there are so many of these types of guys out there, good looking maybe – some of them at least, but so arrogant, so degrading to women.

He has just one picture; a smug face holding up his t-shirt showing off his six pack and Calvin Kleins. He's good looking and he knows it, he thinks the world revolves around him. But who is sleeping with these men? Who is giving them the feeling that this is OK? If it's you, stop it, there are better options out there. I guess this time he thinks it will be me but whatever happens, it will also be the last time for him.

There was no need for seduction with him, Jake had made it clear he was after one thing and one thing only. He wanted to come to my place to 'smash' as he so delightfully put it. I very nearly gave up on him as he was so reluctant to have me in his home, obviously this wasn't going to work otherwise.

I kept on at him that I would be able to get a sitter to come to his but it was just not possible at my place with the baby, how hot he looked and how much of a shame it would be if I didn't get to meet him, finally he agreed, maybe it was the impending threat of the first lock down that changed his mind, or just the fact that his flat mates were away for the weekend and he'd have the place to himself. I was 'allowed' to go over Friday night but I had to leave and absolutely could not be there Saturday morning. That was fine I thought, after all I wouldn't be the only one no longer there on Saturday.

He met me at the door, jogging bottom style shorts, white sports socks and a t-shirt. Jake had gone to exactly no effort. I on the other hand, had put on my best single mum look. Sparkly top, under a denim jacket. A-line skirt, fake tanned legs and a pair of pumps. He looked at me and nodded. NODDED! Opening the door wide to let me walk in, I feel his eyes sizing me up as I walk passed him, I'm a pretty strong willed woman and yet I could feel this arsehole sucking the self-confidence out of me with every second he looked at me.

We walk into his swanky kitchen, the room alone bigger than the student flat, and I shared that with two other people. I already know that mummy and daddy have a hand in paying for this and the spoiled little fuck boy probably doesn't appreciate it.

"Nice kitchen", I say, "it's a big house, how many of you live here?" I already know the answer to this too.

"Just Jimmy, Tony and I, my parents bought it for me, the other two pay rent" That's not quite true either is it Jake, Ma and Pa bought it to save on rentals whilst you are at university here in Bristol and to add to their property portfolio, sure you'll probably inherit it or the proceeds of it but it's not yours yet you smarmy little shit.

Without being asked what I want to drink, Jake hands me a glass of Prosecco. "Thanks" I say a nervous wobble in my voice, fearful but excited at what I am about to do, I hope he puts it down to being nervous in his presence.

"Fancy getting in the hot tub?" He asks out of nowhere, I look at him quizzically for a moment I hadn't been expecting this question and a sudden wave of fear washes over me at the change in my plan.

"I don't have anything to wear" I buy myself some time to think, getting me naked is obviously his intention and that's not necessarily a bad thing but an outdoor exposed hot tub was not in the order of ceremony I had planned.

"You don't need anything, there's a shelter and roof over the tub and the neighbours don't overlook it, we can strip off down there and jump straight in"

This could be interesting, like I said earlier sometimes you have to be prepared to adapt I buy myself a little more time to reformulate my plan.

"Let's have another drink first, I'm a bit nervous" I say draining my glass. He rolls his eyes as if impatient at my request, but he goes to the fridge, gets out a fresh bottle and pours me another, his own glass on the counter barely touched, he clinks my fresh glass then downs his own to show me how macho he is, pouring himself another.

It's not a lie, I am nervous, not about being with him but at what I'm planning to do to him. Even though I had run through it in my mind over and over, being here now faced with the reality was a different thing. Our bodies endocrine system doesn't interpret thoughts in detail, it just recognises anxiety and fear, this produces a adrenal response or the 'fight or flight' instinct. Even though I know this, getting control of it is difficult and I grip the glass and discreetly hold the side of the kitchen counter with my other hand to stop myself visibly shaking. I control my breathing and my heart rate begins to slow a little.

He talks at me, telling me some bullshit about his uni course, he's studying law and when he finishes he's apparently got some cool job to go to in London that his dad has set up for him. Yawn. The hot tub is sounding more appealing now even if it is just to shut him up.

"Show me this hot tub then" His face brightens, he goes to get some towels and puts the freshly opened bottle in an ice bucket. I follow him down the steps into the garden, ensuring I keep looking straight ahead, my brunette hair straightened and long down my back, I position it so it purposefully covers the sides of my face to keep out any prying eyes that might be in neighbouring windows.

True to his word the hot tub is secluded and isn't over looked, I ask him to turn away as I get undressed putting my hair into a pony tail with the hairband on my wrist and slip quickly into the water. He undresses with his back to me, slowly flexing his young gym bunny shoulders, peeling his boxers over his tight butt and shapely legs he's actually putting on a show for me, I can't believe how amazing he thinks he is.

He turns around, his face deadpan, he takes himself seriously and I'm sure he thinks it's my privilege to be able to lay my eyes upon him. His body is completely shaved of any hair, with the six pack he is so proud of flaunting, he stands looking at me, he has got a good body, I'll give him that but my god knows it. He climbs into the pool, sitting opposite me. I resist the urge to drown him, it would be a shame to not feel that hot body before I dispatch him.

I'm still nervous but its under control and I concentrate on sticking to the rest of my plan. Jake doesn't do small talk, he's straight in with the 'compliments' "You have nice tits I thought they would be saggy." What a little cunt he is. I begin to channel the flight response into anger.

"Thanks, you clearly work hard on your body" I say as I hold myself back from the urge to punch him in the throat. I thought this first planned kill would be hard but he's such an arrogant little prick I'm surprised nobody has killed him before, perhaps it's the Prosecco taking affect but I'm feeling less nervous and even a little excited at the prospect of it now.

"Yeah everyday I'm in the gym" He tenses his out stretched arms on the side of the hot tub to show me just how much he works out. We chat for a bit longer and as the wine does its job I start to relax, the revised plan becoming clear in my mind.

"There's a nice jet over here, it hits the bottom of your back and feels so good" Jake professes, I take the hint and slide over next to him. Relaxing into it I lay my head back and sigh "Oh that's lovely"

His hand creeps on to my shoulder, the other reaches across and cups my breast, there is really no subtlety with this boy. Reaching down under the water to find his cock I discover it is still soft but as I play with it, it starts to respond. He lets go of my boob and leans his head back on the side of the hot tub an erection growing in my hand.

I start to work his dick, stroking up and down his length, twisting the shaft as I do, he turns his head to look at me. "Sit on it" He says, matter of fact. I can't keep my mouth shut any longer.

"If that's your idea of foreplay Jake you need to work a little harder" He looks shocked. "We older women expect a bit more than a quick fumble, we have needs to you know?" I'm 6 years older than him but a world apart in maturity.

"Maybe I need to teach you a thing or too about what women want?" He thinks about it, clearly his ego is dented and I can't tell if he's thinking about kicking me out or going with it. He moves his hand on to my thigh in the water and tries to push it between my legs, I grab his wrist and stop him.

Stepping out of the pool I walk back towards the house, glancing over my shoulder my wet footprints leave a trail on the path. Fearful that I have pushed him too hard I say to him;

"How about we go indoors?" A suggestive look on my face

"OK" he nods Some of the cockiness gone from his body language.

He gets out and follows me, wrapping a towel around himself, as I climb the steps back to the kitchen I make sure he gets a good look at my naked body. It's the first time he has seen it in its entirety, I know it is strong and toned, my large breasts still firm, the cold spring air makes my body goose pimple and my nipples stand erect. I see his eyes looking me up and down and his hard cock cannot hide its response.

As he enters the kitchen I pull his towel off him and wrap it around myself, just like that I am now in the control of the situation . "Where's your bedroom?" I ask him.

Naked with his cock bobbing in front of him he takes my hand and leads the way through the house. Out of the kitchen into the hallway and up the plush carpeted stairs, the whole house is a pallet of cream and white, I can't imagine what his parents were thinking, decorating it like this with three twenty something lads living in the property! I assume a regular cleaner has a large part to do with it looking so fresh still.

We enter his bedroom, the doors are open on to his balcony with the curtains flapping in the breeze. "Can you close the window, it's a bit chilly?"I ask, I also don't want to be heard. He closes the windows and comes towards me, I put my hand on his chest. "Lie down" he does as he is told.

I stand over him looking down at his crotch as if inspecting his dick, it's not particularly long but quite thick, I look at it without emotion, watching a flicker of self doubt across his face as I dent his pride by not being impressed. I flick the tip with my finger, making it bounce back and forth. I spit on it and begin to suck, sliding my mouth up and down the length of him, taking it all in, the end of his cock catching the back of my throat, I hold back my gag reflex. Jake sits up on his elbows, transfixed. "Wow"

"You like that?" Momentarily taking it out of my mouth to speak.

"Yeah that's amazing" He replies, wide eyed.

Good, I have his full attention, maybe it's time he learns how to treat a woman properly, I suck on it a few more times. "So you like it when someone makes you feel good? Do you think that woman are just here for your pleasure Jake?" He sits up looking confused and bewildered. I continue "your messages, were pretty shitty, telling me you would consider dating me in spite of being a single mum, doing me a favour? How fucking arrogant are you?" He recoils from me, pulling his legs up, visibly looking scared at the rapid turn of events.

"I want you to leave, you're a fucking psycho, you come into my house and then start giving me shit? You should be grateful to be here you fucking slag" He stands up to approach me but as he does his legs wobble and he has to grip the bedside cabinet to steady himself. His face at first looks puzzled before a flash of realisation washes over it "What the fuck? Have you drugged me?! What the hell have you given me?"

"The Prosecco Jake, when you went to get the towels, I put a few Rohypnol in your glass, you were so busy posing and showing off there was plenty of time for it to dissolve, in about two minutes you are going to pass out" As if on cue he sits down in a flop on the side of the mattress his face now filled with fear.

"You fucking bitch, you fucking drugged me!" His speech has become slurred, he sounds as if he is losing consciousness.

"Yes I did, Jake and now I'm going to kill you, let me tell you why" As I explain to him the error of his ways, he tries to fight the effects of the drug. He flails his arms around around knocking the lamp off the bedside table. I just watch and do nothing, it won't be long now.

The effects of a single dose of Rohypnol can include:- drowsiness, sleep, dizziness, loss of motor control, decreased reaction time, impaired judgement, lack of coordination, slurred speech and confusion. Jake has had four doses, he's already passed the point of causing me any harm and has little control over his muscles, in about thirty seconds it will all be over.

He lays on the bed, sprawled out, his dick now soft, I try to arouse it, perhaps I can have a little action before I finish him off? The body can sometimes produce an involuntary reaction to stimulation. I'm feeling turned on by the power but it looks like the dose is too much for him and nothing is happening. Oh well, that's the end of that part of my fun tonight, as this is my first proper premeditated murder I wanted to make sure I got things right and that things went smoothly. I can always have more fun once I know my plan works. I'm just glad that I have control of the situation this far.

I could still turn back now, no real harm done, he would wake up tomorrow with a sore head and a hazy recollection and that would be all, he'd never find me and the police would not spend much time investigating when there is no evidence of a crime. I take a minute to compose myself. Reminding myself why I am here and I make the decision to cross that line.

I drag him to the bathroom using the bed sheet, the wooden floor makes it easier to slide him along. Once in there I wedge his limp body into the walk in shower leaning him against the tiles, propping his feet against the glass. Taking the Fairbairn Sykes dagger, I cut across his throat, he makes no sound. A ribbon of blood follows the knife as the cut opens up. It's not deep enough though, I've broken the skin but not cut his trachea, even after all the training the first time actually cutting into another human is hard. I grit my teeth and push the dagger deeper along the same line, dragging the blade with both hands. The blood gushes out of him and there is a sucking sound as his body convulses gasping for air through the severed windpipe. The shower fills with blood, so much blood, way more than I expected.

My nerves get the better of me and I throw up, just managing to make it to the toilet bowl in time. My bowels want to open too and I have to sit on the toilet as the blood runs down the wall of the shower and spirals into the plug hole. I have time to get used to these things, my body will adjust as I get more experienced. The terror grips me and I want to run but I fight it, trying to regain control of my faculties. I calm myself as best I can by walking through the rest of the plan in my head, breathing deeply.

Stick to the plan Alys I repeat in my head like a Mantra. First step, I need to get a piece of his heart. I tentatively stab at his chest a few times with the knife my hand trembling as I do, quickly realising that even the sharp pointed blade isn't going to get through his rib cage and breast bone. I'm starting to panic a little, I hadn't thought about this part too much. I clumsily cut into the soft stomach, sawing at it with the blade. Gagging I use my fingers to wriggle inside him and locate the heart. The smell from the cavity makes me wretch again and I pull my hand out as I lurch to the toilet bowl once again, emtying the last remnants from my stomach. I look at myself in the mirror."Get a grip Alys, you've come this far, see it through, nobody is coming, you have time, get control" I say out loud to myself.

I'm a quick learner though and I'm determined to finish my task, I reach the heart, feeling around with both hands I cut it away with the dagger. Keyhole surgery this is not!

Once I have the heart I quickly gather it up and put it into the jar. I look down at his corpse, already taking on a tinge of blue as the blood leaves his body, I allow myself a nervous smile, my plan has started and there is definitely no going back now. The magnitude of my actions hits me and once again I begin to shake as my body is flooded with Adrenalin. I must compose myself, I've practiced and practiced getting control of fear, it doesn't stop the physical response from happening but I am able to keep it under control. Picking up a toothbrush and some paste mixed with entrails, blood and bodily fluids, I write on the mirror:

'And who do you think you are?'

Now that the words are there, I want to run, to get away from here as soon as possible but I feel like I should pose Jake a little better. I arrange some towels on the bathroom floor and drag his wet, blood smeared body out of the shower and arrange him on the towels, his arm pointing to the mirror holding the toothbrush, the other hand holding the first of my cards.

Chapter 3

This was in the paper this morning:

A 'Banrigh Writes' exclusive

There is a new killer in our midst, not this time a deadly virus but something perhaps even more terrifying. A serial killer appears to be at work using the pandemic as their cover, hiding behind face masks and using social distancing to cover their identity.

Perhaps even more unusual, I believe this killer to be a woman. The alleged perpetrator has made the step of contacting me directly revealing several key facts, too gruesome to detail here about three recent murders.

The Police have acknowledged that the crimes detailed in her letter are real however they have asked that I do not go into detail at this crucial stage of the investigation.

I am permitted to reveal one significant detail; at each of the gruesome crime scenes, a Queen of Hearts playing card has been left, furthermore the author of the letter has also signed her name as such.

Currently the three crimes that are being reviewed as possibly being linked are; the murder of Jake Simmonds on March the 6th in Bristol , the second in Brighton on Friday July the 10th of Shaun

McBride and the third Kevin Gower in Leigh Greater Manchester last Friday July 31st.

The time in between each of the crimes seems to be reducing, and any motive is as yet unknown, the police remain open to the possibility of further victims being identified and are searching their database for similar crimes.

The police have advised people to be vigilant and to report any suspicious requests to meet. The police have asked the public to come forward with any detail regarding the crimes no matter how insignificant it may seem.

The number to call is 101 or you can contact the police at:

https://www.police.uk/pu/contact-the-police/report-a-crime-incident/

So why has she written to me? She hints in her letter that she's had enough of society and feels it is time to push back in some way. Now I'm not going to condone killing or violence of any kind and she needs to be stopped, but I've said for a long time if things don't change people are going to snap, it looks like this sadly may be the case here. I will be investigating serial killers over the next few weeks and particularly those rarest of creatures the female serial killer.

Turn to page 14 for the first in the series where I look at what motivates and drives serial killers in general. You can also find dates for socially distanced book signing locations for "Bang to Rights" My expose on domestic violence.

What a start! I couldn't have asked for a better introduction, Banrigh has positioned herself at the forefront as I knew she would, I can use her and her column to get the word out there.

There is definitely no turning back for me now. I have to continue until my work is complete. It'll be all over the rest of the tabloids by tomorrow morning, keen to jump on the bandwaggon and sell more papers, Banrigh will be revelling in her exclusive, so I need to focus my attentions to number four and keep things moving.

Firstly I need a new location, I've got several chats started with potential candidates across the country, I think the Midlands looks promising this time. It's not an area I know well but there are plenty of small surrounding towns and the road network makes it very easy to get in and out.

I scroll through the various dating apps setting my location as Birmingham City centre with a 30 mile radius, to see if anyone new pops up.

Age Range: 30 to 55

The app presents me with a number of choices, I don't know what I'm looking for yet but I'll know when I see it. I take the time to scan through their profiles, some have very little information, many have the same clichéd answers but even from a few minutes of chat you can establish a pretty good picture of someone.

It means I have to start several conversations and do a lot of digging in the background to establish whether they are the right fit for my needs. Whilst I was digging I came across a website that suggest there are essentially 10 types of men you will find on dating sites:

1. **Mr Lonely and desperate**— After his long-term relationship ended, highly likely at his own hand, he was expecting to be driving a sports car with an attractive younger model on his arm, he is faced with the reality of washing his grey skid marked y-fronts in a bedsit sink and is desperate to find anyone to have him. Alternatively he just wants to get back on the horse, any horse, a mail order inflatable horse is probably under his bed.

2. **The Philanderer** - He's in a relationship and he's never going to leave, unless she catches him and kicks him out, where he then is very likely to become number 1. Probably married, the wife definitely doesn't know but he'll suggest on his profile that he's in an open relationship. He'll get what he wants and then ghost you.

3. **The Younger seeks older -** Young, probably ripped and brimming with confidence he thinks he's got what makes a woman tick completely sussed especially in the bedroom. Once he realises you have a brain and depth, he'll be scared shitless and either want you to mother him or run away.

4. **The Perfectionist-** He will never find what he is looking for as it doesn't exist. He moves from relationship to relationship feeling that he just hasn't met the one yet. However when he meets you he'll make you feel like you could be the one before slowly chipping away at your self-esteem until there is nothing left, blaming you for not living up to his impossible goals , the chief of 'Negging'.

5. **The wannabe Sugar Daddy-** His profile says he's 45 but in his pictures he looks no younger than 60. Woman between the ages of 25 and 40 need only apply and the ones at the higher age range better be in good condition. Obviously he deserves you because:

A) He makes a lot of money and will spoil you rotten buying you everything you ever wanted and you'll never have to work again, just attend swanky parties on his arm?

B) He looks like Pierce Brosnan?

C) He's super charming and debonair with friends in all the right places?

Answer: D) None of the above. He is bald, overweight, drives a 20 year old Saab and works in accounts. He may also be a number 1 in disguise.

6. The Phantom. This is the guy that can't be bothered filling out a full profile. Instead he writes something like "if you have a question, just ask." If he can't be bothered to fill it in there are several explanations. A. He has no idea who he is. B He wants to fit himself to whatever you want so he looks good and can get into your pants. C. He'll never meet you, he just wants to chat and feel wanted from a distance basically wasting your time until he ghosts you. You can never pin them down, they message profusely for an evening then nothing for three days or ever again. Also possibly a number two

7. The Fuckboy. How many messages until he goes from normal to perv? I'll give him anything from number two to ten but it won't be long. He has one goal so why waste time getting to know you? Also combines well with number three

Here's how the conversation might go:

HIM: How about dinner?

ME: Sounds great. How about Bills on Thursday night at 7?

HIM: Wow, you are so authoritative. I think I'm getting hard.

ME: Over dinner plans? OK.

HIM: Sorry, horny tonight, I could come over and you could get to know where I'm ticklish?

ME: Have you been drinking?

HIM: No, but I am high. But I like that you could tell something was amiss. I am definitely hard now.

Probably closely followed by a picture of his dick.

8. Mr Vitriolic- He seems nice but every comment has a barb to it and you can sense his rage through the bitterness he exhibits. He obviously has been hurt and doesn't trust women any more and he's basically waiting for you to prove him right.

He'll twist everything you say so that he can then rant at you as to why 'you are all the fucking same' and why none of you can handle a real man. It's the fault of womankind that he hasn't been successful and a woman should know her place and worship her man. Highly possible to be a number one also

9. The Player- He looks the part, the face, the hair, the muscles, probably a dog. He doesn't need to swipe the swipes come to him. How can he pick just one and why should he? It would be almost rude of him to commit to just one woman and he owes women a favour to fuck as many of us as possible. He'll make you feel worthy for a while, keeping you on the back burner, occasionally giving you a stir, that is until he's bored and the next three women come along.

10. Mr Right – This doesn't exist for me but it might for you. He's probably a little embarrassed to be on a dating site and tries very hard not to be like one of the guys above, he's harder to find than you might think and most of you will self-sabotage thinking he belongs in the 'friend zone'

There is fair game for my next victim in all but the last category, depending on how they treat women and their view on the world.

I find Jim. He definitely fits the sugar daddy type. He claims to be 49, he is late 50's if a day. In his first photo , he is wearing a tuxedo holding a brandy glass, his thinning hair pasted to his head and a substantial cummerbund is attempting to restrain his gut.

Photo two, polo-shirt, on a boat somewhere hot, sailors hat perched on his head at a jaunty angle, it's probably taken on a holiday and it's most definitely not his boat.

He claims to be a successful business man who is 'Looking for a princess to spoil' No problem Jimbo I can help him with that.

I swipe right, it's an instant match, of course it is. My name today? Kitty. Soft, girly, old fashioned maybe. He'll like that.

I'll send him the first message it'll get him interested straight away.

"Hi Jim, you look very smart in your tuxedo and on the boat, my name is Kitty, I hope you like my profile"

"Well thank you young lady" he replies instantly, just from the way he writes I can tell he is a sleazebag, I think I might vomit. "May I say you look stunningly beautiful in your pictures, the picture is on my boat that I keep moored in Spain, I don't get out there as much as I would like but I love the water"

Liar liar pants on fire Jim. "That's very kind of you to say, the boat sounds very exciting I'm not much of a sailor but I do like the sunshine! What sort of ladies are you attracted to Jim?" I choose the word lady over woman as I want to play to his old school mentality.

"Ladies like you of course my dear! I like a lady who can appreciate the finer things in life, someone that I can look after and treat well, take out to dinner and the theatre, shopping trips away, that sort of thing" He piles on the less than subtle offers.

"Well you sound like the perfect gentleman, I'd love to be lucky enough to find a man to treat me like that, the guys I date seem to just be after one thing. It's so depressing, what do you do for work Jim?"

"That's very sad to hear my dear, I work in finance, it's all a bit complicated to understand (Patronising cunt) but it's served me well and allowed me to enjoy some of the finer things in life."

" It sounds like you have worked hard, I'm surprised you are not already married or taken, you seem like a lovely man"

I've already used an image search and Jim's Facebook profile picture is the same one of him in a tux. Now I have his surname it's over to LinkedIn. Jim works for an accountancy firm in Coventry. Taking a look at their web page it shows that he is a middle ranked accountant in an insignificant firm. The sort that handles small local businesses not international conglomerates, he is definitely not the big player he is making out to be.

I put his name into the public records website and it transpires that Jim's divorce was finalised earlier this year. It looks like Jim's ex-wife Angela, filed for divorce due to 'adultery with prostitutes' naughty boy Jim, it also lists his date of birth, he's 57.

It takes a few more searches in the public records to reveal that the no doubt long suffering Angela got possession of the house and most of his assets including 40% of his pension, he wasn't rich enough to own a boat before and certainly isn't now.

"My work kept me very busy I'm afraid and I just never had the time to meet the right lady friend. I have some more time on my hands these days so I can focus on providing the right amount of attention. Perhaps it's time you let a slightly (no slightly about it Jim) older gentleman treat you in the way you deserve? Would you do the honour of letting me buy you dinner?"

Bingo.

"That would be lovely, you are very charming ans suave, perhaps I should call you James Bond rather than Jim?!"

"Haha that's very kind of you and far more flattering than I deserve, the pleasure I'm sure, is all mine" You are right about it being more than you deserve and there won't be any pleasure, not for you anyway Jim.

I'm going to have to play this one carefully, he'll be used to playing a longer game strategy and to have at least two or three dates before he takes me home. I don't have the time for that but I don't want him to smell a rat either. I'm sure he will go for it whatever, keen to get his grubby little hands on me but it's better to make sure there is no room for doubt.

I do some more research, this time using the electoral register. Jim pays council tax on a rented flat in Stoke Aldermoor, Coventry.

Google street view shows me what I already suspect, it's an area suffering from social deprivation, high unemployment and high crime. Jim is not doing well since Angela left him. So category wise he's a number one and a number five when it comes to the list, a worthy sacrifice don't you think?

There's no way I'm going back to that shithole he calls home, and it's unlikely that he will want to invite me. Jim will eventually suggest a night in a hotel, hammering his credit card in an attempt to bed me. As much as like to have fun, this old slime ball won't be getting that chance.

We arrange to meet on Thursday evening, Jim has selected the Coombe Abbey restaurant, he revels in telling me all about it, peacocking about how amazing the Garden rooms are and what a treat I am in for. The internet tells me it is an upmarket hotel restaurant, set in beautiful grounds just outside Coventry, Jim you may just have done half of my work for me! easy to get to from the M6 motorway and in a secluded countryside location.

An hour later and my plan is starting to formulate nicely, it's time to find a bike to buy so I head to the Friday ad:

'Yamaha TDM 850 in nice working order overall. The bike has been painted at some point but looks nice and solid. The tank is in good condition, there are some marks to the panels and surface scratches The bike runs and rides well and sounds good' £1350 ono

That sounds perfect. I'll turn up with an envelope full of cash and pay £1100 for it. The wear and tear is good, not flash enough to draw any attention but also with a recent MOT so everything will be working, new brakes too which is always reassuring. The colour is low key blending in with the traffic, there was a Honda Hornet 600 that was in better condition but a bright yellow bike is not what I need right now.

I take a trip to the Sowe Common Sports Ground on Woodway lane, I scouted around as I always do when planning and spotted it on Google Earth. It looks like a good potential place to dispatch Jim. The sports park is at the end of a lane with a row of houses to the left, I park the bike at the end of the row, next to the fence. It's next to a house but in a bit of no-mans land. If the homeowner spots it, they'll think it's someone using the sports park, anyone else will assume it belongs to the house, so it'll be safe for a few days without anyone becoming suspicious.

I walk further down the lane into the sports fields and dip into the overgrowth behind the pavilion building situated close to the perimeter fence. Hiding a bag with a crash helmet, gloves and leathers, deep into the untended weeds and bushes.

On the map I noted that one side of the park butts up against the M6 motorway and there is a pedestrian footbridge that crosses it.

I walk down the lane back towards the houses and call a taxi, giving one of the house numbers. I continue to walk and double back towards the given number as I follow the approaching cab on the app. As it arrives, so do I timing my walk to look like I just came out of one of the houses. The taxi takes me back to the city centre at my request, I get out as we stop at some traffic lights, giving the driver cash with a modest tip, nothing unusual in my behaviour and infinitely forgettable.

I head to the train station and take the train to the Coventry Arena my plan is to head to the other side of the footbridge but taking this long route to cover my tracks.

Once at the arena I use a phone box to call another taxi firm. I ask the driver to take me to Hinckley Road and drop me outside a CO-OP. I walk the mile and a half from there to the other end of Woodway lane. I guess once upon a time before the motorway was built that it was a single connected road, hence being Woodway lane on both sides of the motorway. Whatever the history of it, its given me a handy getaway route.

There is also a fortuitous turn of events, at the end of the lane just before the bottom of the footbridge is a derelict pub called the Craven Arms.

The dictionary defines craven as meaning; contemptibly lacking in courage; cowardly. Perfectly poetic for a man like Jim. I scope out the area, it's a quiet residential road and there is nobody around to see me pull the temporary fencing apart and sneak onto the site, it's a brilliant location for what I need and I can't believe my luck at finding it. I leave my second bag hidden inside the building.

I spend the rest of the week getting to know Jim's background a little better, making sure I know as much about him as possible, I make a plan of action with contingencies in case anything should go wrong.

When it finally comes to Thursday night Jim insists on picking me up and driving me, keen to show off his gentlemanly ways, I give him an address close to the centre of town, I suggest to him I'll be attending our monthly socially distanced team meeting that day so why doesn't he pick me up from the office, sticking with his perfect gentleman image, he of course obliges. I arrange to meet him outside the Friargate building, an imposing office block, housing numerous businesses and part of the city's attempt at some sort of regeneration.

Jim turns up in a Jaguar XK. A cursory glance at the number plate tells me Jim has hired it for the occasion, keen to impress me, he obviously thinks I'll be too impressed to notice it's a hire car.

"Hi you must be Kitty" He steps out of the vehicle moving around to open the passenger door for me. "Hi James" I say giving him my best coquettish smile.

I glide around the car, my business suit clinging to my body, my stockings with the pencil line down the back accentuate my calves, pulled taught by the high stilettos, I can practically hear him panting as I slide across the leather into the passenger seat.

Getting back into the drivers seat he pulls the seatbelt around his portly midriff, the smell of his aftershave overpowering me and I'm glad it's still sunny in the August evening, giving me an excuse to open the window. He looks everyday of his 57 years, sweat patches moisten the already yellow stains under the armpits of his white-shirt, the expensive air conditioning sits unused in the middle of the dashboard as he prods at the sat nav with his podgy finger, clearly with no idea how to use this or the air conditioning.

"Nice car" I purr, trying to look impressed.

"Yes thank you, isn't she lovely? I've not had it long (About three hours I would guess Jim) hence not knowing how this thing works, I like to change my cars often, it's a little treat to myself"

Funny how the only car registered to him is a 2004 Citroen Xsara Picasso...

"Allow me, what's the name of the place again?" I ask him as I switch on the air conditioning, desperate to get rid of some of the ripe smell in this car.

He gives me the address and I tap it in to the satnav, deftly navigating the menu as he asks me "Have you been to Coombe Abbey before?"

"No but I looked online it looks very nice, you are spoiling me" I smile at him giving him a smouldering look.

"You are very welcome my dear and I am sure you are worth it, your face does seem familiar, I wonder if we have met before?"

"I'm sure I'd remember you James, it's probably my pictures from the dating site? I feel like I've met you before too"

"No not that, like somebody famous I mean" He ponders.

"well I hope she's pretty"

"Of course my dear, I can't quite place who I mean but I'm sure you are even more beautiful than she is"

We edge through the evening traffic, my cream silk blouse clings to my breasts, I lean into the back to place my jacket on the seat making sure my body presses against his arm. Jim's eyes flick between my thighs and my chest as we crawl along.

He makes small talk and I start to ask him about his life. He's clearly practiced his bullshit, he's apparently having his house remodeled so is renting a cheap place on the outskirts of town whilst the building work takes place. Planting the seed that if he does actually manage to get me back to his dingy digs he will be able to explain it away. Not even planning on stumping up for a hotel, I'm almost offended.

He claims the boat is in Tenerife, apparently he goes there a lot, judging by the colour of his skin 'Tenerife' is more likely to be the name of a tanning salon on the High street.

The compliments flow out of his mouth like treacle, clawing at my very being. "You smell delicious" he tells me. How he can smell anything over the stench of his aftershave and stale body odour, I'll never know. "You have an elegant jaw line" "You slender hands are very beguiling" I feel like he is devouring me with his eyes. "I want to know everything about you, everything!"

106

I really do wonder if anyone falls for this type of bullshit?

I am grateful when we finally pull into the hotel car park, He opens the door for me and I take in a deep breath of the fresh evening air as he does so. He gestures towards the restaurant and walks alongside me placing his hand in the small of my back, as we approach the doors of reception I see our reflections and I must be at least eight inches taller than him in my heels. He puffs his chest out as he holds the door open, clearly pleased to be seen walking around with me.

"You are such a gentleman, it's so nice to be treated so well" I tell him through the mask, giving him my best doe eyed look. The maître de directs us to the bar.

"Champagne?"

"That would be lovely if it's not too much?"

"Nothing is too much for you my sweet angel" He orders a glass of champagne for me and a double whiskey for himself. Judging by the colour of Jim's cheeks and nose he is no stranger to a wee dram, or six.

After our drinks and another shower of sleazy compliments from Jim, we are guided to our seats in the dining room. Once again he places his hand on my back but this time lower, almost on my arse. It takes a large amount of restraint to not grab his hand and break his fingers. A few more whiskies and Jim might be fancying his chances.

Knowing that he is hammering his credit card to try and impress me, I almost feel sorry for him, still he's not going to have to pay it back so I order a bottle of champagne at £120 not the most expensive on the menu by a long way, he smiles but I notice a flicker of panic behind his eyes as I make the request. I enjoy the moment.

He orders another double whiskey to console himself, clearly drinking and driving are of no concern to him, he also orders dinner for us both, explaining the menu to me as if this is the first time I have ever encountered food, telling me what he thinks I will enjoy. To the chef's credit, he could have ordered anything and it would have been delicious. The food makes up a little for the oily company.

I can't fault Jim for his effort, the charm offensive is relentless, If I didn't already know he was lying through his teeth and if I was looking for a sugar daddy I might actually be convinced by now that he was rich. I soak up the charm and flutter my eye lashes in all the right places, making sure he gets maximum hip wiggle as I leave the room to use the bathroom.

He is on his fourth double whiskey as I return, I'm a little worried he'll actually be able to drive but he seems to be holding it together, the control and alcohol tolerance of a seasoned functioning alcoholic.

It's his turn to leave the table and once he is gone I discreetly pour most of the remaining champagne into the ice bucket, one of us needs a clear head for tonight's activities. As we get to the end of the meal, he makes a pantomime out of paying for the bill slapping his card on top of the leather folder with a flourish and pretending not to care about how much it is.

He escorts me back to the car, his hand is definitely more on my arse and less on my back now, the whiskey bolstering his confidence. "May I escort you home my dear, are you going back to the city centre?" He asks me as we reach the bottom of the steps.

"That would be lovely James but I do not live in the city centre, I'll put it into the Sat-Nav if you like"

"I think we both know that would be easier" He chortles, waving his hand as he talks. He places his hand on my knee as I type in the postcode. I look at his hand and then at him, he smiles wide, blowing whiskey fumes on me through his yellow, stained teeth. I think for a minute he is going to go in for a kiss but then he pats me on the knee and says "all in good time, all in good time"

The drive is terrifying, I do not date to take my eyes off the road as Jim narrowly avoids parked cars and kerbstones several times. I'm concerned that the police will pull us over at moment but somehow we manage to avoid being spotted.

After what seems like an eternity, the satnav finally directs him to turn right into Woodway Lane, I tell him I'm feeling a little queasy from the journey, asking him to drive to the end of the road. "But there are no houses there my dear?"

"I think I'm going to be sick James, I don't want the neighbours to hear or see me, that would be very embarrassing, I don't think I'll make it through the door in time, quickly please James" He looks panicked and pushes his foot onto the pedal accelerating to to the end of the lane, no longer concerned by the location only concerned for the impending damage to the car, I hold my mouth as if about to vomit, my wide eyes staring at him, he slams on the brakes and leans across me opening my door, practically shoving me towards it, his intent to protect the car and his deposit no longer hidden.

I lean out holding on to the door, he exits the driver's side quickly walking around to my side, placing his hand on my back and holding my hair for me with the other. As his hand gathers it up into a ponytail, my hand comes up under his and I step out of the car pushing his arm up into a straight arm lock and as I rotate towards him I place my other hand on the back of his head using the forward momentum of his now off balance body to slam his face hard into the top of the car door frame. He drops to the floor momentarily unconscious, I catch him before he falls completely putting my arms under his shoulders and pulling him to his feet trying to ignore the feel of his sweaty armpits on my bare flesh, he is dazed and confused mumbling incoherently.

I walk him towards the gap in the fence outside the derelict Craven Arms, blood runs from his mouth and three of his yellow front teeth are broken and jagged, as he starts to regain some consciousness he begins to question what's going on. "I'm bleething, whaffss happefing, where arf we?" His speech slurred and distorted by his wounds.

"You tripped Jim, it's OK we can get some help in here" I guide him in through the door and into what was once the bar pushing him down on to a mouldy old bench seat and picking up the stashed bag. I pull out some cable ties and use them to handcuff him. I take off my heels, placing them in the bag and pull on a pair of trainers, they feel like slippers compared to the pinching leather.

Jim starts to sob as he begins to regain full consciousness, taking in his surroundings through watery eyes, rivulets of blood and spit dribbling down his chin. The room is dark and mouldy, lit only by the pocket lanterns I left here and the moon light peaking through the gaps where the boards on the long broken windows have come away or been pulled off, the lights cast ghostly shadows on the walls. The floor is a carpet of rubbish and only a few sticks of broken furniture remain, most of the fixtures have been stripped for salvage or by vandals and one of the walls reports that 'Barry's mam takes it up the arse' The room has that ubiquitous piss smell familiar to all abandoned buildings.

"Wh..wh...what arf we doinf here? Are y..y...y..ou robfing me? I have mo...mo..moo fey, I can get you mofey"

I kick him hard in the balls, he yelps, almost a scream, much higher pitched than I would have expected, he slumps forward off the seat and down onto his knees on the floor amongst the rubbish. "that's a fucking lie Jim isn't it?"

"No, no I haf mofey, I can get you whaffeveer you want," His voice cracked and broken his words more distorted as terror combines with his injuries. His eyes dart around the room as if looking for escape or for a miraculous saviour to appear.

I grip his face squashing it and angling it up towards me, looking him in his eyes, squeezing hard so his jagged broken teeth dig into his lips and cheeks.

"Angela has all your money doesn't she James?"

His eyes widen as he realises I know his ex wife's name, suddenly he understands why he is here and starts to cry as the front of his trousers darken, pissing himself with fear, the gravity of the moment overcoming him. "Dear oh dear, you really are a pathetic man aren't you?" I pull him up to standing hooking my fingers under his chin, the pain forcing him to stand.

"Pleash leff me go, I'm sorry, I shouldn't haff lied" He whimpers, begging and pleading with me. Tears and snot running down his face, I pull him forward by his tied hands, dragging him over to the bar where a solitary hand pump remains, the brass top missing and the wooden handle splintered the screw-thread sticking out of the top.

"The problem is Jim, you are only sorry now that you have been caught, I bet you were sorry when Angela caught you weren't you? The problem with weak little men like you is you think you can get away with everything, that women are stupid and gullible but the truth lies closer to home. You have lived your life treating women like something that is there for your entertainment, for you to use as you see fit, lying and cheating to get what you want, I think today has proven that, hiring a car, throwing money around that you don't even have. What was your plan once you had got what you wanted? Drop me, telling me it was all my fault? I know your type James"

The terror grips him fully now, he knows he is going to die and the smell of faeces fills the air as he shits himself. He looks at the floor in shame.

I hook his hands over the remains of the pump handle so he is leaning across the bar, walking around to the other side to where the bar staff would have once stood. Imagining Jim would be the sort of person who would have letched over the female staff, making smutty comments to the young girls in their first jobs just trying to make a few quid, treating women as a plaything, something for him to enjoy and not to be respected, paying no mind to his long suffering wife at home or maybe even sat at a table waiting for him to return with the drinks.

Still Jim has no understanding of what is going on, not really, men like him never do, he's only upset for himself, not remorseful for anything he has done, maybe with one last hope of living or just out of instinct he struggles against the cable tie, trying to pull his hands up and over, his feet fighting for purchase in the rubbish strewn across the floor. He steps up on to the brass foot rail, somehow still intact maybe too heavy or difficult to remove for the scavengers who have stripped most of the interior bare. As he does I place my hands on his head and with all my weight I jump and pull down slamming his head on to the pump handle impaling his face on to the threaded end of the brass rod.

"Time gentleman please!" I say out loud to nobody. Laughing to myself.

Damn! In my excitement I hadn't really thought about getting to the heart from this position, the rib cage and scapula are going to make it difficult to get to the heart from the back. I walk back around to the other side of the bar kicking his feet off the rail so that his body slumps, grabbing his ankles to rotate his body, His face stays firmly put on the spike. I manage to spin him around enough to get access to the front of his chest, his neck twisted almost 180 degrees which is a strange and gruesome site to behold. I'm surprised at how quickly I have got used to dealing with bodies and how little this horrific scene now bothers me. What was once horrific just a few weeks ago, has almost become normal for me.

I've brought proper tools with me this time and protection in the form of arm length surgical gloves, a paper suit and an apron too. I don't want to be covered in blood or entrails when I make my exit. A scalpel makes much lighter work of the soft tissues than the dagger did and opens up his belly, I'm learning more with each kill and I've been researching anatomy and surgical techniques online. This time I manage to avoid cutting into the stomach or bowel, keeping the stench to a minimum, the smell of shit

115

emanating from his stained trousers is already enough to bear.

There's still plenty of blood though and I wait until the flow subsides, standing on the metal rail to keep my feet off of the floor and out of the rapidly extending blood puddle.

Pushing myself up on to the bar and standing above him my legs astride him, I use a small Bahco Laplander tree saw to cut up through the sternum, the sharp serrated blade designed for cutting branches making quick work of the job. I wedge in a piece of broken wood discarded on top of the bar and with as much force as I can exert, I use it to lever the broken rib cage apart, exposing his heart and lungs. I take the scalpel and cut a chunk of it out and drop it into the waiting jar. I take the other jar from my bag pouring some of the mixed congealed rotting contents into his chest cavity and replacing it with some of his bodily fluids to use next time. Using my gloved hands I smear it around, spreading the entrail cocktail over as as many things as possible, confusing the DNA trail but also tying all of the crimes together, leaving no uncertainty that it's the Queen of Hearts work.

I take the spray can from my bag and write on the wall where the optics once hung.

"And tearing love apart"

Flopping his body back over and onto the bar I skewer the playing card on to the end of the screw protruding from the back of his skull.

Carefully I pack all my items back into the bag then strip off the apron and gloves and shove them in too. I take a minute to reflect, working backwards in my head remembering if I have touched anything or left anything that could give me away, after retracing my steps a few times I'm good to go. I note how much calmer I feel this time.

I linger in the doorway checking my exit, the Jaguar is still sitting in the middle of the road with the passenger door open but undisturbed, still making a pinging sound to let the driver know the lights are on and the door is open, unlike the car Jim's lights are definitely out.

I wait and watch for a few moments in case anyone is outside. …. Slipping out the door quietly and back to the car, wiping down the Sat-Nav screen and everything else I have touched, the fire will destroy them but the heat can burn the fingerprint grease into a permanent record especially if the fire brigade put it out before it is fully consumed.

As I won't be around to watch it, I'm not taking any risks. Grabbing a small squeezy bottle from my bag, I squirt petrol onto the seats, dashboard and roof lining, holding my lighter into the stream. The fumes ignite with a small whumph sound and the bottle becomes a mini flame thrower, once the fuel runs out I chuck the lighter into the car, dropping the bag of clothes and tools into the flames.

With the heat at my back I walk to the end of the road and onto the green metal steps, a small waterproof backpack on my back contains the heart in its jar and the remaining entrails in the other. Walking on to the footbridge crossing the motorway I pause turning back just once to reassure myself that the fire is burning, I can see the orange glow from the car as the flames begin to take hold.

I jog over the footbridge, a few cars whizz along the motorway underneath their lights blazing a trail in the darkness, no chance of them identifying more than an outline of a person should anyone recall me. I take the stairs down the other side into the darkness, moving quickly but careful with my footing, on to the sports-park, a few lights illuminate the path that joins it back to the lane but I choose to jog across the dark field, staying off the track and onto the grass, using the hue of distant light from the houses to guide me. It takes no more than a few minutes to cross the parkland and to find my way to the back of the pavilion, everything looks different in the darkness, disorientating my sense of where I left my bag so I use a small Maglite to locate it.

I pull on the leathers there is a distant explosion, maybe the petrol tank or perhaps a tyre, there is also the growing sound of sirens, probably just fire engines at this stage but time to get out of here. All the unwanted attention will be drawn to the other side of the motorway for a while but there is no point in hanging around, besides the noise even though some distance away might start to arouse the homeowners on this side of the park. I unlock the bike and start the engine, easing out the clutch and rolling quietly away down the lane.

It won't be long now until I'm in the press again, which reminds me I have a letter to post.

Hi Liz,

Thanks for the piece you did on me last month, it was nice to finally have my work acknowledged. I enjoyed your write up and hopefully some of the men out their will sit up and start to take notice. I've enclosed some more pictures for you, I know you can't use them in your work but I hope they will inspire your next article. My story will be revealed all in good time and as it does I'll make sure you are at the forefront of it.

*I chose the last one as he liked to tell lies just ask his ex-wife about him **'Tearing Love Apart'** This time he got caught red handed or should I say red faced? This one was for all the women who have been cheated on and lied to.*

I'll be in touch soon,

Q.O.H

Who do you think you are?

Runnin' round leaving scars

Collecting your jar of hearts

And tearing love apart

You're going to catch a cold

From the ice inside your soul

So don't come back for me

Don't come back at all

120

Chapter 4

As a child our step mother was an avid reader, she loved those books, certainly she gave them more attention than she ever showed to my brother and I. Our own mum had died when Charlie and I were 10, As twins we had always been pretty close unlike some brothers and sisters.

Dad married Carol pretty soon after mum died, she was our god mother and had know our parents for years. I think she had always fancied dad and after mum died he had no idea what to do with us kids, she was suddenly around a lot to console him, I think he was just grateful that somebody was prepared to help him out.

Dad was an oil and gas engineer, so was away for prolonged periods of time on the rigs, I think when Carol made it clear she was still available and pretty much threw herself at him he just went with it, allowing her to pick up some of the slack that mum had left behind. I think he felt grateful and duty bound to her after all the help she had given him I imagine he was pretty lonely too and as she was familiar he just took the path of least resistance.

Their romance was quick, definitely driven and controlled by her and within just three months of them starting to see each other she was living in our house. By the end of month four, she had all but eradicated mums memory from the home.

Her campaign to 'update the house and put her stamp on it' was relentless and a large part of this was the bookcases. She had a huge collection of books and all she seemed to want to do was sit around reading, to be left alone in peace and quiet, this suited Charlie and I, we wanted as little to do with her as possible too.

What had once been a fun house became tinged with mum's death, then when she moved everything of mum out, it no longer felt like our home. She spent all day reading her beloved books and TV shopping, Dad earned good money and we didn't want for anything at home but all we really wanted was his love and time. Don't misunderstand me, she wasn't directly cruel or anything, there was always food in the fridge and she prepared meals for us, we had a cleaner that came every week and the washing was done but there was never any affection, no love other than the consideration of our physical needs. I wonder if dad knew this? I guess he never thought about it.

Charlie and I were mostly left to fend for ourselves, for some reason adults don't hide adult themed books from kids in the same way they do other age inappropriate things and it's easy to squirrel away a book and read for hours without anyone being concerned. We loved all of the gory horror and thriller books that we found.

Whilst most girls my age we're reading smash hits, I was reading James Herbert, Stephen King, Dean Koontz and Shaun Hutson amongst others, I can't remember who discovered this stuff first, my brother or I but we were both vociferous readers. We would read a book each in secret and then spend ages telling each other snippets of the gory details, whetting our appetites but saving the twists so we could swap and read it ourselves, dying for the other to finish it so we could talk about it in detail.

It was around this time I discovered her erotica collection of Anais Nin and Pauline Reage. It was embarrassing at first, reading the graphic descriptions of sex and I used to lock my self in the toilet to read them in case I got caught. I was about thirteen at the time, puberty had already kicked in and I was aware of what sex was from school, however the changing room chats about kissing and fingering were a world apart from the beautifully described acts I was reading about.

I didn't tell Charlie first of all, I wasn't sure what he would think about it, I had no idea how to bring it up anyway or how to describe how these stories made me feel. It was a weekend day and we bumped into each other as I as coming out of the toilet and I dropped the book from under my sweatshirt.

He picked it up and started reading the back, I guess expecting it to be one of the usual horror type novels we liked. There had been talk of sex in some of the books we had read but we always avoided talking about those scenes to each other.

He blushed as he realised what he was reading then looked at me intently, holding my gaze. "Where did you find this?" he asked.

"On the book case in the hallway upstairs, there are lots of them" I couldn't look him in the eye instead staring sheepishly at the carpet my cheeks on fire.

He turns and walks up the stairs and I follow him, my legs feel shaky.

"How many have you read?"

"Four"

I can recall looking at my feet again, my face still hot with embarrassment.

"Why didn't you share them with me?"

"I don't know Charlie, I was sort of embarrassed" I look up at him, he's still holding my gaze.

"You don't need to be, not with me, we're twinnies, let me read one, which one did you read first?"

"This one" I hand him Delta of Venus. "But Charlie, it's... It's very..... detailed"

I try to urge him not to read it, feeling as if my secrets will be exposed, that some how he will know what I have been thinking.

"I'll be fine" He takes the book from my hand ignoring my pleas, smiles at me reassuringly and walks into his room, closing the door behind him.

I lay on my bed cringing, what will Charlie think of me as he reads those intimate stories, will he think the same thoughts, what if he is disgusted by them? What if he tells Dad??

It's dark and late by the time I hear a knock on my door. "It's me, can I come in?"

He comes in and sits next to me on the bed, I look at him, my cheeks flush red again but I need to know so I ask him "What did you think?"

"Alice you were right about it being detailed, I can see why you were embarrassed, but I read it all, I couldn't stop myself. The stories made me feel...excited, it's not like the conversations the boys have at school, they makes sex sound like a gross thing, this makes it sound beautiful"

We've never talked about sex before, I didn't expect Charlie to be this open about it even though we've always shared everything else and been open with each other.

"I know, I like it too, it makes you wonder if it really feels like that, and if it does why are adults so miserable all the time"

"How does it make you feel?" He asks. I don't know where to begin, I'm not even sure I know how to describe it. My face feels like a constant state of beetroot

"You first"

"It makes my heart race and my stomach feel funny, whenever I read about crazy people or murders I'm grossed out but it's fun to read about. Not this, this doesn't repulse me, it makes me feel a yearning to feel like that"

"Me too, it makes my body tingle, I've had books make my hairs stand on end or give me goose bumps, but this is different, it feels nice. It does other things to me too"

It's Charlie's turn to look embarrassed.

"Like what?"

"You know, down there, it makes me feel tingly"

Charlie looks coy and sheepish and then says "Me too, it makes it stick up" I giggle Charlie looks embarrassed for a moment then punches me in the arm and giggles back at me. I push him and he wrestles with me.

I'm not sure how it happened exactly but in seconds we are kissing. Slow, wet kisses, gently exploring our mouths hot against each other.

"Wait Charlie stop, we shouldn't" He stops and looks at me.

"Why?" he enquires? I pause, it feels so natural with him, I love him so why not? I don't know remember what I thought I just remember it didn't feel wrong, and I didn't want it to stop, he was my best friend, my closest ally and protector. It felt the opposite, a closeness that had been missing for a long time in my life and with the one person I trusted more than anyone else.

He rolls me on to my back, his weight feels nice upon me and he kisses me again. We hold each other just kissing like this for a while. It's me that makes the first move. I can feel it 'sticking up' against my leg and I push my hand inside the waistband of his trousers, touching him for the first time. He doesn't resist me, I try to remember what they did in the stories I had read, moving it up and down slowly, scared to hurt him. He rolls on to his side next to me, putting his hand up my skirt and pulls my knickers to one side. His fingers clumsily push at my virginal parts, not sure where to go, so I take hold of his hand and position his finger at the entrance to my vagina.

He too is gentle, edging in just a small bit at a time, it hurts a little as he does, opening me up for the first time and I whimper. He flinches but I whisper to him that it's ok, gently stroking him inside his trousers still. He pushes all the way into me, my pussy resists and it hurts but then suddenly it is inside me and it feels different, pleasurable.

My senses are on high alert and everything is sensitive to his touch. He moves his finger in and out of me slowly, I respond stroking him a little faster, suddenly he grunts and I feel a hot liquid on my hand inside his trousers. He grabs my hand pulling it out, suddenly too sensitive to touch. He takes his hand away from me and we both see blood on his fingers,

Charlie looks scared as if he has hurt me "It's ok I read about it, it can happen the first time for girls, it didn't hurt me" I reassure him. I take some make up wipes off the bedside cabinet cleaning my hand and his.

He looks embarrassed but I have never felt more content than I do in this moment. He tries to speak but I just push my head into his chest pulling him closer to me.

We must have fallen asleep like this and when I awake it's 3am and he is gone. I get up to pee and wander into his room, wanting to feel him close to me again. I crawl into his bed, awaking him a little but he doesn't protest, just telling me to lock the door. Then he is lifting the duvet to let me under, into the warm sanctuary of his arms. We both lose our virginity that night.

Life couldn't have felt more perfect for the next few weeks. We could come and go as we pleased in the house and spent most of our time together. Reading on each others beds limbs intertwined, we both stopped reading the erotica, it wasn't a conscious thing but I think we just wanted to find things for ourselves. Our times together weren't like the descriptions in the book, they were simpler, gentler, arms wrapped around each other kissing with intensity our bodies moving slowly against each other. We didn't spend all our time fooling around, most of our time was just spent in each others company doing the same things as before, whenever I was away from him, I longed to be near him.

My first murder was difficult, I cried for days after that one, I was so petrified after it happened and spent five days locked in my apartment panicking that I was going to get caught but eventually I realised I had got away with it and started to explore how it had felt, the revenge.

Louis was Charlie's best friend, It was the following summer after Charlie and I had kissed for the first time, I was 14 and a group of us used to hang around the Old Town recreation ground in the evenings sitting on the swings or the benches, smoking and drinking, chatting about the usual teenage stuff.

One night I was laying on the big circular swing, gazing up at the stars, I can't remember why

Charlie wasn't there that night but how I wished he had been. Louis came and sat on the edge of the swing, he flirted with me sometimes but only when Charlie wasn't around and had asked me a few times to 'go out with him' I obviously couldn't tell him about Charlie but as far as I was concerned I only had eyes for one person.

We had both been drinking a little and maybe that's what changed it for him. He lay down next to me, I could feel his breath on my neck.

"Why won't you go out with me?"

"You're my brothers best friend, it wouldn't be right"

"Charlie won't care"

"I don't see you like that Louis, you're more like a brother to me"

"Come on, I see you looking at me too" With that he put his arm across my chest and kissed me. I tried to pull away not wanting him to touch me, he was stronger than me, I don't know why I didn't fight harder but I just gave up and let him kiss me. He rolled on to his side, his leg thrown over mine, pinning me on to the swing. Before I knew it, his hand was in the waistband of my tracksuit bottoms and sliding down into my knickers as he did so, I squirmed and tried to cry out but he pushed his mouth against mine so I couldn't.

130

His hand pushed underneath mine as I tried to grab at it, over my recently sprouted tuft of pubic hair and then he was roughly pushing his fingers against me, trying to find my entrance. I squirmed against him, it hurt and I wanted him to stop put he pressed down on me eventually forcing two fingers inside me. I wanted to scream out but the brutal invasion made me freeze, I just let myself go limp my mouth no longer fought his kisses.

After a minute he realised I was not responding and looked down at me as if disgusted, the boy I had known since I was a child transformed into a sneering pig "you're frigid" he said then pushed himself off, "you better not tell Charlie that you let me finger you" I felt violated and humiliated but there was no way I could tell my brother, I could feel the wetness in my knickers and I hated my body for responding to him. I simply stood up and walked away, the tears stinging my cheeks as the voices carried on behind me as if nothing had happened.

I tried to forget about it, showering until my skin was sore, unable to wash away the dirty feeling. , I avoided Louis at school and kept my distance from Charlie for a few days, fearful that somehow he would know. He came back from school two nights later and stormed into my room. "I can't believe you got off with Louis and didn't tell me" He shouted, his face red, angry. "You betrayed me, we always agreed we would discuss it with each other first if we wanted to be with someone else"

"It wasn't like that..."

"James saw you both, kissing on the park, Louis had his hand in your knickers, I think it's exactly like that" He stormed out of my room, his face red with anger, tears welling in his eyes. He marched to his bedroom slamming the door. I tried to follow him but his door was locked, he turned up his music as loud as possible, ignoring my futile knocking.

I went back to my room and threw myself on my bed sobbing, my heart broken. I hoped I'd be able to reason with him, but true to his word Charlie never touched me again. Once I explained to him, he said that I could have stopped him if I had wanted to, that Louis wasn't like that, he could never be sure what had happened and that it was time for us to stop, it was wrong what we were doing anyway. I begged, pleaded, told him that I would never love anyone else but he pushed me away. I needed him more than ever and he had forsaken me.

Our relationship changed from that moment forward, I loved him dearly and just wanted him to hold me but he kept his distance, our book swapping stopped and Charlie retracted more and more into himself and I was left adrift.

I vowed that one day that I would get my revenge on Louis, I had no idea what shape that revenge would take or even if I could do anything. I'd pushed it all deep down inside me and tried to move on with my life when the opportunity to do something presented itself to me.

I had not long finished university and was living in West London, renting a small one bedroom flat. One evening I was scrolling through Facebook on a school alumni page. One of those things you stumble on in the empty weekend hours when you could be doing something worthwhile or fulfilling but instead you worship the screen, flicking mindlessly through endless reams of inane nonsense.

I was reminiscing and having a voyeuristic look at some old school friends and suddenly there he was, my stomach lurched, the old wounds instantly torn back open. I shouldn't have been surprised to see him on the pages but I hadn't thought about it.

He was older obviously, he'd always been one of the cool good looking guys at school, with swagger in his step and a cockiness that said he knew ir.. Here he was now, in a blue suit, shit coloured brown shoes and a shirt and tie, his hair slicked back. I didn't need to read his profile to confirm that he was an estate agent he just had that spiv look about him. There was a group chatting on the page about tonight's meet up, an unofficial reunion for somebodies birthday. Many of my peer group still lived in Eastbourne, from reading the messages I could see that Louis had written 'heading down soon guys, can't wait to see ya all, it'll be good to get out of Tunbridge Wells for a night and see the old Eastbourne haunts, where we meeting first?'

As soon as I knew where he was going to be, something took hold of me and I decided I was going to go and see him, I didn't even know if I was going to speak to him or confront him but everything I held dear had been taken away from me and a big part of that was down to him. Seeing his face and seeing how unaffected his life appeared to be made my blood boil. How dare he think everything was OK when he had stolen so much from me.

That evening I drove back to my home town, I had no plan, just bitter anger in my heart. I waited outside the Dolphin pub on South Street, the first destination for their meet up. My stomach lurched when I saw him walking in, still with that cocky 'I can do anything I want' swagger.

I ducked down in my car and I didn't go into the pub, I just sat there waiting for him to come out. I followed the group to the next pub and the next one after that, finally around midnight he left the group and staggered back drunk to his hotel on the seafront, his arm around a woman I didn't recognise but I guessed might have been from our school days.

I slept in the car that night, parked right on the seafront outside his hotel, facing the front door, it was a restless sleep, jerking awake every few minutes in a panic that I had missed him. By the time the morning came I knew I was going to follow him home and confront him there, so I waited for him to come out of his hotel and I watched him carry his bag to the car.

I followed him all the way back to Tunbridge Wells, how he didn't spot me I'll never know, but I tried my best to drive out of sight, yet still keep up it, the A22 is one long road to Tunbridge Wells so I knew he wasn't likely to turn off and if I stayed back far enough he wouldn't spot me. It was just over an hour until we reached his home, I swear I didn't blink on that journey, concentrating on not loosing him or being spotted, all I could think about was what I was going to say to him, the anger gnawing away at my insides.

The hour had turned my anger into a rage, I sat along the street from his house and waited until it was dark, I still didn't have a plan other than to confront him but figured darkness would be safer, once I was sure he lived on his own I knocked on his door, then I panicked suddenly aware of how vulnerable I was and I stooped picking up a wine bottle for defence from his recycling box as I did so. As he opened the door, I don't know what compelled me to do what I did next, mostly fear at the situation I had put myself in I think, the realisation dawning just as it was too late to turn back.

He peered out looking puzzled and uttered a simple 'Yeah?' I smashed him full in the face with the flat bottom of the bottle, his nose split, blood jetting from his nostrils instantly and the hard glass had left a vicious looking cut across the bridge. As he let out a shrill scream, he stumbled backwards onto his arse, his hands clutching at his face. I quickly walked forwards into his house and closed the front door behind me, the Adrenalin pumping through my veins making my hands tremble and my heart beat audibly inside my head.

As he tried to get up I swung the bottle as hard as I could upwards like a cricket bat, glancing it off his jaw, he fell backwards hitting his head on the bottom step of the staircase and slumped unconscious to the floor.

When he woke up he found himself naked on the living room carpet his hands and feet roped together with his own neck wear hastily sourced from his wardrobe. I'd tied him up whilst I decided what to do with him. My Adrenalin had kicked into over drive and I had to run to use his toilet hoping to hell that he didn't wake up.

When he did finally come round, he had no idea who I was, I was forced to stuff tissues into his mouth to drown out the pathetic sobs, scared the neighbours might hear him, I almost felt sorry for him and nearly let him go there and then, I had no idea what I was doing or what I was going to do I hadn't thought that far ahead, maybe I could talk to him and then let him go?

As I explained to him who I was and why I had followed him, his eyes began to widen in realisation and terror. I tried to calm him down, telling him it would be ok, if he just listened and understood what he had done and the pain he had caused, but he didn't listen, he went into panic mode and struggled furiously managing to get one of his hands free. It was my turn to panic, with his loose hand he lurched at me, I stepped out of the way and as I did, I swung the bottle in a wide arc, the thick glass connecting fully with the side of his head.

I knew before he hit the floor that the blow had killed him, a large dent in the side of his skull leaving me with little doubt about that. I began to hyperventilate, running around in shock I quickly wiped around anything I might have touched. I was crying, I couldn't look at his body and was about to flee when something made me look back at him through the streams of tears, I hadn't meant to kill him, maybe just frighten him or something, then as I looked it suddenly became clear, a switch had been flicked, a line had been crossed. I had done something that could not be undone.

Suddenly a feeling of calm descended, a sense of separation from the bounds and rules of normal life, I had dealt with him, I had conquered my nemesis. All I had wanted was for him to suffer and feel a bit of what I had suffered, to feel the terror at being helpless at another persons hand but it was too late for that now, at least he would never be able to hurt anyone again.

I took a bit longer cleaning up before I left being careful to cover my tracks, I'd seen enough CSI programmes to think about fingerprints but no clue what else I should be doing. I tried to position his body at the bottom of the stairs so it looked like an accident, laying the bottle on the floor under his head as if he had landed on it somehow, I assumed I would immediately get caught, that the police somehow were already on their way but instinct drove me to try to get away with it.

The next few days were a living hell, sitting in my rented flat, constantly moving between twitching the curtains and lying on the sofa, my stomach churning, not sleeping expecting at any minute my door to be smashed in by the police. Watching every news channel and bulletin I could find. Paranoid to use the internet to search for more details in case hits on his name would trigger a flag somewhere and the full force of the law would descend upon me.

I couldn't eat and I was terrified, not once however did I feel guilty for him I only feared for my own freedom, the old adage that time is a great healer rang true. The sensation of fear subsides, the longer the absence of challenge by authoritarian or divine forces the more you relax. Once you realise you may have gotten away with it, you start to become calm. From there it is not a huge leap and again the passage of time to begin to appreciate that if you plan and control, then the risk of getting caught becomes manageable.

As the months past after Charlie stopped talking to me, he became really introverted and angry, jumping on to any cause that he could direct his anger at. He was always civil with me in passing but we never really talked and I couldn't help feel it was me his anger was really towards.

There was not much point being at home so I stayed at school as long as I could each day. Some kids go off the rails but the friends I had were also Charlie's friends and worse they were also friends with Louis. I drifted away from the group, keeping myself to myself. Not wanting to be at home with Carol or feeling the tension from Charlies room seeping under his doorway, staying at school seemed the easiest option. I put all my energy into studying, determined to make something of myself and get away from this town and these people.

By the time I was sixteen I had completed all my G.C.S.E's and started my A-levels, Charlie and I barely saw each other and even when we did we still never really talked. I passed my A-Levels and knew I wanted to study money or rather how to make it. Whenever I could get Charlie to engage in any conversation he would rant on about the corruption in the world, seemingly angry at my choices, he would tell me how evil the world was and how the bankers controlled everything and had all the money. I told him I knew all that so why shouldn't I I figure out how to get some of it, I applied for a place at the London School of Economics and was accepted, it looked like the start of a new chapter for me, a chance to get away from it all.

Then Dad died.

Those days were awful, Dad hadn't been around much with being on the rigs a lot of the time but he had always loved us and provided for us. He was the constant thread of safety holding the family together, someone to turn to and lean on in times of need and now he was gone. I was utterly alone, unable to reach out to Charlie I was totally isolated and the grief took over me. I think it hit him even harder than me, he had always idolised our dad, seeing him as a big hero especially after mum died, he was close to both of them, we both were but he was much more sensitive than me. Where he had been insular and withdrawn before he became practically a ghost.

Carol was still downstairs clinging on to whatever financial gains she could make out of dad's estate, she wanted to sue the oil company even though Dad had died of a heart attack whilst asleep in his bunk. As the executor she harangued me to recruit an expensive lawyer and to stake a claim but I knew dad wouldn't have wanted that so I resisted it. Dad liked his job and the company had been good to him over the years, he'd been able to provide a good living standard for his family and had been proud of what he did. After I refused the house became unbearable, she became more and more bitter towards me picking over the bones of our family possessions. I think she was just sad at his loss too, she waited all those years to have him and then lost him herself.

I confined myself to my room and distracted myself with studying even harder than before, when I wasn't studying I was trying to find solace in others, using dating sites to find empty meaningless sex, craving some attention. I think Carol had expected dad to leave the house to her but thankfully he left it to Charlie and I. Charlie departed for university as soon as he could washing his hands of everything, choosing journalism as his subject, saying that he could only make a real change by letting people know what was happening in the world.

He left me to deal with the settlement of Dad's estate, I left too, I couldn't bare to be in that house anymore, leaving her there with her books, clinging on to the bitter end until she was legally forced to leave. I never went back to that house after that, I just put it on the market and took the first offer we got. Charlie barely even cared when I told him. I took my place at university, I was surrounded by money hungry people and I learned a lot, glad of the distraction, it was great to be surrounded by positivity for once rather than doom and gloom but it was hard to fit in. I felt like a cloud hung over me and I wasn't able to share a large part of my life.

As I had enough to live on from the house sale, I started day trading with my student grant, it was good to be in the big city and meeting new people and for short periods I felt like I was moving on with my life.

Dad had left us a fair bit, after mums untimely death he had got a big chunk as a insurance payment. Working on the rigs all the time he had saved most of his money and the house had been inherited from his parents. We ended up with just shy of £600,000 each but I'd have given back every penny to have Dad back or Charlie talking to me properly.

I went to see Charlie once after Dad died, it felt like maybe a chance to have a reconciliation. I took the train up to see him at his university, booking into a hotel in Leeds and meeting him in the city centre in a pub. I was hoping we could clear the air at least, maybe we wouldn't be romantic with each other but perhaps we could be friends again like we used to be, start a fresh now that mum and dad were gone and we only had each other.

He hadn't told me before I arrived but Charlie had a girlfriend, he brought her along to the pub, it felt to me like it was to prove a point, parading her in front of me like he wanted to make me jealous. I guessed he was really into her, he couldn't stop looking at her, avoiding eye contact with me, she was a show off, she had a necklace that Charlie had bought her that day, one of those hearts that has half the letters on one side and half on the other and when you spin it 'it spells out I Love You.

She kept spinning it, I couldn't stop staring at her the anger and jealousy building up inside me. Charlie looking everywhere but at me. He kept talking about how she was going to shake up the system with her ideas, I couldn't see what the attraction for him with her was? Charlie was a socialist who wanted to use his journalism for the power of good. She was direct action which I'm sure he liked but not a force for good. She was harder, tougher than him; more out for making a name for herself than intent on changing the world.

My brother was a sensitive soul that took everything to heart and I could see she had him wrapped around her finger, doing all the talking and bossing him around.

Unable to bare to see him fawning all over her and unwilling to play along with the charade, I told him I didn't feel well, 'must have been something I ate on the train'. It was true that I was sick, but not in that way, I went back to my hotel room throwing myself onto the bed in floods of tears, just like I had done several years before. I messaged him later that night to say I was too ill to see him, I didn't even stay the night I just checked out and went home on.

That was the last time I saw him.

Five months later he was dead too.

Chapter 5

'Banrigh Writes' Exclusive

KILLER STRIKES AGAIN Calls time on cheater

Murder in Coventry

As you will know from our main headlines, the Queen of Hearts has struck again. I have exclusive information that she has once again sent directly to me. She alleges that he was using a dating profile via an undisclosed app to attract younger women with the pretence of providing for them financially or what is often referred to as a 'sugar daddy'.

According to my investigations he was actually heavily in debt and had recently been divorced from his estranged wife who it is believed, filed adultery as the cause of the demise of her marriage. Clearly a person has lost their life here and it would not be right to speculate but it does make you wonder if he would have become a statistic if his moral compass was a little more in tune.

Police have asked me not to give away too many details of the crime as it may hamper their ongoing investigations but it is believed that the victim was found in a derelict pub, in what was described as, a 'very disturbing scene'. The body had been partly mutilated. I revealed to you last time in my exclusive that a Queen of Hearts playing card was found at the previous scenes.

This rings true in this case and the police have informed me that they believe the four murders are indeed linked. Having examined phone and internet records from the victims, the police believe that she is using dating apps to attract and approach her victims.

The police have asked me not to but I feel it is in the public interest to exclusively reveal a very gruesome detail. The killer appears to be removing her victim's hearts as some sort of grisly souvenir, each time leaving a line from the chorus of a song. The song is called 'Jar of Hearts' and is by the American artist Christina Perri

The chorus contains the following lines:

Who do you think you are?

Runnin' round leaving scars

Collecting your jar of hearts

And tearing love apart

You're going to catch a cold

From the ice inside your soul

So don't come back for me

don't come back at all.

I am aware that so far she has left the first four lines of the chorus, one at each murder. I do not want to speculate but could this suggest that she plans to kill at least four more people?

The police have issued a statement that mirrors these thoughts and warns that 'people should be vigilant when using any form of dating app as this appears to be how she is approaching her victims you should only meet people in public places and ensure that a friend or relative knows where you are going, calling them to check in at regular intervals. Whilst Covid restrictions have been relaxed we should all be distancing as much as possible and only meeting where necessary'.

Their statement also advised not to be too worried, millions of people have safe dates and meet each other every single day. Personally I wouldn't be so sure, I can't help but think if I was a man right now I might be experiencing a little of the fear that woman have felt every single day of their lives from men.

I have of course passed all relevant information from her letters to the police and will assist them as much as possible in their investigations but will keep my readers as informed as possible.

*I too was in the Midlands this week in Birmingham City Centre signing copies of my book **'Bang to Rights'** If you would like to get your hands on a copy, details of more dates are on page 22 along with the second part of my series on serial killers.*

I think about the article and what she has written. She is not the sort of person I would normally want to be associated with, her Wikipedia page presents a ruthless investigator who stops at nothing to get to the truth, it also looks like she doesn't let victim pain or suffering get in the way of a good story. Her recent book has definitely sparked controversy, however she is the only person who can give me what I need. Her Wiki reads like this:

Early life and education

Born Elizabeth Mary Banrigh in November 1991 in Stranraer Scotland Her Father from modest working class background was a local Bank Manager and her Mother a seamstress. She won a part scholarship to the Wellington School in Ayre as a secondary school pupil and graduated with A-Level in English Language and Media.

From there she studied journalism at Leeds university. Graduating in 2014 with a First class honours degree.

Early career

Whilst in her second year of university she made headlines with an article published in the Daily Mail where she exposed the University Vice Chancellor Mark Tweedle in a 'Honey Trap' which resulted in his investigation by the police and expulsion from his job which undoubtedly contributed to the breakdown of his marriage.

The article described how she had intimate relations with the Chancellor in his office on several occasions, that she alleged were cultivated and driven by him, preying on an innocent student. In a counter argument it is suggested that Ms Banrigh was actually the one that pursued the family man who had an otherwise exemplary record. It has been widely reported that Ms Banrigh used her boyfriend at the time to unwittingly expose Mr Tweedle. Whilst police investigated at the time no charges were brought against Either Mr Tweedle or Ms Banrigh.

She started her journalistic career as a trainee with the Mirror group and made her name within 12 months when she exposed the 70s and 80's pop star and Radio broadcaster 'Buck White' as a prolific paedophile. She posed online as a young girl, building up several hours of damning conversations and picture evidence. The subsequent article she published lead to the arrest and investigation of Mr White and to her heavy involvement in the channel 4 Dispatches programme on the same subject. It is believed that her investigation into Mr White sparked the still ongoing, operation Kingfisher started by the Metropolitan Police in 2016.

Current career

Banrigh has written extensively as a freelancer as well as for the Telegraph and Independent and be named reporter of the year, journalist of the year and feature writer of the year at the British Press Awards.

She produced an article on Female genital mutilation within Britain for the Telegraph newspaper that won the Bevins prize for investigative journalism in 2018 being praised for her 'outstanding efforts to expose the truth that nobody wanted to hear'

In 2019 she was awarded the Paul Foot award for her piece 'Behind closed doors' on domestic violence in modern Britain for The Independent. However then the award was later redacted amongst controversy that she had infiltrated a safe house posing as a victim. Potentially denying a place to a legitimate subject of abuse, risking the anonymity of the other residents and extracting their stories under false pretences. She used this information to confront the alleged assailants which could have further endangered the lives of the vulnerable women. When questioned Ms Banrigh said that 'People need to hear the truth about this and the reluctance to expose these men by the women involved simply underlines the depth of fear held by them'

Despite the controversy she retains her column at The Telegraph and has produced a book giving her version of events called 'Bang to Rights'

She has appeared as a guest on a number of Television and Radio panel and chat shows including Question Time, Who's line is it anyway and Radio 4s today programme.

Recently she has been publishing articles relating to an alleged serial killer who has given themselves the moniker of "The Queen of Hearts" The alleged killer has written letters directly to Banrigh revealing details of the crimes. This has caused further controversy amongst other members of the press, questioning whether Ms Banrigh should be publishing these details as it potentially encourages the perpetrator to commit further crimes. The Telegraph has seen an increase in sales when these articles are published and have claimed that revealing the details is 'in the public interest'.

Nice to see I too have made it on to Wikipedia already, no doubt I'll get my very own page soon.

I've headed back to the south coast for a few weeks to what I guess you could call home, I have a cottage that I bought a few years ago tucked into the South downs in Crowlink just West of the town I grew up in. It's my safe haven, ten minutes walk one way and you're in Friston Forest, ten minutes the other direction and you are overlooking the sea at the cliff edges of the Seven Sisters. I can walk or run and clear my head, which is what I was doing this morning. I took a walk out of the cottage turned right and headed out towards the cliffs, the sun was rising up on what was going to be a good day and the sea was calm with barely a breeze.

The track from my cottage brings you out in the middle of one of the dips between two of the 'Sisters'. Once at the cliff tops I bore east heading up over the hilltop and down the other side to Birling Gap which, sits nestled in the hills on the coastline, to grab a coffee from the visitors centre.

I like walking here, It gives me time to reflect and regroup.Four lines of the song in, four more to go, the Queen of Hearts will be retired soon after that.

Sitting on one of the benches overlooking the sea and down on to the pebble beach, I observe a guy walking his dog, the dog barks at him and he is trying to catch it to put it back on the lead. The dog is a scruffy looking leggy thing, mostly collie and probably some greyhound, he looks like he is living his best life, having fun barking and running into the sea every time he gets close. The man with the lead is getting more and more agitated as the dog goads him, I can hear him shouting at the dog although his words remain indecipherable over the sound of the sea and gulls swooping over head.

He appears to give up and walks off, stomping up the pebble beach his shoulders tight and his hands bunched into fists at his sides. I can see he is fuming from where I sit, his face red under his baseball cap.

I smile as the dog bounds out of the waves after him, approaching him from behind nudging at his hand with his nose as if to say I'm back now. He leans down and grabs the dog by the collar and as he does punches him hard on the top of his head! I can hear the dog yelp from where I sit which is a good thirty metres away.

The metal steps lead up from the beach, it's a few stories up the cliff face and into the car park. I finish my coffee and walk out of the café standing as if looking out to sea, another walker just taking in the view. The man with the dog passes me, as he does I bend, pretending to tie my shoe lace, the dog sniffs at me and I hold out my hand to stroke his head but the man yanks on his lead. "Fucking come on you prick". The dog cowers, he drags it past the bowl of water left purposefully for dogs and ties him up outside the café as he goes inside. I walk over, dropping down onto my haunches, holding out a gentle hand the dog tentatively sniffs it and allows me to stroke him. I can feel lumps under his fur that don't belong there, and there is definitely some matted blood on one of his legs. Lurchers are usually skinny but there is something hungry looking about this dog.

I pick up the water bowl and carry it across to him, fuck the guy, he can think what he likes. I leave it there and watch the dog drink greedily for a moment before I walk off in the direction of the Belle Tout light house.

I pause for a while by the coastguard building pretending to be looking at the boat and as I glance back to see the man untying the dog, he looks puzzled by the bowl but pays it little attention. He walks towards me, intent on taking the same path up to the clifftop lighthouse, yanking violently on the dogs collar anytime he so much as strays an inch from walking at heel. He passes me without acknowledgment, i estimate him to be mid twenties, he is not ideally dressed for a cliff top walk, his outfit is more suited for swearing loudly outside McDonalds. He wears the ubiquitous Adidas tracksuit bottoms that hang half way down his arse; I wonder if he knew that this trend emanates from the American penal system, and was once a signal in prison to demonstrate homosexual availability whether he would still wear them like this? He doesn't look cool enough to be openly gay.

On his feet are Black Air Max trainers with an over inflated shiny sole that were probably designed for the basketball court not the South Downs. His outfit is completed by a hoodie and a baseball cap and one of those small Nike shoulder bags worn across the body, big enough to hold his fags and weed probably.

I wonder how these two came to be together, they seem an unlikely couple, following at a short distance the sound travels from his phone conversation and I get the gist of what he is saying.

"Allright bruv, yeah man I'm up at Beachy Head in'it?.......... Yeah kicked me out mate, she's a slag, ...constantly giving me ear ache.......Banging on about getting a job an that, couldn't be doing with it fam, girl needs to let mans do his owe ting and stay out of mans business, you get me?........... Yeah yeah, I know, she was happy when she was smoking mans weed though in it? complaining that I don't give her any money and stay at her gaff all the time..........nah mate......Needed to show her who's boss though so I took her I-pad mate, sold it on e-bay hahahaha, I took her fucking dog too but nobody wants to buy the thing, I thought dogs was worth money these days with lock down but they needs to be a pedigree or somat...... it's mental, doesn't do anything I tell it......That's where I am now mate, I'm out near Birling Gap, had to take it for a walk it was driving me nuts in the house........Yeah safe cuz I'll pop round later we can get blazed and shit, cool cool, catch you later...."

He lights up a hand rolled cigarette from his pocket, the unmistakable sickly sweet smell of cannabis drifts to my nostrils on the light breeze, the dog dragging along behind him reluctantly. As he passes the lighthouse he pauses on the cliff edge, stupid enough on a chalk edger notorious for erosion but even more stupid with a dog on a

155

lead, the dog could chase something and easily pull you over.

The cliff tops are surprisingly quiet for this time of year, lock down keeping the tourists at bay and even the locals seem to be in scant numbers. We have this peak to ourselves with a couple of brightly clad walkers climbing the next hill ahead, their backs towards me, the lighthouse normally used as a holiday retreat, is still closed due to the pandemic.

I increase my walking pace and approach behind him, careful to stay out of his peripheral vision. The dog turns to look at me and comes to sniff my outstretched hand I reach out unclipping the lead from his collar, as the lead goes slack and drops onto his shoe he spins around "What the fu...."

Before he can finish his sentence I plant a front kick square in his chest, resisting the urge to shout "THIS IS SPARTA" and instead I just say "You shouldn't hit dogs" the surprise on his face turns to terror at the moment just before he disappears out of sight and plummets the 140 metres to the rocks below, his scream absorbed by the cliff edge and the sound of the waves below. I scan left and right, the dog is behind me happily sniffing at something, unaware of his new-found freedom.

I lay on my chest and edge forward on my belly, peering over the side of the cliff I can see the body bent backwards over a rock, one of his legs is clearly broken and the white bone of his femur pokes out through the torn fabric of his tracksuit bottoms combining into a mess of tissue, skin and blood. The contents of his skull are now decorating the yellowy white chalk in a crimson explosion as the the incoming tide laps hungrily at the edges of the rocks, already licking at the blood that is trickling to meet the incoming waves.

Maybe he'll be spotted by the chaplain patrols that service this area trying to save the lives of those considering taking theirs, just another sad suicide victim who has chosen to take his life at this notorious stretch of coastline, no doubt pushed over the edge by the Covid crisis. Or perhaps he'll be washed out to sea to become fish food and a missing person statistic.

Taking off my backpack I pull out the drawstring from the top and tie it to the dogs collar, no need for two victims of the cliffs. Casting my eyes over the hills to make sure nobody has seen anything, I give the makeshift lead a gentle tug and say "come on boy and he trots in behind me, I'm not sure if dogs can but I'm convinced he's smiling at me.

We head back the way we came, passing a few walkers and the occasional runner, exchanging the obligatory countryside 'good afternoon' greetings. Nothing to see here, just a woman and her dog out for a walk.

Entering back into the sanctity of the cottage he sniffs around and then makes a beeline for the armchair by the unlit fire, the suns rays casting a spotlight beam onto it. Circling around, prodding at the fabric with his paws he makes himself comfy before curling his long body into a ball more akin to a cat than a dog. The chair is where Barney sits, Barney was Charlie's childhood teddy bear, one of the few remaining things I have of him. A picture of my brother sits on the mantle, "Charlie" I mumble thinking of my brother for a moment, the dog lifts his head and looks at me enquiringly as I place my hand on my brothers picture.

"Make yourself at home why don't you? That's Barney you are sitting on, do not eat him! he was my brother Charlie's bear" I show him the picture as if in explanation. I gently remove the bear, stroking the dog as I do and place him on the shelf out of harms reach. I'm sure his ears prick up again as I say Charlie's name and he looks at me with those sorrowful eyes long dogs tend to have.

"I guess that's what we'll call you then, Charlie it shall be, it'll be nice to have a Charlie around again for a while" He flops his head onto his paws and closes his eyes as I stroke his ears.

Being a woman on a dating site is very different to being a man. Most men seem to have zero selection criteria and it appears they swipe yes on more or less everyone. Sure there will be those that are sizeist, racist or have a certain type, and some that actually do respect women and take their time making careful assessments but for a large number it's apparently open season and regardless of whether the woman is looking for a particular thing or is obviously out of their league, they will indiscriminately swipe to the positive.

They definitely don't read profiles, certainly not until they have a match and in many cases not even then. Some use the classy opening gambit of a picture of their dick, others try two or three lines of chat before sending the same or asking for nudes. It can be disheartening and scary for a woman trying to pick out the wheat from the chaff. It seems that somewhere along the way these men have missed out on the education of the art of seduction or perhaps the anonymity of the internet gives them the confidence to behave how they truly are?

A male friend once gave a good insight, he said; men are predominantly visual creatures, that's why most pornography is aimed at men. Women tend to prefer to read erotica than look at pictures. Because men want to see the visual, they think by sending it out they will get the same in return. There will be women out there that break the mould and do like it and send pictures back or respond to them, so for every fifty dick pics they send they might get one hit back, for those that don't understand any other way to approach women this is a success. Especially if all you are looking for is sex.

Focusing on one person in a single city at a time would be time consuming and risky. To ensure I have enough potential targets I have to maintain multiple conversations across multiple areas. The dick pic senders actually do themselves a favour as they make it too difficult to engage in any form of sensible conversation, it's too much work to try to get past the smut, besides I've already taken one of these boys down in the form of Jake.

In order to find people in the right places, I go through a lot of chats and the circumstances and timing needs to be right. I've been chatting to Julian for a while, I wasn't sure about him at first, he seemed pretty nice to be honest, paying me compliments and cracking jokes, I normally ghost these guys after a while as I need to be sure that my victims are at least partly worthy.

I'd actually been chatting with him for a few nights but decided he was too innocuous to kill we exchanged a few more messages and then I focused on the other hats and I left him alone.

Literally thirty minutes later I got the following message from him;

"Did you get cut off??"

I left it, no need to reply it's a dating app not a marriage contract.

No more than six hours later I receive the following gem;

"I'm so sad that you haven't messaged me, I thought we were perfect together, like really good for each other, you could have just messaged to say you were busy, or you would talk to me later, or been up front and said you didn't want to chat. It's women like you that give other women a bad name, leading men on. I'm gutted you didn't bother to reply"

Men like this are also far too common, I stopped politely declining because of guys like this, you would say "Nice chatting but I don't think we're compatible" or something along those lines and they would turn out a tirade of abuse as if you had left them at the alter.

Not once either but all the time, making it my fault that I had somehow rejected them, going from what appeared to be a nice exchange straight to instant poison; "You fucking bitch" "Go fuck yourself you slag" "You look fat / ugly / undesirable in your pictures" These men think it perfectly acceptable to tell you where you are going wrong and why you are not worthy of

161

them, not that there would ever be any reasonable grounds for this type of behaviour but these were all decidedly average men in the physical stakes, none of them blessed with sparkling personalities either.

I had to message this dick head back straight away. "Hi Julian, I'm so sorry, my phone ran out of battery last night and I went to bed, I'm sorry if you were upset"

"Ah hey, that's Ok, what are you doing today?" Literally no apology, no mention of his outburst.

Let me tell you how this would go if I pulled him up on it, Julian would not accept any of this as his responsibility, instead he'll slip straight back into being charming and lovely he'll dismiss it as a misunderstanding that of course is down to me not him and that it's just me being silly, trying to make me doubt that it had happened or question whether it was just me overreacting. Or 'mansplaining' to me in great details as to why, by his standards not replying as per his unwritten guidelines was my fault.

This would set the scene for the whole relationship. This is the sort of guy that fits into a number of categories, firstly he can be charming, he knows how to behave in all the right places, if he meets your friends they'll love him at first, 'so polite, so engaging'. But behind closed doors he'll chip away at your confidence, challenging what you wear or how you behave, gaslighting you.

If you don't know (and if you do, forgive me for mansplaining) gaslighting is a form of abuse, It's the act of manipulating a person by forcing them to question their thoughts and memories and even the events occurring around them. A victim can be pushed so far that they can question their own sanity.

Being in that situation you might start question who you are, losing sight of your own individuality or begin questioning your own judgements, you'll lose self confidence and become anxious. You might start apologising in advance for fear of upsetting the person but you'll position it in your head as if it's you getting it wrong because that's what you have been manipulated to believe. You might find it increasingly hard to make your own decisions and start drawing away from friends and family to save hiding things from your partner in case you get it wrong and make them angry.

Of course it's not done in an obvious way, it's a cleverly orchestrated regime that slowly drip drip drips, eroding your confidence. It won't be a direct "I don't like what you are wearing" More a "Oh you are wearing that today?" Or I thought you were meeting me at 10?" When you know you said 10.30 but it'll be so cleverly played down you'll start to wonder if you did say 10.

They might be prone to losing their temper, screaming and shouting at you then just a few minutes after an outburst appearing fine and happy, playing down the whole situation as if you are over reacting. Often these covert narcissists don't even realise they are doing it but that's exactly what they are. They can only view things from the perspective that the world revolves around them. Their self absorption leaves no capacity for interest in other people unless it serves a purpose for them. They have no ability to understand what you are feeling or experiencing but they will happily tell you what they think you should be feeling and why you are wrong for not feeling it.

It's not just in dating that this happens, these people exist within families and the workplace too. If you have a parent like this your self-esteem and perspective of the world could be extremely skewed ending up with you having a subservient personality where you put everyone else before yourself, you'll be drawn to these types of men again and again.

Julian is absolutely perfect for a potential kill but he's up in Sheffield, I can't be in that direction for a few weeks so I'll need to keep him hanging on, I'm going to have to keep chatting to this arsehole for a while.

I set diary reminders to make sure I message him at certain times so as to ensure he remains interested, I keep a coded spreadsheet of all the people I am chatting to so I can quickly reference anything that comes up in conversation, there is no time to flick backwards and forwards through messages so I just populate the spreadsheet with al the usual details, age, height, location then columns for interests, things we have talked about, likes, dislikes that sort of thing, it's surprisingly easy. I also have to admit to cutting and pasting the same things to lots of them at the same time. It helps if you can have the same conversation over and over to weed out what you need to know.

I've had another guy on my spreadsheet for almost a year, he's not one that I found on a dating site he's actually an Uber driver or was until he got arrested last year after two women accused him of assault. Uber were forced to pay out an undisclosed sum in a private civil case as the court deemed they had failed to protect the women but he was never individually prosecuted due to a lack of evidence.

He was actually using his brothers Uber account so whilst his brother was banned, there is nothing to stop this guy working anywhere. I've been watching his movements online, I know he is working as an unlicensed minicab driver because he advertises on his Facebook page, offering airport pick-ups and regular cabbing services.

I have a small flat in West London that I bought as an investment a few years ago, I love living by the coast but I keep it for whenever I want to be in the city and not have to travel back, sometimes you need some culture and to be around people, before the pandemic anyway.

I have a cleaner who keeps it fresh for me, dropping in once a month to empty the Roomba and keep the dust at bay. It's surprisingly easy to hide in a city too, people notice less as their senses are overloaded with everything around them, that said London is awash with cameras on buses and tubes, with the shops and main streets also covered with CCTV, some of the ones right in the heart of the city even have gait analysis that allows them to track a person from how they walk! It's a difficult arena to plan in but nothing is impossible, it just takes organisation and an eye for detail.

Another reason I know he is working as a mini cab driver is because I've been in it. I wanted to check him out before I took action. So early in lock down I booked an evening trip with him to drive me to Gatwick airport. It's was an hour trip from my place in Chiswick.

When he arrived I tried to sit in the back but the doors were locked, no doubt to force me sit in the front, purposefully my legs are on show in a short skirt, partially to see what he will do and mostly because why the fuck not? I throw my backpack into the backseat and make no effort to talk just looking at my phone screen, he started the conversation with the usual taxi chat

"Going on holidays?"

Clearly I only have a small backpack so this is a stupid question.

"We can't fly due to Covid so obviously no"

"Oh yeah I forget, do you work at airport?"

"No, I'm collecting somebody who has been isolating in France, they have just been allowed home"

"Boyfriend?"

"Just a friend"

"Do you have boyfriend?"

"No"

"Shame, pretty girl like you should have boyfriend, such a waste"

"Erm ok"

We sit in silence for a while, anytime we stop at traffic lights he turns to look at me, shifting his body to face me, leaning in and invading my body space, I can feel his eyes boring into the side of my head but I pretend not to notice.

"You have pretty eyes, nice sexy blonde hair, you look like woman from TV"

"Right, thanks"

"What you do for job?"

"Finance"

"Smart city girl, I knew it, looks and brains yes, I like smart girl, what kind of men you like?"

"I don't have a type, it depends on personality"

"I can take you out, show you a good time"

Having combat skills and the ability to potentially disable somebody with a few moves, does help you to feel a lot safer, however I'm still creeped out by this man. What if I wasn't able to defend myself? How would a vulnerable female feel right now? She's not going to straight up blank him as she's in his car and it's dark outside, he is in control of the vehicle and could probably over power her, I play the role to see how he reacts.

"I'm sure you are really nice but I'm not looking for a boyfriend right now"

"Why not, I nice guy, I take you nice place" His thick Eastern European accent and simplified language makes it sound even more seedy, he looks away from the wheel, looking at me, I imagine him grinning under his mask.

"I'm very busy"

"Everywhere closed now, no parties but I know a place we could go" He doesn't give up

"I really don't want to, I'm sorry"

He leaves it alone for a while, turning up the radio to Kiss FM and nodding his head in an attempt I guess to look cool. I can feel his glance flick from the road to my legs repeatedly. The car feels oppressive, sitting just inches from him.

"You like music?" He persists

"Everyone likes music"

"You like this music?"

"It's ok, not really my thing, it's a bit upbeat for this type of situation"

"Ah you like the slow, sexy music" He changes station, selecting smooth FM.

"You like this?"

"I don't mind what you play, I just want to get to the airport thanks"

"No problem I get you there, you safe with me, I look after" I very much fucking doubt that Pavel.

"Why you not go out with me? You lesbian?" Whether I am or not Pavel is irrelevant, it's because you are a slimy sex pest who has no idea how to treat a woman. Part of me wonders if I should feel sorry for him, how has he got to the point in his life where he doesn't know what is appropriate or not, does he not have a mother or a sister? The pity subsides with his next line;

"Men need sex, pretty girls show all the goods to tease men but not give out, this is bad for men and bad for you"

I hear the threat in his voice, If I was vulnerable I'd be terrified now.

"You think because I wear a short skirt that I am asking for sex?"

"I say you like men to look, you want men to look but you don't want to give, I say very bad, very bad, nice girl not behave like this you English sluts all the same" He shakes his head.

"I'm sorry you feel like that, I want to get out now please"

"I take airport, not safe here" The central locking button is on his side of the car but I can reach it if I have too, it's about the same distance to his windpipe but he's not going to try anything at fifty miles an hour so I resist the urge to punch him in the throat.

He keeps on driving ignoring my request to stop, quietly I'm glad he did, a trip back from here would be a pain in the arse but for anyone else his refusal to stop would be terrifying.

Luckily for him he drops me at the airport, by the time we get there I am in no doubt that the girls testimonies were all true. I pay him and lean in to the back to get my bag, he puts his hand on my boob and looks directly at me, his thick set eyebrows leering over the face mask. "Call me, I give good time"

I firmly pull his hand off twisting his arm and bending the thumb back towards the wrist, enough to make him let out a startled yell but not enough to break it. "Fuck off you pervert" I close the door and get out. Heading to the train station and back to the South Coast with a name to add to the long list. Pavel Terzic you are definitely one for the future.

Chapter 6

I'm in Cardiff this week.

Paul catches my eye, immediately obvious from his pictures that he is ex-military, police or perhaps both, in every picture he is involved in some sort of sporting activity yet never smiling, he is too manly to look like he is enjoying it. He approaches these sports like a challenge, showing enjoyment is for the weak. His stoic expression shows just how strong and masculine he is. In one he's stood on the top of a hill or mountain somewhere, maybe Scotland or the lake district, all the right gear on, In another a kayak on a Loch, looking determined with his muscular arms bulging.

If I was actually interested in looking for dates then this sort of guy might seem like a good choice on paper, shared interests and he would at least be able to keep up with me physically, however I'm wary of these types of guys for several reasons; first of all, they have skills that can make my life difficult, secondly they are not necessarily bad guys, sure the military and police are heavily patriarchal organisations and breed individuals that think like that but they can also be reliable and loyal. Thirdly if he's actually Police that's attention I do not need, he looks so good though and after Jim I think I deserve some fun.

His profile reads:

Interests: I'm into skiing, horse riding, mountain biking and climbing, kayaking, and hiking maybe we can go adventuring together

Sounds more like something you would read on the side of a Tampax box to me Paul but OK.

No kids and no psycho exes waiting in the wings. It's important that we have a physical and mental attraction, that's what makes everything tick. I have had enough meaningless relationships and wants to find 'the one'

He's never held down a relationship long enough to have a meaningful ex or children, either he's been totally committed to his job or cannot form meaningful relationships.

Ideal first date: A nice walk followed by a coffee, let's get to know each other.

He's not normally what I would go for as a choice of kill but he looks hot and I fancy getting my hands on something good, clearly Jim was no action and was never going to be, Paul on the other hand could be a whole lot of fun.

I start the text chat, same M.O as before, get as much information from him as I can so I can do some research, he is indeed ex-military having served in the Royal Marines for 15 years, definitely a tough one, thankfully he's not in the police, he is away a lot overseas doing 'private security' that can mean a multitude of things, protecting people, protecting property, killing people for money that sort of thing.

He asks me for my number so we can chat properly rather than texting. I like that. I'll also be able to get more from him in less time. He has a nice voice, I detect an accent hidden in there but I can't quite place it. He's cagier than most men, clearly his military background has trained him to not give up much information but I glean enough to get his surname and birthday. He's charming but distant, no silly banter from this one, he flits from serious conversation to dark humour and as soon as I try to probe deeper into anything about him, he bats me away with a joke. It no doubt reflects what goes on inside his mind, I quite like him.

The conversation flows a little like this:

"I love outdoors stuff too, I guess with your military background you're good at survival stuff? I'd love to do some wild camping!'

"I was in the woods camping with one of my buddies recently and he had an accident"

"Oh no that's not good, what happened?"

"We were tracking some deer and he fell and smashed his head, I called an ambulance as he wasn't breathing"

175

"Jesus Paul, that must have been awful, what did you do?"

"Well when I spoke to the ambulance woman she said not to panic and to make sure he definitely wasn't breathing before I did anything else. So I went back and broke his neck" He pauses for dramatic effect and then bursts into laughter.

"That is sick! OMG I was actually believing you, arsehole"

"I know sorry, I couldn't resist it"

I guess camping is off the agenda then! I've got one for you... I took a kid wild camping the other week, it was dusk and the kid said to me, I'm scared of the dark, I said to him, how do you think I feel? I've got to walk back alone! "

"Hahaha that's an old one but a good one, Yeah I can look after you in the woods, pretty much anywhere to be honest, if you are ever caught in a fire fight in Helmand province, I'm your man"

"I'm sure you can, I guess you have seen some things in the Marines? Must have been tough?"

"Yeah you know how it is, it's just something that you kind of get used to, squash down to the back of your mind and try to forget about" (I know all about that Paul, we're not that different you and I)

"Is that healthy? Sorry I shouldn't pry"

"It's not something I talk about much, once a Marine, always a Marine etc. I guess also once you have shot someone, it feels like an easy way to resolve all future arguments!"

"Paul you're a sick puppy... I like it"

Talking of puppies I've had to put Charlie in a local kennel for a few days. Having a dog is not part of my plan but until I can find a decent home for him I need to make sure he's ok.

As always I'm digging whilst we're chatting, It turns out that our friend Paul does have an ex or two, using image searches I find him alongside a couple of women on Instagram. Researching these and their Facebook pages is too easy and after a while there histories start to reflect what I can safely assume is the Paul period of their lives. Sentimental posts about just wanting to love somebody, why does love hurt so much etc., then later more vitriolic posts about alcohol and the effects on relationships. It looks like Paul may not be as sweet as he seems.

Why is it that we now as humans and especially women, express ourselves through these internet mediums? Do we expect or hope our partner will read the posts and somehow be inspired to rectify their behaviour? Do we want someone to rescue us? Maybe it's a bit of both and more, perhaps we use them simply because they are there. I read long into the night, their time lines run consecutively, and it looks like Paul went straight from one to the other, perhaps even with an overlap.

One of the women's early relationship posts remain, they look happy together her smiling looking longingly at him, Paul looking manly as ever, a protective arm around her shoulder that also says 'my property back away' He clearly likes a drink and reading some of the emotional outpourings in seems that the alcohol plays a regular part, perhaps awakening the demons in his past.

These types of guys have often been through a lot in their careers and the PTSD they are left with creates personality issues rather than them being arseholes at heart. That doesn't excuse shitty behaviour though, you've had a tough time yes, don't take it out on some poor unsuspecting woman who just wants to love you, get help if you need it. If it keeps happening, you have to ask yourself how keen you are to actually seek help and how much of it is just you? I think it's time Paul was taught a lesson.

Military boys are drilled to be gentlemen and he's not going to push the agenda on the first date. If I throw myself at him, it won't appeal to his expectations and it'll put him off, so as I'm not going to get him into a one date situation, the walk with a coffee scenario is a good option and I can take the dog. The outdoors location means not many people will see us which is always a bonus.

We arrange to meet in the Brecon Beacons national park, (of course we do Paul, how very military) Just under an hour from Cardiff. He suggests a walk to the top of Pen Y Fan, I know it well, one particular climb is known in military circles as the 'Fan Dance' and is part of the SAS selection process, having the dog means I need to opt for a car for this journey, I pick up a recently serviced Volvo S60 in some sort of dark blue colour as it has all wheel drive capabilities and is boringly forgettable.

I collect Charlie from the kennels in it and the dog seems to like it, refusing to stay in the back he positions himself in the passenger seat, staring out of the window. "We're not going to push this one off a cliff, I've got bigger plans for him, so be nice to him for me, I hope you like walking as we're going up a big hill"

I wonder If Paul is like many other ex military boys, fond of a macho challenge and intimidated by a strong woman, It'll be interesting to see his face when I tell him I easily completed the course well under the required 4 hours 10 minutes. The route he has selected is a less arduous one and will take us to the top via a forest walk and then back down to the Old Barn tea room where we can refuel.

He turns out to actually be good company and the dog warms to him instantly, the two of them tussling on the ground in the car park. Paul is polite and friendly and constantly cracking those dark jokes. He sets out at a good pace and I match him, I think he expected me to fall behind so he could be the hero, when I'm able to keep up his attitude towards me changes and he views me in a slightly different light offering me more respect, direct feedback is how these guys work.

The walk up is as beautiful as ever, the rolling grassy hills of Wales, moss covered rocks and jagged outcrops, the light ever changing and the view glorious. As we get higher banks of cloud and mist occasionally waft across our path in the cooler October air. The view is of lakes and distant villages, Charlie is having the time of his life and I'm glad he's enjoying himself, Paul slips into the alpha roll, telling him when to wait or come back, surprisingly the dog responds.

We stop at the top and Paul puts his arms around me from behind, it feels natural not pushy and rests his chin on my shoulder pointing out landmarks in the distance, the dog sits in front of us at his feet also taking in the view. For a moment it feels perfect, like something people with normal lives do. I take this opportunity to point out the Fan Dance route and tell him I've done it. He's impressed, Paul that is, not the dog, my story about a charity event seems to wash and I ask him if he's done it. He nods "A few times"

"I suppose you wouldn't tell me if you were special forces trained would you?"

"I wouldn't you are right, but I'm not, just straight up marines those SAS (he pronounces it sass as if one word, rather than individual letters.) boys don't like to recruit us, I think we're too tough for them, they are mostly paratroopers, marines prefer to do some thinking before we do our shooting, para's are not renowned for their brains" He laughs to himself. Slipping into well worn military ribbing that would be more appropriate in the barracks than on a date but I smile and nod agreeing with him conspiratorially.

Even though he has bridged the gap of intimacy with his hug, he doesn't attempt to kiss me, he offers me his hand a few times as we climb over styles and negotiate the brooks running over the path, immediately withdrawing it once the help is no longer needed. He is the perfect gentleman but remains distant, mysterious almost, he's the sort of guy that would make you feel physically secure but emotionally bereft.

We chat about the world, the global pandemic, politics in the UK and America, he doesn't ask me anything too personal and deflects my attempts to get inside his head, I learn that he has a small cottage in the Forest of Dean that's more or less off the grid and that he is away again soon for a month for 'work'.

we make it back to the Old Barn in time for dusk, we sit in the Volvo and chat over hot tea and peanut butter on toast whilst Paul feeds the dog with a sausage he insisted on buying for him.

"You haven't told me where your name comes from? Hatta that's unusual"

"It's Scandinavian, my dad was from Norway, he was a fisherman, my mum grew up in a fishing village and sometimes the boats would come in to the village to stay overnight in stormy conditions, I guess they fell in love etc. He drowned at sea before I was born so I think my mum chose my name as a tribute to him"

"Hatta I know who you remind me of now! You look like that crazy newspaper woman, the one who is always on some crusade or another, she outed that pervy old pop star as a kiddy-fiddler, you know the one"

"Elizabeth Banrigh? I don't know whether to be flattered or insulted"

"She would be pretty if her face wasn't constantly sucking on a lemon about something or other, you are prettier of course, you just remind me of her a little bit"

It's not the first time I've heard this said. It's fine looking like someone famous normally but not if you want to be anonymous.

"Maybe I should change my hair?" I'm enjoying making him squirm, thinking he has offended me.

"It looks good to me, I like it, don't change anything just because of some nut job in the newspaper, anyway sorry I mentioned it, to make up for it, can I buy you dinner this week?"

"I'd like that but I thought you were away soon?"

"I'm here this week, I'm staying at the Park Plaza Hotel for a couple of nights before I fly out, I've got some work being done on the cottage and the builders start tomorrow so I figured I'd get a few days in Cardiff, I got a mate to drop me in rather than bring the Land Rover, I can catch up on some admin and buy some new kit, you're welcome to join me for dinner if you fancy it. I'd have invited you for a swim in the hotel pool but it's still closed after lock down.

"I'm not sure I'd have taken you up on the swim, although I admire your effort at trying to get my clothes off" I smile. He cocks his head raising an eyebrow. "I would love dinner though"

"The hotel has a good restaurant, we can try somewhere else in Cardiff if you want but this lock down is making it tricky and everything closes early."

"The hotel restaurant is fine, it's the company I'm interested in, not the surroundings" I weigh up my options, the hotel poses a lot of risk, a big chain will have security camera's everywhere and whilst masks will be OK in the communal area's I'll need to take it off for dinner. My plan was to get to his cottage. I need some time to plan properly and to figure out how to make this work but the risk is exciting me, not to mention the thought of fucking him.

The Plaza has five floors of rooms facing front into the street and back across parkland and towards the castle. Paul is in room 227 on the second floor, facing out of the back of the hotel. I book a room for myself. 1st Floor also the back of the building. I need to be able to check out the hotel properly without arousing suspicion, masked up, made up and a different wig, I should minimise the risk of bumping into Paul.

It's a pretty standard city centre hotel, the décor is none offensive and it's 4 stars make it respectable without being boutique. It sits in a central location in Cardiff which means I need to ensure my exit routes from the city are memorised and planned. There are plenty of options but also a lot of risk factors to consider.

Sitting in the hotel bar I watch him leave, I head up to the second floor, his room is three doors away from the stairs and a fair distance from the lifts. A stairwell at each end of the corridor gives me options to slip out once I've had my fun. I take the stairs down and back to the lobby. Then up to the lift and to my room, before heading back down the other stairs.

I take the lift up to the top floor, checking for roof access or alternative exits, there is nothing of note up here and the roof is not an option, besides escaping across rooftops looks great in movies but is a quick route to capture or death unless you know exactly where you are going.

Security cameras survey the lifts, corridors and staircases, as I wander around I make a map of their positions around the hotel, working out how I can avoid most of them with a mask. There is going to be a lot of exposure but I'm ok with that, I'll ditch this look once I've dealt with Paul, the CCTV will only catch glimpses and I'll ensure my camera time is limited and at poor angles, I'll book the table for dinner so I can choose where we sit and arrive before him so he just assumes I've been seated.

This is going to be fun!

Paul looks every bit the military man, white shirt, two buttons undone at the neck, sleeves neatly rolled to just below the elbow. Black trousers pressed and his shoes polished to a mirror shine. He smells delicious, citrusy and his skin is tanned, weathered but not haggard and his facial hair is on the right side of trimmed without looking contrived, short dark hair and piercing steel blue eyes. I deserve a treat and he looks like one.

I've opted for a black jump suit, belted at the waste, accentuating my long leg line and unbuttoned enough to entice but on the demure side of exposure. Black pumps and a clutch bag, a Jeremy Hoye necklace around my neck I picked up in Brighton before I killed Shaun, it's a chunky jagged silver heart locket, with a memento of my brother inside. The blonde hair hangs loose on my shoulders, replacing the brunette wig I had used to check out the hotel, The long hair also strategically covers my face from a number of angles.

The food in the Laguna restaurant is actually pretty good, the conversation flows easily and his eyes almost mesmerise me across the table, I turn on my best flirting body language, I play with my hair my wrists turned towards him, touching my neck and ear lobes, we subtly interpret these signals. My gaze holds his then lowers showing submission and desire, I know how to exhibit these signs and he knows how to read them. As the meal progresses our hands touch across the table, feet casually brush then intertwine, I am signaling my intentions and Paul reciprocates.

We both refuse dessert, opting for coffee, Paul has kept his alcohol intake under control tonight it seems just a glass of wine with dinner and he orders a single malt with his coffee. "Would you like one" He asks as the waiter hovers.

"Please, anything Speyside nothing too peaty, a double with one cube of ice please" The waiter nods and heads off to the bar. "How about we have those in your room?" It's a risk but he is too much of the gentleman to push it now, he would wait until his return in a month, men that work away are used to waiting, I remember my dad was always patient.

"I'd like that, lets wait for them and we can head on up"

We sit in silence, staring at each other, chemistry doing all the talking, the waiter brings back the drinks, Paul stands and moves to the back of my chair, gallantly guiding me to my feet. We walk across the lobby to the lift carrying our drinks.

Still no chat as the lift carries us to the second floor and we exit and walk to his room in silence the anticipation growing inside me. He opens the room with his key card, holding the door as he gestures for me to enter. His room is identical to mine, he closes the door gently turning to face me, taking the drink from my hand, he places it on the desk alongside his own, he pulls me too him, his eyes close as our lips touch and we kiss, gentler than I imagined, his tongue flicking into my mouth entangling with my own, his beard feels soft against my face, he tastes of whiskey

187

and it combines with the citrus smell of his aftershave.

His strong hands slide down my back, under my bum and he lifts me up effortlessly, I wrap my legs around his waist and he carries me to the bed, lowering me gently onto the duvet. He kicks off his shoes and pulls his socks off, then unties my laces pulling the pumps off in turn, planting a kiss on each foot as he does, his eyes staring deep into mine and then down over my body, fuck he is good!

Unbuttoning his trousers he lets them fall, his dick obviously large, straining against his black jersey shorts. He unbuttons his shirt, defined pecs and a suggestion of abs on display as the white shirt contrasts against his tanned skin and dark trimmed body hair. He climbs on to the bed straddling me, leaning forward to kiss my lips then my neck, one hand unbuttoning my jump suit. He reaches the belt, unfastens it, slides it out from under me and drops it on the floor.

I sit up slightly pulling the suit down over one shoulder and then the other, revealing my black lace bra, he stands again tugging at the bottoms of the trousers and I lift my bum as he slides the garment over my legs to reveal the matching panties, he drops his shirt to the floor exposing his broad shoulders.

I feel his gaze on me a hungry look in his eyes, I part my legs slightly, giving him a subtle invitation. As he climbs on top of me again, he pulls at my nipple through my bra with his teeth, gazing up at me as he does, looking to see my reaction, I put my hands around his strong shoulders feeling the muscles change shape as he works his way up my body.

He uses his leg to open mine more forceful this time pushing the weight of his groin against me. He kisses me deeply then rolls me over, allowing me to be on top for a second, the lights outside cast shadows that dance across my body from the movement of the trees outside the window. I see him looking closer now with intrigue at the scars that mark my body, his fingers tracing some of them, but soon distracted by my breasts as he cups them through the bra with his strong rough hands, that feel good on my skin. Propping himself up on one elbow to reach around and unfasten my bra, struggling with the clasp we share an awkward glance then a smile as he manages to unclip it.

With my breasts free, we exchange a wry smile, "Like the view?" He nods.

"It's pretty good from up here too" His chest is taught, the muscles well defined. He pulls me to him once again and rolls us so I am back on to the bottom. He likes to be in control, typical alpha male, it's OK though I'm enjoying letting him be. His kisses passionate now, full mouthed, biting, nibbling, our tongues entwined. Raising his hips he pulls off his shorts and I use my feet to help him, he pulls down my knickers then lowers himself on to me both naked at last,

The simple act of flesh on flesh creates an instant reaction in both of us, he lets out a soft moan and my pussy spasms. He raises himself up just enough to slide his hand down over my belly, pausing when he feels the patch of hair. Then gently but firmly he moves his hand down between my legs, creating a v with his fingers to apply pressure either side of my pussy. He pauses again, pushing the palm of his hand against my clit firmly. God he's good at this. My pussy is starting to ache and his cock throbs against my thigh. He kisses me deeply again, pulling away, just enough to make eye contact. He draws his hand back up my pussy, so that the tips of his fingers are brushing the clit, then slides his hand back down, bringing his fingers together and confidently pushing his middle finger deep inside. He verbally confirms what I already new. "Hmm, You're so wet!". The feeling and the compliment, make me buck my hips involuntarily. He makes a deep sound, in his throat, like this is the best feeling he's had for a long time.

I try to focus, my turn to explore him, even though he's now alternately sliding his finger out from my pussy and up to my clit, and back down again, in slow rhythmic circles. I slide my hand between our bodies and find his cock, which gives a pleasing twitch as my fingers wrap around it, feeling my way along his length, down to the base and all the way up again to the tip. My thumb glides over the helmet of his cock, seeking out the tiny wet spot, sliding the wetness around feeling its viscosity between my fingertips. My hand caresses him, fingers stroking his balls, running along the shaft length and nails lightly tickling the tip.

He's lost for a moment in his own pleasure, finger deep in me, his breathing a little ragged. He doesn't want to give in to the feelings too soon, this pleases me. He kisses me again, more gently, savouring the moment. I want his mouth on me, I stop stroking him, and find his hand, raising his fingers to my mouth, I taste myself, his eyes sparkle, clearly turned on by this.

"I need to taste you now" he slides down me, kissing my body as he goes, pausing to take each nipple in his mouth in turn. I'm already soaking as his tongue makes the first tentative contact, tasting the hot sticky juices as they coat his mouth and lips. He runs his tongue over my clit, seeking his way under the hood and rolling the delicate pink bud around, then back down to the entrance of my pussy, probing, trying to get inside me, as he does I moan in response.

I feel greedy, I want it all and I want it now, kissing him I wanted his mouth upon me but as soon as I feel him, its not enough and I want him inside me. I want to feel the sensation of his thickness expanding me.

I pull at his head and he understands, kissing his way back up my body, again pausing to nibble momentarily on each nipple.The urgency takes over and I can't resist reaching down and trying to push his cock deep inside me but he locks his hips and resists me. The longing drives me crazy and I let out a moan. He silences me, by kissing me. Then, holding himself steady with one arm, he uses his other hand to edge my pussy lips open with the tip of his cock, rocking just an inch inside. I can feel how big he is, even from this, and I'm longing to feel him in me.

I grab at his hips trying to reach his bum to pull him forwards but he's strong, in control, and enjoying the power. "Do you want my cock?" He whispers.

"Fuck me! I want you now". Even he can't resist that.

He slides it all the way in, and I gasp, it's thick and hitting the deepest point. He makes a guttural noise of pure pleasure, and finding my mouth kisses me hard. Still I'm hungry for more, I lift my legs, pulling my knees up and allowing him to plunge even deeper. But he pulls back again! "No!!!" I whimper. He returns to just an inch inside me, probing my pussy, I want it in me so badly.

"Again, I want you, again" I bite his ear lobe, trying to pull him back into me. He's struggling not to lose control too, I can feel the muscles in his back ripple with the tension and little beads of sweat are beginning to pool in the dip at the base of his spine. The feeling is too intense and I squirm and try to raise my hips to him but he resists me again. The torture is bliss.

He leans in biting my left nipple and as he does, slides all the way in to me rolling his hips forward so that he penetrates further. This is so deep, I moan loudly, not caring if anyone in the rooms around us can hear. The feeling is so intense and I know I'm right on the limit of the line between pleasure and pain.

We rock like this for a while, occasionally sliding his length to the tip, but mostly burying himself into me, like he wants to push through me to find the point of ecstasy. His weight pushing down on me, the sensation of safety and submission combine. I feel like he is in control, but I'm surprised that I am willing to trust him not to go too far he reads the situation well.

Sex is the one time I allow myself to submit, to feel weak, but with this guy there's something else. I roll on to my side, legs bent up, I watch in the mirror on the dressing table as he slides into me, my gaze flicking from the wetness that glistens on his length back to his face to watch the expressions change, it's almost a shame to kill him.

His cock feels amazing and I tighten my pussy to grip and respond to his thrusts, the desire rushes through me. His hold on my hips is getting more urgent, and I wonder if he'll leave bruises, to carry with me for the next few days, a memory of this night.

I want more, I don't know where this urgency is coming from. I shuffle around on to my knees and position myself on the bed so we are now facing the mirror. I tell him to pull my hair, talking to him, telling him to watch himself fucking me.

I push myself into an upright position so I can kiss him over one shoulder and we look at each other in the mirror, all the time I'm talking, telling him how amazing his body looks, how good his dick feels in my pussy and how sexy he is, I want his complete trust and focus.

We move together like this, he pushes me back on my knees my head down further on to the bed. His hands grip my waist thrusting deep into me, fucking hard and fast until his body glistens with sweat and his muscles look taught.

I respond moving with him. He pulls me back with his hands on my hips as the end of each thrust becomes deep and I instinctively pull away from him.

"I want to cum, but I need you to cum first" my demand quickens his pace, he's breathing heavily now, and I can feel heat starting to build in my body. He starts to moan, the sound brings my orgasm to the fore, the last few thrusts take on an urgency and then suddenly he stops and with one final thrust I feel him explode inside me, pumping as his legs tremble "fucking hell, that's amazing' He exclaims. My own pleasure rippling through my body, quivering with him, my legs weak, my body no longer in my control as I lose myself to the sensation washing over me. Paul lets his weight collapse as the waves subside. Panting, he mouths in my ear "that was so fucking good" Our bodies hot and sweaty against each other. We lie entwined as our breathing returns to normal. Lying next to him, I feel momentarily safe and I drift off for a few minutes.

After a while I feel him move away from me gently and slide off the bed, my head close to the end I glance down and see the belt of my jumpsuit. My hand drops casually to the floor and as he passes me on route to the bathroom I pick it up, fitting the end through the buckle loop, and just as he opens the bathroom door I silently stand reaching to pull it around his neck. As it is about to go over his head, something makes me hesitate, stopping me in my tracks, Fuck! I actually like him.

As I pause Paul catches sight of me in the bathroom mirror, standing behind him a looped belt poised over his head. Instinctively he drops a shoulder rotating his body, he swings his arm back, catching me in the head with his elbow. I stumble backwards falling off the other side of the bed with a crash, the bedside lamp clattering and breaking on the floor. I pull myself up "WHAT THE FUCK ARE YOU DOING?!" He rages at me, he lunges across the bed to grab me, but I jump back and bring my knee up into his face as he does, my knee goes numb as I feel his nose break against it and the blood trickles from it, this takes the forward momentum from him and he thuds into the mattress with a loud yelp.

He winces, taking a second to blink and wipe the tears from his watering eyes, as I dart past him heading for the door he pushes himself up, throwing himself over and grabs my hair pulling me backwards onto the floor. I scream knocking the desk chair over on the way down, it hits me in the back, winding me. Paul leaps off the bed, straddling me on the carpet, punching me square in the face. "WHO THE FUCK ARE YOU?"

"GET OFF ME" I scream He pins me down holding my hands above my head, His face inches from mine "WHAT THE FUCK IS GOING ON?" I buck upwards with my hips and rotate, making my arm long as I do, his centre of balance changes and I slide out from under him, his grip on my wrist doesn't loosen and I stand and try to wrench myself free, kicking out at him as I do, a cacophony of yelps and grunts as we struggle for supremacy. On his back he yanks me down on top of him, shortening the range and reducing the impact of my blows.

He bear hugs me too him, I sink my teeth into his shoulder tasting blood and he roars in pain. He rolls side to side, eventually over powering my attempt to stay on top of him and he sprawls onto me, not making the same mistake this time, he inches up my body using his hips, digging his toes into the carpet, legs spread wide to control my wriggling. I try to keep moving using my Ju-Jitsu knowledge, changing his centre of gravity to attempt to roll him once again but he too knows how to fight and is keeping his centre of mass low.

He pushes under my chin pressing hard down with his forearm across my throat angling his elbow to create a lever between my shoulder and jaw. I struggle and writhe, bucking my hips but he weighs a lot more than me. An untrained person would have no chance holding me down but he is no ordinary civilian. I'm trying to escape but each time I move the pressure increases, my fingers claw at his face with my spare hand, maybe I can gouge an eye or force a finger into his nostril, anything to loosen his grip and buy myself time but he controls my arm with his other hand, the edges of my vision start to close in as he squeezes against my carotid artery, I think I am going to pass out.

The door flies open with a crash and two security guards wade into the room, clearly alerted by the noise or summoned by a concerned guest, one immediately dives onto Paul rolling him off me, the other pounces across the bed joining in the fray as they try to control him. He struggles furiously, shouting at them that it's her not me, they ignore his pleas but he's not going to give in easily and they three of them crash into the corner of the room, Paul's face is bleeding and is a picture of rage. He throws one of the guards off of him and makes a lunge for me again but the other guard grabs him around the waist rugby tackling him onto the bed.

I gasp for breath my eyes streaming, jumping to my feet and sprinting for the door, grabbing my clutch bag as I do, I run naked along the corridor, the carpet soft against my feet, the sounds of pain and breaking furniture echo behind me.I slam into the door and onto the cold concrete of the fire escape steps, using the banisters to swing down one flight then a second, through the door of the lower floor, not caring if anyone sees me, pulling the key card from my bag opening the door to my room. I kept the room just in-case and I push the door closed behind me, I can still hear shouting and thuds from the floor above through the ceiling, I catch sight of myself in the mirror blood around my left eye the skin already starting to turn purple, my mascara stains my cheeks in streaks.

I laugh, maybe I'm hysterical maybe it's the Adrenalin or just the exhilaration of the moment. I mouth into the mirror "keep going girl, you've got this, winking at myself as I do. I pull on the running tights from my bag, no time for underwear, on with the already laced trainers and I push my head and arms into the black hoodie. I pull the leather gloves on, shove my handbag into my backpack, the room is already cleaned for prints and the only items were the ones I'm wearing.

My jumpsuit and pumps will have to be left behind. Perhaps the police will get some DNA from them but I'm not on any databases so it won't lead them anywhere. I open the door into the hallway, and the noise increases momentarily, Paul is clearly still putting up a fight and I hear footsteps on the corridor and stairs above as more staff join in the fray.

I wipe both sides of the door handle for any prints with my sleeve and close it again.Opening the window wide I position myself on the sill pausing for a few seconds to gauge the distance. Leaping off the edge into the tree a couple of metres in front of my window grabbing an armful of branches as I reach it, my whole body hurts with the impact, the impact of Pauls blows starting to take effect. The branches stretch but hold my weight and as the downwards momentum lowers me, I let go grabbing the next branch down, reducing the height of the drop like this branch by branch I land in the bark chippings at the base.

Without looking back I pull up the hood and start to run, it's more of a limp but I do not think there is any permanent or serious damage and as I get into a rhythm my legs reluctantly begin to work. I head towards the castle and to the river, hoping that to any passers-by I look like a late night jogger out for their daily exercise. The night is filled with the sound of sirens as I head across the park and onto the riverside trail, I stop momentarily to catch my breath, checking back to see if anyone has followed me. It looks like I'm in the clear. The Adrenalin is wearing off and the pain is starting to kick in.

It takes me an effort to make it the two miles down the path where the bike sits waiting. I just want to sleep it's probably a bit of concussion combined with exhaustion after the exertion of the past twenty minutes, as my heart rate subsides I embrace the pain like an old friend, it hurts but I can handle it.

There are bike leathers and a helmet stuffed into a dry bag and weighed down in the river under the bridge, which I retrieve, I don't bother with the bike suit, I was planning on getting out of the city tonight but riding a bike in this condition is going to be hard work, I still have three days rental to the apartment I stayed in this week and I don't relish the thought of a long journey now, I can lay low there for a day or two until I recover a little. my temple throbs against the helmet as I manage to squeeze it onto my head.

I sink the bike suit once again inside the dry bag and then fire up the bike. I circle back towards the city centre, I can't resist taking a route back past the front of the Plaza, the street is all but blocked off, with police vehicles on both sides of the road their lights bouncing off the glass of the buildings, making it look like a monochrome blue Las Vegas. The city is quieter than normal due to social distancing but there are still plenty of people straining to see what is going on. The traffic is backed up but the bike makes it easy to navigate through, the slow pace allowing me to fully take in the scene.

Four officers are escorting the handcuffed Paul from the foyer and into the waiting van, I slow to watch but don't stop, my black visor obscuring any chance of recognition. He has stopped struggling, although his blood smeared face looks like thunder his piercing blue eyes still radiate through and he looks even more rugged and handsome. I almost want to reach out to him, to tell him it's all been a terrible misunderstanding and suggest we just crawl back into bed. I can't imagine he would go for it right now though. He looks pretty pissed off. Thankfully they've given him his shirt and trousers to put back on, saving him the indignity of a naked frog march.

Five more minutes on the bike and I'm in the underground car park of the apartment block on Bute Street. I keep my helmet on as I take the lift up to the apartment and I'm grateful that I don't encounter anyone.

In the apartment I pour myself a vodka from the bottle of Stolichnaya I left in the freezer and hold the cold bottle against my swollen eye and lip. I'm exhausted and need to sleep but first I need to shower and dress my wounds, apart from my face I have a few cuts and bruises on my body some of which will no doubt add to the collection of scars I already carry, but nothing is too bad and the apartment first aid kit has enough supplies. The vodka will do as a painkiller for now.

The hot water of the shower beats a tattoo on my throbbing head, I try to reflect on the events of the evening, what evidence may I have left behind? I'm too tired to think, I'll hole up here tomorrow and go through everything in detail, if there is anything I need to destroy I'll be well placed to do it. My mind drifts and my body aches. I let the water wash over me, turning the shower to cold to help reduce the swelling.

I pull on a robe and head back into the living room. I put on the 24 hour news channel but nothing has reached them yet. It'll be a few hours before Paul has calmed down enough to make rational sense and to be able to explain what was actually going on, I guess he's going to miss his

202

flight too. For now the police probably think it was a domestic incident, No doubt they'll stick him in a cell tonight and interview him tomorrow. I'm sure his solicitor will get him out quick enough once they realise what is going on.

I turn off the TV, pour myself another drink and head into the bedroom. As I slide into the white sheets. I reflect on how less than an hour ago I was laying next to Paul my body still throbbing from an orgasm. I smile as I fall asleep.

Chapter 7

After I reconciled myself with the death of Louis, I decided that if I was going to do it again, I needed to make sure I could do things better. Graduating university with a first, I took the money dad had given me and put it to work with everything I had studied at university. I started my own investment portfolio spreading my risk and kept up the day trading with a much bigger stake.

Charlie had left his share of dads money to me, he took the time to make a will, naming me as the sole beneficiary. His single other request was to have his ashes scattered on the Isle of Wight, the last family holiday we ever had with Mum and Dad together. He left me a long letter too:

Dear Alys,

Every time I try to love someone they are taken away from me. First Mum, then you then Dad and now my heart has been wrenched from my chest a final time. The pain and humiliation are simply too much to bear again. I am tired and weary.

I always loved you and still do with all my being but know we could never be together, I realised long ago that you were telling the truth about Louis. I didn't understand why you would not have reported it but I see now how difficult it must have been. It broke my heart knowing that I rejected you and was not there to support you. Even If you could ever forgive me, society would not forgive us and allow us to be together, like everyone else in this life they would just hound us and destroy us.

You were always stronger than me, stay strong for both of us. I'm sorry I couldn't be. ..

That broke me, the feelings I had felt then but never really processed as a young girl came flooding back to me; the person you love with every ounce of your being is just there, right in front of you and yet you can't get to them, they have shut you out, closed the door on you, they hear you but refuse to listen, the harder you try the more their disdain for you grows, the more you push, the more out of reach they become.

You cling to the tiniest sliver of attention, maybe they are changing their minds, some false hope that they will see you again as they once did, trying different ways to win them back, giving them space but that doesn't work, writing to them, pouring out your emotions via thinly veiled social media posts in the hope that they will read between the lines and come and save you from this anguish and pain. You pretend to be breezy, friendly even hoping that your change of demeanour will pique their interest once again. Then the anger, how could they have loved you if they can hurt you like this? How dare they get on with their lives and appear to be ok with everything? Was it worth so little to them? Why are they so cruel? Why is life so cruel? Next comes the self-hatred, what did I do wrong? Why am I so undesirable? Was it my fault what happened? It must have been me.

Had I been an adult then could I have done something differently, persuaded Charlie that it was true, made him understand? Why if he had realised, didn't he reach out to me, did I cause that? Was I so distant and angry that there was no way back for him? Was it my fault Charlie had taken his own life? He'd been taken away from me once before and here I was being forced to mourn him all over again.

I felt vulnerable and alone, at that point I considered taking my own life, sitting with a bottle of pills on the sofa, trying to find a reason why not, a point to all this pain and suffering, who would care anyway if I just ended it all?

It was the end of Charlie's letter that stopped me doing it, it was probably that letter that lead to me confronting Louis too. I wanted to be strong like the way he saw me, everyone in my life had continuously left me and now the last person who I had in my life had done the same. If I was going to carry on then I could provide for myself with the money I had but nobody was going to protect me, I needed to learn how to protect myself.

I was able to work a few hours a day playing the financial markets, applying the knowledge I'd been building over the last few years. With a decent size stake and a solid strategy I began to make regular modest amounts, careful with my investments, not taking too much risk and reinvesting my money so each time my profit was greater and my stake grew bigger.

Able to work from anywhere and with nowhere to call home, travel became an attractive proposition. My thirst for knowledge had not diminished and with spare time on my hands, I knew it was time to take control and stop allowing people to use me as a victim.

I found a close security course in Israel designed for bodyguards. The course lasted for just six days but it was a revelation, I stopped feeling vulnerable and scared, I gained control of my fear and learned how to focus the Adrenalin, sure the first few nights laying in a foreign land with the eerie sound of the muezzin wafting over from the Muslim side of the city were hard, my bruised body aching, the fear and self-doubt gnawing away at my insides making me want to run away, but to where? Each night it got easier and the sounds started to become familiar and eventually reassuring.

I enlisted in more courses, this part of the world has seen years of military action and there are no end of battle hardened veterans willing to impart their knowledge in exchange for money. I studied Krav Maga a military self defence system devised by the Israeli army, learning how to fight with just your body against knives and other weapons, dirty street fighting tactics inflicting maximum damage as quickly as possible.

I headed into the dessert and learned to use evasive driving skills in both cars and on motorbikes, on the street and off road, in pursuit and whilst being pursued, how to follow and detect if you were being followed.

It was hard being on my own but I guess I was used to it, I'd really been on my own since Charlie had turned his back on me. Sometimes I would cry myself to sleep, hating myself for being weak, I was determined not to be weak anymore. I focused on developing and controlling my emotions and taught myself how to channel sorrow into anger and anger into hate.

After several months in the Middle East I headed to America and trained mixed martial arts for six months at the Jackson Winklejohn gym in Albuquerque considered to be the best of its kind in the world. I spent a lot of time getting my arse kicked but I turned up everyday and persevered until it I was able to defend myself enough to be a match for most ordinary people, drilling strikes and blocks time after time until they become instinctive.

I made several trips to Mikes gym in Marbella, Spain. a purpose built facility aimed at the obstacle course and parkour community. Here I got fitter and stronger than I thought was ever possible for my body. I learned how to use it too, hand eye co-ordination, balance and movement. The more I pushed my body the more I began to enjoy the pain, these were feelings that were in my control. I climbed and ran in the mountains and I kayaked and dived in the sea, I gained a focus that I had never known before. I had always studied hard in my life but not like this, not with such single minded determination. At night I would sit in a restaurant or bar or in my hotel room, nursing my aching body and I would read online courses and books about covert information gathering, on computers and how to hide you trail and stop yourself being tracked.

I'd pick up the occasional lover for sex along the way, either someone from whatever course I was undertaking or by hanging around in local bars. It doesn't take long for men to come sniffing no matter where you are in the world, I used the experience as an opportunity, listening to the bullshit they would spin in order to get what they wanted, how they try to manipulate and undermine, praying on your self confidence to make you feel weak and dependent on them, I had some fun not only with sex but occasionally kicking the crap out of the ones that tried to take advantage or wouldn't take no for an answer. I had female lovers too, finding comfort in their tenderness, compassion and respect. Where men were indifferent to me being closed emotionally, happy to just have sex, the women seemed to want to get to know me and to care for me. I wasn't prepared or able to give anything of myself at that point as my anger and pain were too focused and those relationships ended as quickly as they had begun.

Most real life fight situations are not like a Hollywood movie, a quick kick to the nuts or a palm strike to the nose is usually enough to put most people down or at least make them change their minds about what they intended to do, it's usually enough to send them scuttling back to their mates with a flea in their ear. The single most important piece of martial arts advice I ever received as a woman was this: 'You always win, the fight you are not in' Basically, incapacitate as quickly as possible or at least buy yourself time and get the hell out of there. The best weapon after a gun is a pair of running shoes.

I was using my lovers just as much as they were using me and I made them work hard to get what they wanted, each one becoming a lesson, learning how their minds worked and the things they would say in order to get what they wanted, practising my body language and unspoken signals to lure them to me, learning the lies and half-truths that would spew from their mouths.

I was in Thailand learning Muay Thai and scuba diving in the rest periods on Koh Lanta Island off the West coast, when I was forced to kill for the second time. I was letting my hair down at the Liberty Beach bar, after a morning of diving in the clear blue waters surrounding the Island and an afternoon getting out smarted by local fighters half my age who had probably worn boxing gloves before they wore shoes.

After several drinks, I was headed back along the beach, gazing at the moonlight reflecting of the perfectly flat sea, on the way to my beach to my hut. The golden sand, still warm from the days sun underneath my feet. I quietly sang the chorus from the last song I had heard at the bar a few minutes earlier, swinging my shoes in my hand.

Suddenly I became aware of someone really close behind me, my heart leaped and before I had time to think he had tackled me to the ground and was laying on my back, pushing my head into the sand as his hands pulled roughly at my fisherman trousers. Despite everything I had already learned, and even though I had been drilling the same moves over and over for hours on end, my body froze my mind dragged instantly back to the fourteen year old me in that park in Eastbourne.

Whoever he was, dragged at my pants until they were my down around my mid thighs his hand trying to force a way between my legs, as his

212

hand touched my vulva, I felt his breath on my neck, finally something inside me snapped and I threw my head back catching him full in the mouth and he let out a scream, my instincts kicked into action and I wriggled free before he could regain control of the situation. I was about to flee, the Adrenalin coursing through my veins sending my flight instinct into overdrive but my now much more developed fight instinct kept me rooted to the spot.

He faced me, arms out as if to block me, then he lunged at me at waist height in an attempt to tackle me to the ground once again, I anticipated his movement, perhaps it was muscle memory having been practicing all afternoon, or maybe my brain spotting the opportunity, whatever it was, as he lunged forward I launched off one foot, driving the other knee upwards as I did so smashing a jumping knee strike under his chin, knocking him flat on his back, I don't recall if he made a sound and he could have already been unconscious I didn't wait to find out as the rage descended.

I was upon him straddling him, punch after punch reigned down into his face, my fists relentless. It wasn't just him I was punching but Louis and every other person who had ever made my life miserable. I don't know how long I was hitting him for but by the time I looked down, there was no longer anything recognisable about his face as human. I dragged his body into the sea, the salt water stinging my blooded and battered knuckles. I walked calmly back to my beach hut aware of the silent tears running down my cheeks. Not tears of sadness but of relief, relief that I would never have to suffer at the hands of another again, my destiny now mine to control.

The police came the following morning, I'd watched them visiting each beach hut and listened to their questions as they interviewed each dweller, they kept it brief talking to them from the beach as the residents sat on their decks or on the steps up to them. I was scared but prepared. I stood in my doorway my hands resting at shoulder height on the door frame so not to expose my knuckles. I'd heard them ask for passports as they came down the beach so I'd already laid the document on the deck in front of my feet. I played the part of the scared tourist to perfection, horrified to hear that someone had been killed, were we safe? Should I call the embassy? what if they came back?

As I knew already from listening as they had made their way along the beach, the police seemed to have already put it down to a local rivalry, suggesting that the body belonged to a known criminal who had probably crossed the wrong person, keen to reassure me and the many other tourists that bring revenue to the Island that this was an isolated incident and everything was fine. They were sure to have the culprit apprehended soon and we should carry on without a concern but just to reassure us, they would be patrolling the sand at night. They didn't even bother to check my passport before they went off to the next hut to repeat the same reassurances.

Despite the instinct to pack up and flee, I stayed for a few more weeks, preferring to stay close and watch how things developed than move away and suffer the paranoia of being chased down. The marks on my hands were easy to pass off when combined with the ones on my legs from training, after all it was not unusual to see people from the fight schools sporting a variety of cuts and bruises.

The police hung around the beach smoking and chatting for the first few nights probably grateful for a change of scenery, Eventually the tourists in the huts had mostly been replaced by new ones, the excitement died down and the police drifted away.

I spent time processing how I felt, dealing with the emotion of taking a life, but also the life of someone who had intended to hurt me, perhaps even take my life. Lots of training I had done was designed to desensitise you to the act of violence, it had certainly helped at the time but was harder to process in the aftermath. I also thought about how I had reacted to the police, beginning to understand how easily we can present an external persona whilst terrified inside, learning to keep calm when paranoia is tearing at your insides is hard but

I continued my travels, embracing everything new that I could learn. Anything that might improve my chances of survival became of interest to me, if it was something I could use I devoured and practised it relentlessly until it was right, my life suddenly had a purpose like never before. By the time my trip was finished I could track someone physically or electronically, defend myself in most situations and take evasive action in a crisis as if it was instinct. My pain focused into anger and by the time I returned I was able to detach violence from emotion completely.

By the time I returned I was a changed person, both physically and mentally. In total I was away for the best part of three years.

They let Paul out yesterday within the 24 hours they can hold him without charge. His face was bruised he was sporting some butterfly stitches on his nose and eyebrow, his solicitor drove him home.

Paul wasn't wrong, his cottage is remote, Charlie and I went on a road trip. Following the car without being detected was hard, especially as his spider senses would have been on full alert, but my training had prepared me for this. I had a rough idea from our conversation which area it was in so I was able to get ahead of the car and wait for it to pass by. I doubled back staying at a distance and came around a bend just in time to watch it turn into a narrow track half way up the valley, Charlie barking as if to tell me Paul was in the car, Instead of following I headed up to higher ground, the dog looking at me puzzled before settling back down on to the seat.

I was able to spot the solicitors car through my binoculars winding and bumping slowly along the track, splashing the sides of his executive saloon with mud, the low road suspension not enjoying the journey. Following the track I could see a solitary property with an old Land Rover parked outside and a builders van. I mark the location on the OS app on my phone.

Nothing on the news over the past few days and it's time to leave, I've taken the bike from the underground car park and dumped it, a quick trip to the river was all that was required, wheeling the bike along the footpath, under the bridge where I stashed my kit the other night. I don't often return to the same spots but this was nicely sheltered, quiet after dark and easy to get to. I park it side on and then push it in. A quick splash and then nothing. It'll be years before it's recovered.

I head back to collect Charlie from the apartment. I can't envisage this place appearing on any investigators radar, but I'll still clean it for prints and the owners will be organising a Covid deep-clean for the next guests. If it does come up at any point, there will have been so many people through the apartment leaving more DNA that it'll be worthless as evidence anyway. I drop the keys back into the letter box as I leave.

Charlie snuggles into the seat of the Volvo for the last time, we head up into the hills again and park up at the same location I watched Paul from yesterday. Dressed all in black, I put a muzzle on Charlie "Sorry buddy, I can't have you barking until it's time" He looks at me with those forlorn eyes that make my heart melt.

The journey down the hill is not too bad, using the moonlight as much as possible to find the way, our breaths clouding in the cold night air the OS app guiding me to the pinned location. I let Charlie off the lead, he busies himself sniffing for rabbits and responding to nocturnal animal activity but he stays close, waiting for me to catch up. I'm going to miss him.

The back of his property is open to a small patch of woodland which gives me cover, holding Charlie's collar, I take off his muzzle and stroking his ears, giving him a final hug I whisper too him, "Go and find Paul, he'll look after you" He licks my ear and face, pawing at my leg as if to say 'come with me' "Good boy off you go" I throw a handful of treats towards the backdoor and he trots over, sniffing out the snacks. I retreat, using the trees for cover, looking back to see the dog silhouetted against the muted light cast by the back door window.

He let's out a solitary bark and then sits down. I see the curtain move and I turn and walk purposefully back the way I came, once I'm a few hundred metres away I break into a jog. My wounds throb a little as the blood pumps around my body and my ribs ache as my lungs expand and contract. Back at the car, I scan the property with the binoculars. I can see them both framed in the light from the doorway looking out into the night as if letting me know they are OK.

I've let myself get too distracted, firstly by the dog and then hesitating with Paul, I have no intention of trying to finish him off now, not because I'm fearful, he's a formidable opponent but you can take anyone out if you plan it right. There is something about him, something intoxicating that draws me too him, I'm not sure I could go through with it and that is dangerous, I have a plan to stick to and besides who would look after the dog?

I must stay focused. Those two have taken up too much of my time already, I need to get back on course. I head back to Crowlink to heal and to revise my plan.

Chapter 8

I've kept the narcissistic fuckwit Julian interested with messages over the past few weeks, I fancy a trip to Sheffield and move him into the spotlight. I make my usual arrangements and suggest we meet up.

I check the spreadsheet to see where we left off and look at the last few messages

"Hi Julian, sorry I haven't had chance to message you since yesterday, I've been busy at work. I'm hoping you still want to meet me, I know we've been chatting a while and I've not been able to meet but I'm free this weekend. I wondered if you're available this coming Friday?" Passive and apologetic enough I think.

"Well, well you have been a busy girl haven't you? But I'm willing to forgive you, I'm sure you can make it up to me, I could make myself available on Friday" Grit your teeth Alys, grit your teeth.

"I'm glad you are, where shall we meet?" I'll see what he comes up with and suggest somewhere else if it's not appropriate.

"I'm thinking of a nice restaurant I know called Rafters, I doubt you have been there, it's quite upmarket, it's difficult to get a table there especially in the current climate but I should be able to pull a few strings, give me half an hour and I'll see what I can do" The conversation has already started with him showing me how much better he is than me and how grateful I should be.

Logging on to the restaurant website, I see It is less than a mile from his house, that will work nicely. They also have space for Friday night, so let's see what he comes back with.

Twenty minutes later he texts back. "Good news, they were full but I had a word with the manager and they have found me a space" Not us, him, they found him a space because he's the alpha. I want to play along so I ask him;

"What should I wear? Is it very glamorous?"

"Well it is quite expensive so you'll need to look the part, maybe send me some pictures of what you intended to wear and I'll let you know whether I think it's suitable, nothing too slutty I don't want people to think I'm paying you! I'm joking of course, I'm sure you will look delightful!" It's exactly this sort of comment that appears throw away but will leave a woman panicking about what to wear, concerned for his approval rather than her own sense of self esteem and self worth.

"I think I have just the dress"

"Why don't you send me a picture first?"

"I think it'll be OK, I've eaten out once or twice before"

"Hmmmm ok I'm sure you'll look great, but don't show me up, I am a regular there and have a reputation to uphold. I'm looking forward to meeting you finally, it seems like we have been chatting for ages. You are always so busy, I'll have to have words with that boss of yours!"

We arrange the details. Julian lives in Fullwood, a salubrious area of Sheffield. I'm not sure how he would react to being pushed to take me back to his on a first date so I need a plan to get me there. He thinks I live in the centre of Sheffield so it's two or three miles further to mine than his, I have an idea that should work, if it doesn't I know where he lives so I'll just turn up later and kill him then.

We arrange to meet at the restaurant, as I arrive in the taxi, he is standing outside with a face mask on. I arrive five minutes late, on purpose of course, just to piss him off. He looks smartly turned out, well groomed and immaculate

"Hi Julian, I like your suit"

"You are late, but thank you"

"Am I? Oh well I'm here now, it's only five minutes, shall we go in?"

I nip the chance for him to belittle me in the bud, I'll give him plenty of opportunity for that later, the restaurant is formal, with tables laid with starched grey cloths to match the fabric of the dining chairs, and we are seated next to the window, the glass ware sparkles form the candlelight all ready flickering, the cutlery is laid out in rows, a nice throw back to the more traditional dining rooms that seem to have been replaced by bare tables and cutlery in a tin bucket. Julian has good taste it would seem, the six course tasting menu looks exquisite.

He turns on the charm, talking slightly louder than I would expect, then I realise he is performing to the tables around us, he wants them to notice him. The staff clearly know him, greeting him in that 'hello sir, how are you today' voice through a fake smile when what they actually mean is 'oh great it's you again you patronising prick'.

Surprisingly he actually compliments me on my dress, I've gone for a plum velvet cocktail dress, black stockings and classic black patent heels. The neckline allows for just an inch of cleavage, subtle but drop dead sexy. My heart necklace frames my neck, my brother always close by.

Julian couldn't be more charming, that is as long as the conversation is about him. He asks me about work and how I can afford to live in S1, One of the more expensive parts of the city. I start to make up a story about a finance role, it's always easier to lie when there is an element of truth so I tell him about trading stocks and shares, his face grows redder, either annoyed that I potentially earn more than him or that he thinks I'm showing off. I trial off "Anyway I'm

224

sure it's not as exciting as what you do, my job really is just buying and selling it's not complicated like your job" The anger seems to subside and he launches into a well practised monologue about the importance of his work and how difficult it is for most people but how his superior intellect can cope with it, how the place would fall apart without him blah blah blah. I can't even remember what he does but I dare not ask as he'll know I've not been paying attention.

I notice a few glances from the other diners which I read as embarrassment, Julian notices them too but instead of picking up on the vibe, seems to enjoy the attention mistaking it for admiration.

I bring up a story I had watched on the news this morning, a father had drowned with his daughter in his arms trying to cross the Rio Grande from Mexico to America. I said to Julian, how awful it must be to be that desperate, how I had nearly cried seeing the lifeless bodies on the banks of the river, the fathers attempt at a better life resulting in the end for both him and his daughter. I pause to hear Julian's thoughts on it, expecting him to agree with me, instead he launches into why these 'low life scum' will always fall short of the mark, how life is survival of the fittest and how Trump is absoultely right to build the wall to keep out the vermin.

I eye the shiny silver steak knife, in the middle of the row of cutlery as he talks, imagining cutting out that flapping tongue but I manage to keep myself in check, as he waves his arms around I slide it off the table into my bag, that will come in handy for later.

Unsurprisingly he quickly manages to make it about him, how he had very little help to get to where he has got to, managing to somehow compare his decidedly middle class first world life to a destitute man in Mexico and make himself seem worse off, I see one woman over his shoulder look at me with what I can only describe as pity.

The food makes up for the bombastic company and by the time I get to the sixth course, my taste buds have been truly stimulated, unlike my ears.As the waiter deposits the English strawberry mouse with white chocolate in front of me I knock it into my lap, covering the dress in the dessert and meringue, the glass dish dropping on to the carpet. The customers and staff turn to look at the unfolding scene as the waiter does his best to help me clean up, apologising profusely. I snatch a glance at Julian's face, I've always wondered what the colour puce looks like, now I know. He stands up, walks around to my side of the table and grabs my arm, literally dragging me from the restaurant, as we stand in the street he snarls at me through gritted teeth.

"I have never been so fucking embarrassed, wait here whilst I go and pay" Well that went better than planned, I thought it would annoy him but the exit was even more than I could have hoped for.

I stand there with the mousse staining my dress waiting for him to come out, wondering how I would feel if this was actually happening to me, would I walk away or simply stand and wait? Would I behave differently to any other woman if I wanted to impress this man and if it had been an accident? What would be going through my head; Would I think it was my fault because I spilled the dessert and his reaction was justifiable? Did I deserve to be spoken to like this?

His face is the same colour of purple as he exits the restaurant "What the hell was that? I'll be ashamed to go back in there ever again"

"I'm sorry It was an accident, I just knocked it over, these things happen"

"These things don't happen to ME"

"Look I'm sorry, it really was an accident, I didn't mean to embarrass you. I'm sorry if it ruined the evening but I can't just stand here in the street, I need to get cleaned up"

"Well it did ruin the evening, I can't believe you have done this to me."

"Done this to you? I'm the one covered in mousse! I guess I'll just get a taxi. Let me pay you back for the dinner to make it up to you"

"I never let a lady pay don't insult me further. I live five minutes walk away, you'll come back to my house, I can't have you standing here any longer embarrassing me with everyone gawping at you through the window. You can come back as long as you promise not to break anything, I'll give you a tracksuit to wear and you can get a taxi from there" Bingo the plan is working.

He doesn't even wait for me to answer, he grabs my hand and strides off in the direction of his house, forcing me to totter along beside him on my heels, It's going to be really difficult not to kill this man in the next thirty seconds but I refrain from letting my instincts take over. I'm going to make sure I really enjoy this one.

His house is a modern detached property at the end of a cul-de-sac. It's a large place probably four or five bedrooms, clearly Julian has done well for himself, I also happen to know that his grandfather left him a house that he sold to pay for a big part of this one.

From the outside it's very neat and tidy, too modern for my tastes and it's a bit 'building by numbers' but appealing none the less. He leads me in to his porch then into the large open plan lounge. "Stand there" He commands. Turning the lights on as he strides up the stairs. I look around the living room, it's like a show home with not a thing out of place. The furniture is a mixture of modern and vintage yet the place lacks character, everything is muted and somehow characterless. He returns carrying a towel, "you can take off your shoes here and use this to stop anything dripping on the carpet. Go upstairs to the bathroom on the left at the top, It's easy to spot it's the one with the open door, I'll bring you something to wear in a minute, try not to damage anything else please" His anger is palpable in the room, his knuckles white as he grips the towel before passing it to me, for a fleeting moment I think he might actually be about to hit me. A man so used to being in control faced with a situation so far from it.

I take the towel from him, kicking my shoes off onto the expensive looking carpet as I head up the stairs, aware of his eyes glaring after me. "I'm so sorry Julian" I say glancing back at him with an embarrassed look on my face. I close the bathroom door behind me and I hear him follow me up the stairs and go into one of the other rooms, He angrily opens and closes draws and makes a big show of rattling around. I imagine he is picking out his shittiest clothes to give to me, a further tool in his humiliation of me.

I peel off the dress, dropping it on the floor, I'll collect that later, the family bathroom is large with a bath and separate walk in shower, tiled from floor to ceiling again it's modern but soulless. I turn the tap on in the bath letting the noise drown out my activities.

I take off my bra and panties along with my stockings and jewellery dropping them in the corner onto my dress, the feeling of being naked in a strangers house, knowing what I am about to do turns me on, the element of the unknown and the excitement starts my Adrenalin pumping.

I look at myself in the mirror and mouth the words 'number five'. Funny how not that long ago I was standing in Jakes bathroom feeling terrified and here I am feeling almost calm.

I open the bathroom cabinet, taking out a bottle of shampoo. "Julian! Help, Come quickly" I hear his footsteps hurrying along the corridor. "What is it now? What have you done?" His voice is agitated and angry and he shouts the words as if in a rage.

I open the door letting it swing wide into the room, one hand holding the shampoo bottle behind the door as I stand there in front of him, naked. "Will you help me get clean?" I purr giving him my best coy eyes. I can see his brain working overtime, he's annoyed and likes to be in control yet in front of him is a naked woman asking him to touch her body. I don't give him time to decide, using his hesitation to seize the moment, I step forward and pull out the shampoo squeezing the bottle hard, a jet of the soapy liquid hitting him in the eyes, he yells out in surprise and grabs at his face.

"My eyes! Oh my god, you crazy bitch what are you doing?"

As he flaps around I grab the bottoms of his trousers legs and yank towards me pulling his feet from underneath him, they slip easily on the shampoo covered floor and he lands with a yelp of pain on his arse. He claws at his face in panic, unable to see, yelling and screaming.

The beauty of a detached house is it's a lot harder for the neighbours to hear, still I need to shut him up just in case, besides I've heard enough from this dick head this evening to last me a lifetime or should I say the rest of his? I drag him by his collar on his heels not allowing him to stand up and pull him all the way into the master bedroom. There is a dressing gown on the back of the door, I use the belt to tie his hands behind his back and to the leg of the bed. His eyes are streaming but he has cleared his eyes enough to be able to see again, he doesn't stop talking

 "Oh my god, I know who you are, you're that crazy serial killer bitch, HELP... SOMEBODY HELP"

I kneel in front of him pinching his face, holding his mouth open,

"You can't stop saying nasty things can you Julian, maybe we should wash your mouth out?"

This time I squeeze the shampoo bottle directly into his mouth , emptying the remaining contents into it, he thrashes against me but I manage to get plenty in and he chokes and gags on the liquid soap, spitting it out onto the carpet and retching. He manoeuvres himself around so he is on all fours coughing and spluttering, I take a pillow from the bed and strip off the case and find a pair of socks in one of his drawers, I stuff the socks into his mouth and pull the pillowcase over his head.

"I'll be back in a minute, make any more fucking noise and I'll kill you"

I'm going to kill him anyway but the human mind will comply when faced with great danger if it thinks there is a chance of survival. He'll does as he is told for now in the hope that he can survive until a better opportunity arises.

Julian has 'kindly' left me a sweatshirt and some tracksuit bottoms on the bed, they look like they have previously been used for D.I.Y or painting, still they will do for now so I pull them on. I pad downstairs enjoying the feel of the soft carpet between my toes, my handbag sits by my shoes and I locate the key for the car I parked in the cul-de-sac yesterday.

I take a cap from the coat stand in the porch pulling it down over my face and jog out to the car, the wet pavement cold on my feet a stark contrast to his plush carpet. I grab the holdall from the boot, slinging it over one shoulder and jog on tip-toes the few metres back to his house. As I enter I can hear him moving about, no doubt trying to move the bed to free his hands. I pick up my handbag and run up the stairs catching him half under the bed attempting to lift it with his shoulders. I jump onto the bed flattening him into the carpet the bed frame crashing into his ribs.

He whimpers, gasping for breath the pillowcase still over his head. I leave him there enjoying the terror he must be feeling hearing me walk around the bedroom. I place the holdall on the bed and unzip it. Taking out first the leg spreader. I attach the leather cuffs to one ankle and then the other, the two foot long bar forcing his feet apart.

Next it's the handcuffs, the dressing gown belt is too difficult to undo now, the knot tightened by his struggle. I take a knife from the bag and cut at the toweling fabric, taking his left wrist behind his back and fastening the cuffs on, collecting his other hand as I do and cuffing that. I drag him out from under the bed and pull him awkwardly to his feet, the bar making him stand spread-eagled. Shoving him down on to the mattress, I take the scissors from the bag and cut away his clothes, he whimpers and twitches as the cold steel glances against his skin, the sharp blades making light work of the fabric.

Once he is naked, I take the dental mouth prop from out of the bag; a tool used by dentists to keep the patients mouth forced open. Pulling the hood from over his head makes him blink against the light, his eyes are still streaming the skin red around the lids, his face is a mixture of soap, snot and tears. I pull the socks from his mouth, grabbing his hair and wrenching his head back as the prop is forced in, he looks almost comical with his cheeks extended and his mouth forced wide.

Along one wall of the bedroom is a full length mirrored wardrobe, so I position him sat on the edge of the bed facing the mirror. "Do you know the story of Narcissus Julian?" He shakes his head. As he sits perched on the edge I begin to tell him the story:

"Narcissus was a beautiful young man that many people fell in love with at first sight, however in return he only showed them disdain and contempt, sound familiar Julian? One day the nymph Echo saw him and instantly fell in love"

As I say the words I slowly walk up and down parading in front of him watching him in the mirror as I tell him the story. He makes sucking, grunting noises trying to swallow the saliva being produced by his overstretched lips.

"She tried to hug Narcissus but he rejected her telling her she wasn't good enough and pushing her away. That's what you do isn't it Julian? Get women to like you then crush them with words?"

He shakes his head vigorously and tries to speak, his eyes have reached the pleading stage. I ignore him

"Echo roamed the woods in despair until she wilted away and all that remained was an echo sound. See Julian, he had robbed her of her identity until there was nothing left of her. That's what you do to women. Nemesis the goddess of retribution, and just for the point of clarity Julian. that's me in this story"

I turn away from the mirror at this point looking straight at him, "Nemesis learned what had happened and decided to punish Narcissus for his behaviour. She led him to a pool and when he saw his own reflection he fell instantly in love with it, however he spent so long staring at his own perceived beauty that he stumbled into the pool and drowned. Now Julian those Greeks were pretty good at coming up with creative ways to kill people but what Nemesis should have done, in my humble opinion of course"

I lean right in inches from his face for full effect "Is cut out his nasty, spiteful, vicious tongue"

He lets out a stifled scream, the stretched open mouth making it hard to form the sound.

I walk around to my hand bag, and pull out the steak knife from dinner.

"I had always planned to cut your tongue out Julian, the way you speak to women should be an example to everyone of how not to treat another human being, then I saw this knife at dinner and just thought how perfect it would be."

His eyes wider now, he attempts to stand, the leg spreader and hand cuffs making it difficult, he falls back onto the bed in the vain hope of rolling off to the other side, there is no escape.

From the holdall comes the tongue forceps. I show them to Julian and then push him on to his back straddling his body, I inch up using the weight of my thighs to pin him to the bed, squeezing my knees on either side of his head to keep it as still as I can. He thrashes from side to side but I hold his face with one hand and grab the tongue with the other pulling hard with the forceps.

Then with one, two, three strokes of the serrated blade I cut through the tongue. He begins to choke as the blood fills his mouth, I climb off him and drop the pink lump onto the bedside table, there is plenty of blood but he's not going to bleed to death immediately, pulling him back up to sitting, facing the mirror. "See now Julian, you can't say anymore horrible things to people can you?" I don't expect an answer.

"Of course that bit was just my own adaptation of the story, the real ending was drowning"

I grab his right ear digging my nails into it, using it to pull him off the bed, he stumbles forwards trying to keep up as the leg spreaders make it hard for him to walk, reminiscent of him dragging me along in my heels.

I lead him into the bathroom, he tries to resist but has no force with his hands cuffed and his legs spread, he see's the bath full of water ready and waiting for him, with one last effort he tries to throw himself backwards, I allow him too then just as he reaches the furthest point I use the momentum to fling him forwards, his chest smashes into the edge of the bath and I plunge his head under the cold water. His legs kick out as the water turns to pink and Julian's life ends like Narcissus.

'You're gonna catch a cold'

it's not the most impactful line from the song but it's the one he is getting, I need to get to the heart, the steak knife is an option but it'll take ages. I've given myself the luxury of some tools in the bag. I flip him over, positioning him on the floor face up, removing the dental prop as I do. I find an extension lead in one of the bedrooms and run it from a socket in the hallway to the bathroom, I plug in the small angle grinder and cut into him, making light work of his chest, it's very messy though and by the time I'm finished I have blood up to my elbows, the bathroom tiles displaying impressive spurts and splatters of blood and tissue, globules of flesh slide down the wall and land in the bathwater, spreading out like Halloween bath bombs, the police forensics will have a field day. Once I'm through the bone I use the steak knife to hack part of the heart out dropping it into the jar, a liberal spreading of entrails form the other murders chucked around the bathroom creates a fantastically gory scene fit for a horror movie.

I drag his corpse to the bedroom, leaving a bloody skid trail along the carpet, I reposition him on the bed, facing the mirror, I pick up the forceps and write in large letters across it using the lump of tongue to spell out the words, finally I leave the card positioned between his bloodstained lips.

Once finished I admire my handiwork one last time before I begin the clean-up routine, Julian has turned blue, his ankles fat where the blood has started to pool no longer pumped by his heart that sits in my bag.

Chapter 9

'Banrigh Writes' Exclusive

Another Murder – Queen of Hearts strikes again. Gruesome findings in Sheffield.

Monday October 26th 2020

It appears that the Queen of Hearts has struck again. The following statement was issued by the North Yorkshire police:

'A man is his late 30's was discovered dead in his own home on Sunday the 25th of October in the Fullwood area of Sheffield. The victim displayed injuries that are consistent with those found at other crimes attributed to the self-styled Queen of Hearts murderer. Forensic experts estimate the crime took place sometime between 8.30pm and 11.00pm on the evening of Saturday the 24th. The victim's family have been informed and the police urge anyone with information relating to this case or any of the other murders to come forward'

His name is yet to be released as the police continue with their enquiries and background investigations, looking into what may have made him a target.

Fullwood is and affluent suburban area and local residents described the news as 'Shocking' and 'Deeply worrying' the events in their otherwise quiet cul-de-sac. One neighbour we interviewed said the victim; "tended to keep himself to himself but had never been any trouble and always looked well presented' she thought he worked in the central Sheffield area. It is believed a cleaner raised the alarm upon discovering the body on Sunday morning"

This Friday the 30th of October I will be presenting a special live edition of Crimewatch for the BBC. The programme will feature re-enactments of the events leading up to the first four murders in the hope that public may be able to provide further information as to the identity of the killer. The police will also issue a further statement on yesterday's murder.

I shall also be sharing details from the correspondence sent to me by the killer and reviewing it with a criminal profiler as well as speaking to a number of criminal psychologists to build a picture of the type of person we could be looking for.

We will also look at the victims in an attempt to understand how the killer may be selecting her victims.

The murders have taken place as follows:-

Bristol   Jake Simmonds March 6th

Brighton   Shaun McBride July 10th

Manchester   Kevin Gower July 31st

Coventry   Jim Whittaker August 13th

Sheffield   Julian Tyrell October 24th

It is an honour for me to be able to present this one off special of the Crimewatch programme, which was axed in 2017 due to falling viewer numbers however has been brought back for this one off special due to the huge amount of public interest in this case. The broadcast will link detectives from all five police forces working on the cases. Detectives will be on hand to take calls, emails and texts. You can follow the show live on Twitter with the hashtag #QueenCW The number to call is 08081 570000 The police urge anyone with information relating to any of the crimes, no matter how insignificant it may seem to come forward.

The programme will start at 9pm on BBC 2

I send Liz another letter:

Dearest Liz,

Great to see you have a TV special coming up, looks like my work is helping you with your career too, I wouldn't want you to have to present the show without a little update from me so feel free to use this letter. I think you and I are quite similar in a lot of ways Liz, we're both driven to get what we want and know how to use men to get it.

241

Just so you know it's me, I wrote the words on the mirror using Julian's tongue.

I cut it out to stop him saying anymore spiteful words to women, men like him need to realise that they cannot just destroy women's lives to feed their narcissistic egos.

No doubt they'll want you to paint me as a monster but I trust that you will do the right thing and let the public know that there is a bigger message here and it's time that us women stood up for ourselves.

Good luck with the show, I'll be watching you.

Q.O.H

Things are going to plan and already I'm ready for number six, London will be the perfect location, especially with the Crimewatch programme being filmed in White City, the desire to do something right under their noses is too tempting a proposition. Unknowingly they have given me the perfect situation to pick up my Eastern European friend again and take a little taxi ride.

I buy a used car ten or so miles along the coast road from my home in Seaford. I fill it up with fuel and take the drive cross country along the A22 to East Croydon and get the train into Victoria, from there I take the District line to

Chiswick Park and walk the rest of the way to the apartment on the side of the river. It's always good to cover my tracks even before anything happens.

I arrive on Thursday and apart from picking up some groceries from Marks and Spencer and a wander up the high street for a few items , I stay in the flat. Friday morning I go for a quick 5km run along the riverside towards Hammersmith, over the bridge, returning along the other side and back over Kew bridge, a takeaway breakfast and coffee on the way and I sit on the balcony to finalise tonight's plan.

The easiest way around London is by bike...pushbike. The apartment comes with an underground car park which also houses a cycle rack, there are around twenty bikes in the rack many of which are dusty and seldom used. I take the rubbish down to the bin room in case I encounter anyone and take the opportunity to check out the different bikes. I find what I'm looking for, those four number combination locks take minimal effort to undo and after fifteen minutes I've got the number of a half decent mountain bike. I have my own here but using my own kit would be fool hardy, I want to be able to return it as if nothing has happened so it doesn't lead back to here. In the case I'm not able to get it back in a few days, I doubt they will report it stolen for a while judging by the layer of dust that sits upon it. I make a note of the number and re-lock it and use the pump from my bike to make sure the tyres are firm. It's just under three miles cycle ride to where I want to be a very easy distance.

You can move easily around a city dressed in black like some sort of urban commando, you just simply have to wear running or sports gear and nothing will look out of place. I pack my holdall with black running tights, black trainers and a hoodie, I need something else to ride the bike in but also something that might look like I've been working in a cool media environment. Skinny stretch jeans, grey New Balance trainers, white long sleeve top and a black denim jacket, topped off with a helmet and a black face mask, the air quality in London is pretty dodgy after all.

I take the lights from my own bike and a decent lock, no point getting stopped by the police or worse, run over. The risky part of my plan is I do not know where I'm going to end up, I'm a strong runner so as long as were in central London I'm good, that is as long as I don't pick up any injuries and everything goes as it should. My plan is to run back through the streets like I did in Cardiff, just another late night runner pounding the pavements. I need a few more items for the back pack, a beanie and a head-torch, lighter fluid and a zippo, a small first aid kit with field bandages, you can never be too careful, some cable ties and a small bottle of whiskey.

On a lanyard around my neck I hang a push dagger, it's a short two inch blade with a handle that fits between your fingers so you punch to stab with it, ideal for short range combat where space is at a premium, like in a car. The last items in the bag are the jars, one full of gloop, the other empty in preparation.

With everything ready I try to relax for the rest of the day. The nervous energy makes me fidgety and I can't concentrate on any one thing for too long, TV on TV off, crossword puzzle, read a book, flick through a magazine nothing really holds my attention for too long. 9pm finally comes and I switch on the TV and an ominous and oppressive sound transports me back to a childhood bedtime. The Crimewatch theme stirs my adrenal gland, the military paradiddle of snare drums, conjures an idea of a national anthem of some far off eastern-block regime, kettle drum combined with brass brings back memories of sitting on the sofa at home with Charlie and Dad, hiding behind cushions being scared by real life crimes. I imagine the people watching tonight will be scared, for a change I imagine it will be the men in the household rather than the women but men tend to have that innate sense of belief that it won't happen to them, I imagine them sitting on their sofa's saying to their wives, girlfriends or mates that 'no woman could overpower me' how wrong they are.

The re-enactments are interesting, they have of course picked up the locations of each of the meetings and show some CCTV footage from each of the venues, the expensive restaurant I met Jim in has the highest quality and Elizabeth makes reference to the fact that some witnesses have mentioned there is a passing resemblance between the killer and herself. I'm impressed by some of the police work, on the same murder they managed to work out that I took a bike from the other side of the field but then their trail runs cold.

There is a lot of speculation about how I might be attracting men and they touch on some of the photo's I used to lure in my victims, even doing a good job of pointing out that the group ones don't even contain the same person.

The psychologists make an interesting but generalist assessment; 'wronged by men, unhappy childhood, possible sexual assault, angry' nothing that you wouldn't expect. Banrigh makes comment at this point and asks the psychologist why he thinks the particular victims have been selected, she labours this point, asking which men in society should be careful and what message the killer is trying to send. The psychologist looks uncomfortable with the line of questioning and the co-host tries to interject, Banrigh continues on regardless, pushing the point by asking the questions;

'Would this be happening if the patriarchy wasn't so entrenched in society? Do you think that this killer is a product of society rather than just of a bad childhood?'

The psychologist glances around the studio as if to say this line of questioning wasn't discussed and tries to form an answer but looks out of his depth, before he has finished she makes another statement, animal rights campaigners use violence to get their point across, protesters rise up violently against oppressive regimes, terrorists make their demands know through acts of violence, for years men have used violence to get what they want, from waging war on each other to beating their wives into submission, is it unsurprising that women are finally starting to consider violence as a way to be heard?" she segues to the next section without waiting for his answer, underlining her point beautifully.

Twitter goes crazy at this point with a split between those of the opinion that Banrigh is right and we need more people like her, a few even suggest that they support what I am doing! The other half are outraged that she is using the platform to apparently push her own agenda. Controversial as ever Liz and never one to miss an opportunity to further your career, what's more you are bringing my plan together beautifully.

It's a two hour special, they report of calls coming in of possible sightings on the days in question but I know I have all my tracks covered so I'm not worried, it's surreal to watch actors taking the same steps and to hear the presenters talking about me, It's strange but I feel surprisingly calm not stressed about getting caught, of course they won't reveal everything they have but the basic elements of the lead up to, and aftermath of events, they are focusing on make me think they have very little to go on in the first place. I appreciate the reassurance BBC thanks very much.

As the programme is drawing to a close, I leave the apartment and head down in the lift to the carpark. I unlock the bike, attach the lights and head off into the city, along the river first before heading North across Chiswick High Road and onto Goldhawk Road which takes me all the way to Shepherds Bush, I head off through the back streets and come out at the impressive Janet Adegoke leisure centre where I park my bike. I walk the remaining three quarters of a mile to Television centre. The thrill of standing outside the building where no doubt the officers looking for me are still taking calls is exhilarating, talking of calls it's time to give my taxi driver friend a ring.

He answers the phone and I slur into the receiver, "Can I get a cab please?"

"Sure no problem, where are you"

248

"Television centre, White City"

"Where you want go?"

I've figured on a location that gives me enough
time to pretend to fall asleep but close enough to
keep him on his patch and an area that I should
be familiar with myself.

"Notting Hill"

"Sure thing, what's your name?"

"Tina, how long will you be?"

"Ten minutes, no problem, I be there soon" I
know this is not true as the tracking device I
stuck under his car seat back in August tells me
he's at least twenty minutes away but when was
a taxi ever on time?

"Ok I'll be outside"

I hang around in the shadows across the road
from our watching him on my phone waiting for
him to arrive. I call him back again "Five minutes,
bad traffic sorry, five minutes"

A take a mouthful of the whiskey, the darker
spirit having a stronger smell on the breath, and
swill it around spitting it out on to the pavement.
A couple of splashes onto my top for maximum
stench and I'm good to go. I let my hair down
taking off the hat and stuffing it in my bag and let
the long blonde tresses rest on my shoulders, I
leave the face mask off.

249

Pavel pulls up outside Television centre in his Skoda Octavia so I stagger over the road to the drivers side, attempting to open the back door, it's locked and as I pull on the handle I make a big scene of falling backwards on my arse into the road, giggling as I do.

Pavel gets out of the car, gives me his hand and helps me up. "You is Tina yes? Let's get you in car, I look after"

I giggle and nod as he guides his arm around my waist and leads me around the front to the passenger seat.

Opening the door for me as I take a stagger first backwards then lurch forwards into the car. "You no be sick in car?" He brushes my hair away from my face. "You very pretty lady"

"No I'm good, honest, I'll be fine, giggle. I put my finger onto his lips and make a shhhhhush sound, giggling as I do" He walks back around the front of the car, I adjust my jacket so that my tits push out between the lapels giving him an eye full., the headlights reflecting back off his stonewashed jeans as he passes along the nose of the vehicle.

Back in the drivers seat, he leans in close. "Where you go?"

I breathe my whiskey breath over him as I slur "Ladbroke Road, Notting Hill please"

"Sure thing beautiful, did you have good night?"
He asks as he pulls away from the kerb, I smile
and nod, I"I like this tune" I say in response.

"I like your sexy hair, I like blonde very much,
you go home to your boyfriend?"

"Not tonight" I mumble as if sleepy closing my
eyes.

I lie my head back on to the headrest nodding my
head in time to the chilled music and slowly stop
moving letting my head roll off towards the
passenger side window as if drifting off to sleep.
I keep one eye open looking out, following the
route he is taking. He drives us under the A40
Westway takes a right and doubles back on
himself down a small industrial road called
Stable way. This road is deserted at night, filled
with lock ups and garages, half repaired cars and
bits of disassembled engine litter the edges. He
weaves his way slowly down the road avoiding
the potholes in the road surface long overdue a
resurface, until the car is under the Westway
flyover.

It's a desolate area which is probably a hive of
activity during the day but at this hour devoid of
anyone save the nocturnal adventuring of foxes.
He pulls over to the side and switches off the
engine, I hear him unclip his seatbelt and then I
feel his hand on my thigh, sliding up my leg, he
reaches across with his other hand and pushes it
against my breast mashing it with his palm, as

251

his fingers reach the buttons of my jeans I open my eyes and look at him "What's going on?" I look shocked.

"Shhh it's ok, keep quiet" I move my right hand onto his, grabbing his wrist I pretend to resist him, his other hand reaches for my throat and as he grabs me says

"You keep quiet, you do what I say now, I not hurt if you do as I tell"

He pushes harder into my throat, his thumb and fingers gripping my windpipe, opening the passenger door he climbs over me pulling me out of the car by my arm and neck. There is a gap in the fence that leads to the dirt amongst the concrete supports of the flyover, dimly lit in patches from the light cast by the motorway lamps above. Gripping one arm he forces me through the hole and I stumble onto my hands and knees, his foot slams into the small of my back flattening me into the ground. Straddling me his face kissing my neck I can smell his breath and feel it hot on my skin, I squirm under him, struggling to make him think he is in control

"You like that huh, you girls all same, get drunk and have no self respect, I have many girls like you in my car"

Reaching under me he pulls the fly buttons undone and drags the jeans down to my ankles. I pretend to resist, gripping hard and pulling back at the waist band, as he wrenches the fabric from

252

between my fingers, my hand reaches under me defensively as if to protect my vagina, distracted by trying to pull my hand away he doesn't notice the other sliding up under my top to reach the dagger between my breasts, my fingers wrap around the gripped handle and I pull it from it's sheath.

He pulls at my panties and I rise up onto my elbows wriggling forward kicking with my feet trying to get some purchase to move away from him, he grabs at my shoulder pulling me back towards him, wanting to roll me over onto my back, as he does I use the momentum of his force and I swing my arm jabbing the short blade into his face, then two short jabs into his neck. He screams grabbing at his neck with both hands and I thrust up with my hips forcing him to fall off me, still clutching his hands to his wounds. I rise pulling up my jeans buttoning them as I stand over him, wiping his disgusting spit from my neck. He lies face up, his legs pushing into the dirt trying to slide himself away from me.

"You fucking rapist scum bag, there's no need to explain anything to you"

And with that I drop onto him with both knees, my fist jabbing at his torso with the double edged blade, puncturing his flesh in a new place with each blow. He stops moving, his blood pooling in the dark earth around him.

My breathing begins to slow as the yellowy light casts multiple shadows on concrete structures around us. I walk back to his car and open the boot looking for tools I can use to open his chest. There is a wheel brace and jack neatly stored in a moulded tray inside the spare wheel under the boot carpet, both of which I take, as I pull out the tray, I find a small leather folder, I sit on the edge of the boot, the interior light is inadequate but I can clearly see that the folder contains Polaroids of girls, unconscious naked or semi naked either in the car or on the ground, I doubt I'm the first person he has brought to this location, these are clearly previous victims he has taken advantage of, I count at least twelve different women.

I take the jack and brace back to the body. Cutting along the line of his ribs with the dagger, like opening a tin can I open a flap of skin, using the wheel brace I push his stomach down and wedge it in raising up his rib cage, I force the folded jack into the space, making squelching noises as it forces the air and fluid out of the space. I attach the handle and begin turning it slowly, the jack opens and extend its arms so that it pushes the rib cage up, stretching it out against the spine, there is a satisfying crack as the sternum splits and I hack his heart out with the small dagger.

I drop it into the earth and stamp on it with my heel. I walk back to the car once again retrieving my bag. Back at the body the bits of squashed heart goes into the jar, I use the contents of the other to smear around swapping the contents for some of the contents of his stomach. Dragging his body up to the edge of the concrete pillar I position him face down pointing at the opposite wall. Taking the paint can from my bag I write the words:

"From the ice inside your soul"

I squirt some of the lighter fluid onto what is left of his clothes. I take a couple of glugs from the whiskey bottle, I've earned this drink and the fiery spirit warms and stings my throat reminding me of the recently applied pressure. I pour the remainder of the small bottle inside his body cavity, strip off my jeans and top, using them to wipe the blood from my skin as best I can and once I have redressed in my running gear I pack the jars into my bag. I take the Zippo lighter, the flame momentarily casting movement onto the brutalist concrete, and squirt some more of the fluid through its flame, it ignites into an orange jet like a mini flamethrower and as it hits the body, the fumes from the lighter fluid and whiskey igniting instantly, the flames grow rapidly as the fabric catches fire, next his hair burst into flames the intensity encouraging his flesh to burn too. It takes a long time for fire to consume a body

255

properly although it's unlikely anyone will find anything until morning at least by the time the police arrive any of my DNA will be destroyed. I put the bottle and can back into my bag and take out the playing card. After taking a copy of the pictures on my phone, I rest the photo album against the wall underneath the graffiti and slide the Queen of Hearts card into one of the empty spaces.

The flickering light of the burning corpse guides my way back to the car. I close the boot and passenger door and sit in the drivers seat. I drive the car back to the end of Stable lane and just before it turns onto the main road I park it across the lane, I spray the rest of the fluid onto the seat and onto my blood stained clothes, leaving the whiskey bottle and the cans of fuel and paint.

I pull on the beanie and the head torch, taking the Zippo I flip open the lid with a satisfying clink, spin the wheel causing the flint to spark and ignite the wick. Just like in the movies, I drop the lighter into the passenger foot well and again the fumes combust immediately.

I wait a minute to ensure the flames have taken hold fully, the burning vehicle will attract attention and raise the alarm but the road will be blocked and the flames will disguise the burning body further down the lane hidden by the flyover giving me time to get away before the police realise I have been busy again.

He had driven us less than a mile from where he picked me up and it's an easy jog back to the bike, I smile to myself as I peddle the bike. If I've felt guilt or remorse for my victims before I feel non for Pavel. Using the side roads through the suburban estates and rows of houses I cycle all the way to Old Oak road in Acton, I then follow the main roads back to Chiswick, If CCTV picks me up I'll be just another late night commuter on their way back from work with nothing to link me to the crime.

Back in the underground car park I lock the bike up in the same spot with the combination lock, removing my lights, I give the bike a cursory wipe over and head up to my apartment. Taking the vodka from the freezer I drop two ice cubes into a glass and pour myself a large measure. I take a shower washing the residue and blood from my arms and face and the dirt from my hair.

Once I am clean I run myself a bath getting myself another drink whilst the warm water grows the bubbles, I take the I-pad and drink and slip into the comforting warmth. Luxuriating in the watery blanket I flick through Twitter reading the comments that still rage on, it appears that the tide is turning in favour of Liz, with woman shouting down those that criticise her, most men seem to have seen sense enough to leave this debate to the girls with the few remaining ones stupid enough to try to mansplain their opinions rapidly silenced with withering put downs, it seems that The Queen of Hearts may not be abhorrent to everyone.

A new hashtag has spun off away from the original #VBV violence begets violence, with some women calling for those that are being oppressed to speak up and for women to rise up against their oppressors. It seems that Liz has started maybe more than she expected. Still I imagine her book is getting more publicity, this won't do her tour any harm either.

The following morning I awake after a good nights sleep, looking in the mirror I note that I have finger mark bruises on my neck where Pavel tried to choke me, I'll stay here for a few days and watch how the media frenzy pan out, there might even be a chance to pick up another victim in the capital if I'm extra careful.

The news breaks around five with BBC news 24 carrying the story first. They reveal that there has been a sixth murder, police as yet unable to confirm that it is the work of me, but that early evidence suggest it might be and that is has taken place within spitting distance of where they were filming last nights show. The press feeding frenzy for this one is going to be immense and will elevate me from this week's click bait to household name.

By 7pm there is another newsflash, apparently a woman has stabbed her husband of twenty years in the neck at the Leicester Tesco supermarket home wares section, the weapon is thought to be a pair of kitchen scissors, early reports suggest the woman may have been known to social services and a previous victim of domestic violence, the reports are as yet unconfirmed.

In a turn of events that I didn't see coming by 8pm Elizabeth Banrigh has been arrested under suspicion of inciting violence! I can't imagine the CPS will be able to make that one stick but I guess they need to do something to quash a potential uprising or copycat incidents.

The Twittersphere explodes and it's impossible to follow all of the items trending, there are still those posting the #VBV hashtag with others demanding that they #freebanrigh and yet more are talking about the murders, I've even got my own #QOH hashtag.

By 10pm it appears the Tescos chap is 'in a stable condition and his wounds are not considered life threatening'

The Sunday papers don't know what to run with as their headlines, The sun goes with 'Slash, Ban, Wallop!' The Daily Mirror comes up with 'Scissor Sisters' and The Guardian opts for Red Queen attacks White City. None of the others are as imaginative.

There is nothing new inside, scant information on my crime scene as it's too early for the police to release anything, they'll want to be extra careful with this one as they have egg on their faces already, plus they'll be keen not to be pour anymore fuel on to the social media fire.

Things are calming down by Sunday night and the The Tescos story isn't developing into much with the victim not wanting to press charges and the woman claiming to know nothing about 'Elizabeth Banrigh' it doesn't stop one hack running this story;

Journalist Arrested after woman attacks husband with scissors

Mark Bayard

The newspaper columnist and freelance Journalist Elizabeth Banrigh was arrested yesterday at her home in Notting Hill West London after several complaints were made to the BBC and television watchdog in relation to comments made on Friday nights live broadcast of the Crimewatch programme. The programme was supposed to focus on the ongoing police enquiry into the 'Queen of Hearts' serial killings but several viewers have complained that Banrigh high jacked the show to push her own agenda, potentially inciting violence. Social media was reported to have been trending with the Hashtag #VBV for violence begets violence, stealing a quote that was originally intended to demonstrate that violence was not the answer. Ms Banrigh has been released without charge and the police made the following statement; 'Ms Banrigh was helping us with our enquiries in relation to an ongoing investigation, she has been released without charge at this stage, due to the sensitive nature of the case, there is no further information available at this time'

Banrigh declined to comment on the incident stating that she would 'set the story straight' via her own written word. The Independent whom she writes a column for stated that 'Ms Banrigh was released without charge in what appears to have been an overzealous approach, where she was treated somewhat harshly, she will be maintaining her popular column and will be expressing her side of the story in her next installment.

This is not the first time the well-known journalist has helped police with their enquiries, as a university student she was interviewed regarding a relationship with the vice chancellor, it was that story that started her journalistic career, it was widely reported that she may have used a 'honey trap' to trick the academic into it, there was some speculation at the time that another incident involving the death of a student was also connected. More recently she was interviewed in relation to acquiring information under false pretenses, when she posed as a victim of domestic violence. She subsequently produced a controversial book on the events which has been the feature of an ongoing book tour.

So far no charges have been brought against Ms Banrigh in this or any of the other cases.

Banrigh Writes

Elizabeth Banrigh

Contrary to what has been widely reported in the press this week I was not arrested at my home last Saturday, but asked to assist the police in relation to an incident which they felt may have been caused by a misinterpretation of my wording on last Fridays Crimewatch programme. It transpired that the alleged incident was completely unrelated and no charges were brought against me. The police acted fairly and professionally in my dealings with them.

Once again the gutter press have shown their inability to produce quality journalism and I suggest if this is the highest calibre of work they can produce that they leave it up to us professionals. Sadly the sensationalism of my situation overpowered some of the excellent work conducted by the police and investigative team working on the Queen of Hearts murder and subsequently may have allowed further vital information to go unreported.

It would be remiss of me not to address the issues that were raised by a few callers to the BBC. My line of questioning around whether the phenomena of a serial killer could have been caused by the nature of how our society currently treats women was intended to spark debate not to incite violence. The quote violence begets violence was originally quoted in the Bible (Matthew verse 26:52) and later used in a speech by Martin Luther King in the form of Hate Begets Hate, in both examples it was used to demonstrate that violence just leads to more violence and nothing is solved, only by resisting the urge to fight fire with fire can we create change. Mahatma Ghandi said it a little clearer when he said 'An eye for an eye will leave the whole world blind"

Women should come together to elicit a change but do not sink to the same level as your oppressors, rise up and use your voices to be heard, use your intelligence to elicit change and educate your children to create a better future.

To get back to some proper journalism the murder that took place on Saturday has still to be attributed to the serial killer in our midst, there were some differences particularly in how the killer selected the victim but there are a lot of elements that point to the same protagonist.

The victim is reported to be Pavel Terzic a man previously known to police In connection with two incidents of sexual assault on women in the London area. Readers may remember that a civil case was brought against the online car service Uber for failing to protect the two women and out of court settlements were made, no charges were ever brought against Mr Terzic.

It is not yet clear if the killer targeted him specifically or if it was coincidental. Due to the meticulous manner in which she has conducted her other crimes I personally find the first explanation the most likely.

In light of recent events I will be postponing my book tour until sometime in the new year, I will continue to bring you news on this and other stories however I am currently working on a number of highly sensitive investigations that require my dedication all will be revealed all in good time.

I imagine she has been told to wind her neck in or lose her job, that carefully crafted statement reads more like political spin than cutting edge journalism, it looks like she has outlived her usefulness to me, in a journalistic sense at least, However she has provided me with more than enough opportunity to get what I want so I think I'll wish her well with a final note.

Hi Liz,

Loved the Crimewatch special, I thought you made some salient points about violence but it appears your superiors disagreed and forced a retraction, sometimes you have to lose a battle to win the war. Strange to think we were working so close to one another and only a short amount of time apart, we could have almost bumped into each other.

So number six has been ticked off the list! You will be interested to know that Pavel had a folder of photographs, containing graphic images of a number of women, the judicial system failed to stop him previously, I have succeeded. As you are all too aware the damage done by people to others is life changing and sometimes life ending. I've attached their pictures and maybe you can do something to help? Sounds like you have your hands full with your other investigations but maybe you'll fit this one in.

Two more to go and then it will be time for the Queen of Hearts to head off and I'll be bidding you farewell, until then keep up the good work.

Q.O.H

Chapter 10

Striking again now might be best option, the further down the path I go the harder it gets, the more you do the more opportunities there are to get caught. The Police will be pushing harder than ever now that the public interest has reached maximum furore, getting the next one done quickly will leave them struggling to keep up and create more panic.

The psychological pundits that are popping up on the breakfast and chat shows will no doubt make a big thing of the fact that the frequency is increasing, my need to kill is becoming greater, they are wrong but it doesn't hurt to let them think this is the case.

Trying to pick someone fresh up on the dating sites is going to be difficult, people will be on high alert, that is unless I've already been chatting to them. I have a couple of London guys on my spreadsheet. Ideally I need a straight up booty call to bypass the dating stage, easy enough yes but I also need to work out escape routes and make sure I have a decent plan.

I trawl through the existing candidates, nobody is quite right. There is a guy I've been talking to for a week or so, he's a serial cheater with a wife and kids at home, That in itself might be a problem, he'll want to come to my place or meet in a hotel, after Paul I'm a little wary of hotels and it takes a lot more planning not to mention adds in a lot of unknown factors.

I check out Tinder, it's definitely the best option for Mr Right now, If I start today I can build up a quick enough picture and by tomorrow or Thursday I should be able to set out a strategy. There is nothing to tie me back to either of my properties and as long as I don't get followed the chances of them catching me are slim. As soon as I'm done with the last two I'll be gone and any trail will run cold.

Changing your identity is not easy but with money you can do most things, it's finding the right people to do it that is the hardest part. It may or may not surprise you to learn that the kind of places to meet those types of people are not in the worst parts of a city but in the best. Things like identities cost money and people with money are happy to pay it. If you want to find a gun or a fake passport, don't go to a council estate, go to a private members club. I won't mention any names, it pays to be discreet with these sorts of things, but even once you have found one finding the right contacts still won't be easy and it may take you years of being a member to even start to have the right conversations; you can't just bowl up and ask if anyone can get you a new name.

It takes a subtle approach, questions about less high profile criminal activities like off shore banking and how to avoid a little tax here and there, find the people that are happy to chat about such things conspiratorially over a single malt or an expensive cognac and you are on the right track. Next maybe a casual word about a news item wondering how that wanted person got out of the country 'But how does one go about getting a fake passport? I'd have no idea where to start' a few drinks later and you'll know if the person you are talking to is of use or not. Give it a few more weeks and a lot more confidence building and then have a quiet word about a 'friend' who could do with the type of thing they were talking about. If you have played it right you might just get an introduction to the person who actually knows the people that will get you what you need.

Money will change hands several times before you actually see anything and lots of it, but you are paying for discretion and a quality product. Once you have completed one successful transaction and trust has been earned you can then move on to bigger things and meet a wider circle.

A great route if you have the time and money or you can just go on to the dark web like I did! The dark web can't be accessed via the normal search engines, you need to understand a few things first. You'll need what is called a Tor or onion server, this protects your location and the location of anyone you are connecting with from prying eyes, it's also a good idea to log on to a VPN first, this stops anyone that might be looking (say a government agency or the police) knowing that you have even logged on to a Tor server which is suspicious in itself.

Once you have an idea of which web addresses to look for you can then start to use it much like the traditional internet. When I first started using it the main location to buy and trade was called 'The Silk Road' this was closed down but like all these sorts of things, a similar thing popped up a few days later.

So you might be thinking how do you know what you are buying is legit? How do you stop yourself meeting someone in a car park with a brown envelope full of cash only to find yourself waking up in a shipping container on your way to become a prostitute in some undisclosed South American brothel?

Believe it or not these people actually have ratings, criminals are as keen to do business as anyone else and therefore they will leave good reviews for each other on the quality of their product and on the discretion and quality of their postal packaging. I've bought over 20 identities and never met one seller. I buy card details and load them onto other card chips, so whenever I tap my card on a reader it's not my details or anything I've ever set up but some other unsuspecting person who's card has been cloned.

Of course I can afford to pay for what I need but whenever I'm in QOH mode I need to ensure there is no trail to me.

Both my properties belong to companies that are 'shells' those companies belong to other companies and so on and so forth. If I wanted to sell them I could and the money would be available to me but I'd never be spending it under my name. Of course I have a completely legitimate side should I ever need to return to it or get interviewed as a potential witness. Alys White lives a very normal life in her home town, she makes a reasonable amount of money as a trader, pays her tax, pays her bills from her bank and keeps her nose clean. On paper anyway. If anyone went to investigate her physical location they would find a very happy family of Somalian refugees who are awaiting asylum and thus can't work, who have a fully paid for house, regular food delivered, internet and all bills paid from a secret benefactor, but nobody is likely to want to track her down because she is very boring and I keep her that way so that if I ever need to I can disappear by simply becoming me again.

Tinder comes up with a couple of options and I start the messages in the same way for both of them.

'Hey you look fun, let's see if you are. Ten questions:-

Beach or Mountain?

Bike or Car?

Smart or Casual?

Comedy or Thriller?

Watch or Play?

Beer or Wine?

Cat or Dog?

Night or Day?

Boxers or briefs?

Lights on or lights off?

The questions get the conversation started straight away and can give a real insight if they play along. The last two give plenty of opportunity for flirtation and will weed out the ones that get too excited too quickly.

Michael replies with:

"How about I drive my 'car' to the top of the 'mountain' with 'bikes' on the back and we 'casually' roll down with our legs sticking out shouting wheeeeee, in a 'comedy' way it'll be a real 'thrill'. We can ride all the way to the 'beach' and 'play' in the sand, 'smart' idea? of course I'll probably 'whine' that we left the 'dog' at home (he's a 'boxer' by the way). We'll be having such a fun 'day' that it will get dark and we'll need to turn the lights on to find our way back that 'night'. I hope this description wasn't too 'brief'...

Funny guy, I like that. Michaels profile is OK, there isn't much to make him stand out as someone that could be worthy of killing and I don't have too much time to dig so I'll focus a bit more on Joseph.

His profile is subtle but hints at someone who has just joined and maybe a phantom who'll want to chat but never meet, he has very little on there including his pictures, a couple of long distance shots and a torso shot but no detailed head shot, his profile is almost like mine.

Joseph comes up with standard answers:

"Mountain, Car, Casual, Comedy, Watch, Beer, neither, Day, Boxers, Lights on, these were tough to answer as I like lots of things but I get it's just for fun. I notice from your profile that you like outdoors things as do I, I'd be up for mountain biking. I said neither to pets because I don't really have time with work. What were your answers?"

I'm an environmentalist so I like to recycle, a quick copy and paste and I insert Michael's comments as my own answer;

"How about I drive my 'car' to the top of the 'mountain' with 'bikes' on the back and we 'casually' roll down with our legs sticking out shouting wheeeeee, in a 'comedy' way it'll be a real 'thrill'. We can ride all the way to the 'beach' and 'play' in the sand, 'smart' idea? of course I'll probably 'whine' that we left the 'dog' at home (he's a 'boxer' by the way). We'll be having such a fun 'day' that it will get dark and we'll need to turn the lights on to find our way back that 'night'. I hope this description wasn't too 'brief'..."

"That's hilarious, it makes my answer look a bit lame now, you are very funny"

"Thanks Joseph, so tell me more about you, what are you looking for on this dating site? Girl of your dreams, a booty call, something in between?"

"Well I never say no to a booty call but I guess I'm open to meeting the right person if it happens, in the meantime hanging out with cool people is nice"

My Facebook search turns up something interesting, his profile is there but it's only three weeks old, I instantly smell a rat, this guy is up to no good. I use the image search of him on the beach, it takes a while but eventually I find him Richard Wilkins, married to Kerry, two kids six and four. Naughty boy Joseph or should I say Richard it looks like you have created a fake profile so you can play away from home. I think you have just made the top of the list, that was a very easy find.

The chat goes backwards and forwards, he is flirtatious but casual, he keeps it always on the right side of respectful, each time he answers he takes his time, this guy knows what he is doing. I dig around a bit more and he seems pretty normal except for the philandering.

"Look I know this is forward, but do you fancy a drink this week? Socially distanced of course" I throw caution to the wind and take the bold approach.

"Forward is good and sure that would be fantastic, I live in Southwark not far from London Bridge, we could meet near there if that suits you, there's plenty of bars still open and if it's not too cold we can go for a walk along the Embankment?"

"That sounds great" I reply.

I was wondering how we were going to meet, the flat in Southwark seems strange, is he divorced or separated but not updating his profile? If so why the fake name? What's your game buddy?

We arrange to meet the following night, outside the Refinery bar, just off Southwark Street in a relatively new complex of apartments, complete with bars and shops. It's a few minutes walk from the river and to the Millennium bridge.

I plan my route, first I'll take the tube from Turnham Green, it's one stop on from my nearest station so I can walk there. The easiest way would be to get off at Embankment station but that's way too obvious and risky, I'll use a cloned card to tap in and out of the stations and a different one to hire a Boris bike. I'll cycle the bike along the river and drop the bike off at the Santander bike stand on Northumberland Avenue just before the Golden Jubilee Bridge. I can walk from there and it is always prudent to put in a quick 360 degree circuit of the area so I can to check for anything out of the ordinary. I don't have his address and there are no apartments in the area registered to either his fictitious Joseph name or his Richard profile, There are several registered to a private equity firms and companies so it probably means it's being rented by his employer which would make sense.

I want to be sure though, so I dig a little deeper.

"Nice area to have a flat in Joseph, what do you do for a living?!" I ask.

"I'm a computer engineer, it's very boring but I build main frames for corporations and financial institutions. It's not actually my flat, the company rent it for me as I'm in London all the time, I bought a place a few years ago over in East Finchley as it was 'up and coming' it's still up and coming apparently! I rent it out and just stay here most of the time or head down to see my parents in Sussex"

More lies, from Facebook it looks like his family home is in Arundel West Sussex but with his wife and kids not his parents. Clearly this guy is a player. He does appear on the company website for Spectrotech as an engineer though so the flat is probably legit. I guess he meets women in London and heads home to the family at weekends, naughty naughty.

Hiding any change of clothes or escape kit is going to be difficult as I don't know exactly where he lives, so my plan is to get naked before I kill him, that way I can put the same clothes back on. I'll need a change before I head home and to make sure I drop off CCTV radar. There's an easy place to hide things in public that people rarely ever look in and I know where there are several of them dotted around the city. The good old bright yellow winter grit bins sit innocuously at the side of roads or pavements ignored by everyone until needed. A bag placed there after dark is highly unlikely to be discovered, I'll make an on foot get away down the river, pick up another Boris bike and head to Green Park, there is a bin there that I can stash my bag in.

A quick change behind the trees after dark will go unnoticed. I'll put the already worn stuff in the back pack and dispose of it into anyone of the city's hundreds of thousands of commercial waste bins that require a standardised key, I'll cover it in bleach of course, before I ditch it. From Green Park I'll take a few different tubes and change directions. Coming out of one station, walking to another and heading back into the underground again. Tapping in and out with different cards. Finally back to Acton or Hammersmith where I can make my way back to Chiswick if everything feels safe.

I take the tube as planned and disembark at Victoria, the escalators bringing me up into the twilight of the autumnal city early evening, I find a bike and take a leisurely ride past Buckingham Palace, drop the bag and cut through St James Park, past Nelsons column and down past Charring Cross station to the Embankment coming out on the opposite side of the river to where I need to be. I work my way along the river until I get to London bridge. I decide to leave the bike here instead. I'm early and I have time, something about Joseph has been bothering me on the journey over and I want to check something out so I walk over the bridge and sit outside a small coffee truck in Borough Market.

I pull up Facebook and look at the profile of Richard Wilkins, I check it again not sure what I'm looking for, I flick through the images again and then the messages on his posts, it all seems perfectly fine. Then it hits me, it's too perfect, it almost looks like it could be staged, the pictures of him with his kids are all the same age. There are pictures of the kids on their own at different ages but the family together have all been taken at the same time, they have been careful to change locations and outfits but now I am aware it's easy to see.

I start to check out his friends, all of their profiles are set to the highest security and show nothing, for all of your friends to be on the same settings is very unusual. I dig into Richards wife, same story. Electoral register search and there is no Richard and Kerry Wilkins.

The colour drains from my face as I realise this is a trap! Richard is a profile built to make me think Joseph is cheating on his wife and to lure me in, the Police must be working with the dating site companies to flag up this profile to any new users registering, a background check on anyone showing an interest before the messages start will quickly flag up if anything suspicious is going on, 99% of hits will bare nothing, my complete lack of background would have set of all the alerts, very clever.

I'm so annoyed at myself, in my eagerness to get the job finished I've nearly walked into a trap. They could be tracking this phone right now, I've logged in via Tor and VPN on an unregistered laptop from the flat but if they are tracking hits to his Facebook page they can track the Wi-Fi location I am using. I switch the phone off. Standing calmly from the table I turn and walk towards the river, heading through the cobbled streets and past the Cutty Sark. A lady with a buggy passes and I stop her to ask directions, as she is pointing out the route I hastily drop the phone into the pushchair.

It's unlikely they would have struck before the meeting, waiting to the last second to be sure they had me but they are probably tracking my movements to know where I am. I should go immediately just get out but I need to be sure this was a trap, I should have been more careful, when it seems too good to be true, it usually is. I walk down the river towards Shakespeares Globe and the Tate Modern, I need to calm myself, my breathing is erratic and I'm shaking.

If they are watching they would either be in a building or a vehicle, they don't need wired bugs anymore, he would have simply placed his mobile phone on the table and they would have listened through the microphone, they will have other officers all over the place in plain clothes acting as normal passers by or diners but they will also have a tactical unit somewhere to make the strike with armed officers at the critical moment.

Seeing an armed response vehicle in the centre of any big city is no longer unusual but seeing a vehicle full of tactically dressed officers will still stick out. It's this I am looking for, I walk in a large square around the area until I've completed a full circuit, then I move inward a street and complete the same process, there's just twenty minutes now until our arranged date, I need to be sure, if I walk away because of paranoia I could miss a perfectly suitable kill.

Another street closer and still nothing. I'm all the way in with seven minutes to spare. The bar sits on a pedestrianised area off of Southwark Street, it's a well presented area with stone benches and trees breaking up the route, restaurants and bars line the sides with residential apartments above. It's all modern glass and chrome the festoon lights from the bars reflect off the buildings making it feel almost Christmas like.

I'm directly opposite the Refinery restaurant where we are due to meet, and I dip into a salad bar, I scan the alfresco dining and drinking area outside of the bar and spot him, close to the outer fence, his face highlighted in the light of the flickering heaters that adorn the patio area, it would be an easy place for the police to surround if they wanted to grab me here.

I order a smoothie and wait, the baseball cap from my bag firmly on my head and mask in place. Nothing happens, 7pm, the agreed meeting time, arrives and passes, nobody moves, I wait five more minutes, still nothing, did I get it wrong? Maybe I'm getting too twitchy with the end in sight, still it pays to be cautious. It looks like everything is OK after all.

I am just about to leave and head over to introduce myself , when I hear it, the slightest crackle of static and the quietest words saying;

'Stay in position stand by'

There is a woman sitting at the same window bench as me, one stool away, looking out over the same scene, I glance towards her and as she brushes her hair from out of her face I catch sight of an ear piece, it's tiny, not noticeable until you actually look for it.

I stand up and walk to the counter placing my tray and cup upon it. gripping tightly to stop my hands from shaking. "Could I get a flat white coffee to go please?" The police officer pays me no attention her gaze transfixed ahead of her focused on her fellow officer awaiting my arrival.

She sits right by the door, my only means of exit and she is probably armed. I collect my coffee, pay and walk to the door, passing right alongside the police officer as I do, my heart is in my mouth. I use all of my training to control my breathing the fear of capture running through me, it takes every bit of my resolve to resist the urge to break into a sprint.

I turn immediately left walking past her in front of the window, and towards Southwark Street, I reach the corner and turn left again, past the Pret a Manger sandwich shop and keep on walking, dropping the untouched coffee into a waste bin. I reach the end of the next block and am heartened to see a row of Boris bikes resplendent in their silver and red livery, I walk towards them, eager to unlock one and make a hasty retreat.

As I unlock the bike, I glance to my left and I see it, parked on the forecourt of an office block set back from the road tucked against the side of a Marks and Spencer's is the police tactical unit, exterior lights off and lurking in the shadows but the weak interior light inside enough to make me aware.

I look directly at the vehicle, again my brain screams run but I ignore it, the officer in the front seat stares directly at me, it's like slow motion as I see him raise his hand and point, 'do not panic' my inner voice tells me, I wheel the bike and walk it off the curb, mounting it and begin to peddle up towards London Bridge, the brightly lit Shard looming high on the skyline in-front of me. The inner voice speaks again 'do not glance back', convinced that any second the screech of car tyres and slamming of doors will be upon me and looking back will just cement my guilt, I hear the siren fire up, clearly the commanding officer in charge of the operation has got the information from the van driver and has made the call to break cover! No point staying cool now, I peddle faster making a right turn across the flow of traffic into Great Guildford Street, a cabbie flashes me and I wave a thanks as I peddle onward, I chance a look to my right as I do, still no sign of movement behind me but the siren increases and I can hear two more coming from different directions. By now they are circulating my description to all units and will be closing a net in around me. Hopefully they are trying to track the mobile phone, even switched off it will emit a signal, maybe they will follow that. Pretty soon some unsuspecting mum will have an exciting story to tell her friends at playgroup tomorrow.

A left turn into America Street and I come face to face with a motorbike courier, his headlight fierce in my eyes. I stop in front of him blocking his path my lips moving but too low for the sound to be audible to him. He emits a muffled "What?" I shrug and walk to the side of him leaning in closer and I point, talking inaudibly again. He takes off his helmet "What's going on, what you saying?" he asks.

"Road blocked up ahead some sort of accident"

He kicks the stand onto the bike probably to reroute his satnav, I snatch the helmet from his hands ramming it into his nose and as he falls

back in surprise I step towards the back of the
bike my hand pressing into his chest using the
momentum to push him off the still running bike.
I ram the helmet on my head and throttle the
bike hard kicking the stand off and using my foot
to fire through the gears. I head off back towards
the way I have just come, the police van almost
hits me as it comes around the corner at the
same time.

If the biker manages to flag them down, which is
highly likely with a bloody face and a random
push bike lying in the street, it'll be a matter of
seconds before my new vehicle and direction are
reported. The bike weaves through the traffic
back towards Southwark bridge, I take the bike
onto the bridge and look down over the edge
with the idea of dropping onto a boat it's at least
ten metres to the water though so even allowing
for the height of the boat it's like the equivalent
of diving off the high board in a swimming pool, I
don't fancy my chances of landing on anything
moving from that height without breaking
something and probably falling into the water,
the idea of drowning in the Thames with a
broken back does not fill me with joy.

Southwark bridge is a metal construction on
concrete plinths, I climb over the rail, not
bothering to look if anyone sees me, time is not a
luxury I can afford, I clamber down the cast iron
framework dropping on to the plinth. At this
height I've got a lot more chance of making the

leap. It's going to take a decent jump forwards but that's better than a downward plummet into the watery abyss. Like a brightly lit beacon of hope I can see a Uber Boat coming, one of the cities river bus services. I press myself back against the bridge pillar, I can here sirens growing increasingly louder above me, it'll be a matter of seconds before they are on the bridge and spot the bike, as the boat pulls level I push myself forwards with just a few steps available and I jump onto the top of the Uber boat trying to land silently, the top is slippery and I lose my footing but I sprawl quickly on to my front spreading my weight to grip on board, making as little noise as possible, keen to avoid alerting the commuters below.

The boat passes under the bridge, the blue lights of the arriving police van lighting the water buffeted by the boats wake. As we appear from under the bridge I glance back, thankfully nobody is looking over this side of the bridge, the officers I can see gathering around the bike and looking left and right along the bridge and not into the water!

It'll take at least a few minutes for them to figure out where I have gone, perhaps assuming I've ditched the bike to make it look like I've jumped and headed off on foot or commandeered another vehicle. The river is well lit but the reflected light and the darkness of the water will make me hard to spot and unless they look this way immediately I should be fine, I keep low and flat, hoping the dark will shield me.

The next stop is Tower, It's just a few minutes down river, I cling on trying to use my body to grip, the roof is relatively flat but with a slight curvature and the construction material is hard to gain purchase on. I dig in with my toes and try to distribute my weight as the boat rocks on the current. After what feels like an agonising length of time the boat begins to alight at the jetty, the second it docks I sit up and slide off, landing in a roll, and immediately into a jog. The startled ticket collector calls out as I leap the barrier but I'm quickly lost in the melee of people.

I need to think, the first thing to do in a crisis is stop and plan, only then can you make rational decisions. I pull a face mask from my pocket and sit for a minute on a bench, picking up a discarded coffee cup as a prop, serial killers tend not to sit drinking coffee when on the run from the police as far as I am aware. The facts are this; that was a police set up, I encountered the police twice, once in the salad bar and once getting the bike, they were not waiting to arrest me at either point, it was only a visual recognition that sparked the chase therefore they were not following me up to that point. This means the Chiswick property is safe.

I cannot take the risk of public transport, certainly not from a main hub, for all I know the police may be monitoring the main hubs with gait analysis software, it can identify you as accurately as a finger print just by the way you walk. I have no idea how advanced this technology is or how widespread, I saw one of the crime shows on TV where the police were using it to follow pick pockets on Oxford Street, it might not be widely used but I can't take that chance, however I'm aware it only works if you are on foot.

I need to get out of the city quickly preferably without the tube. I can hear at least one police helicopter in the air, if they get another visual on my location and the chopper picks me up, there will be no escape. I have an idea, I'm off there radar for a few minutes and they'll expect me to flee, why not hide in plain sight, head back towards the point of escape?

I walk as casually as my trembling legs will allow over Tower Bridge, the familiar towers stand tall as I pass them over to the other side of the river and down the steps passing the oddly shaped city hall building, I walk with purpose along the river following the small crowds, thinned by the Covid restrictions but still busy enough to use as cover. five minutes down the path and I'm at the Hays Galleria, a beautiful arcade with a high domed glass roof filled with designer shops. It might not seem like the ideal time to do some shopping however I can buy myself some time and I can change my appearance.

I wander into the first boutique I see, the shop assistant alert and eager to help, desperate for customers having been closed for several weeks. "How can I help you madam?" The shop assistant enquires.

"I need something smart but chic for an interview" I say through the face mask.

"Were you thinking a skirt or trousers madam?"

"Trousers I think, I want to appear serious not flirty" I reply

"Absolutely, keep it business-like and wow them with class"

She selects a few items, handing them too me; "we're not supposed to try things on due to the pandemic guidelines madam but I'm sure we can make an exception" She says in a conspiratorially lowered voice gesturing for me to head into the back room ,obviously keen to make a sale.

I head into the dressing room drawing the curtain behind me. "Would you like a coffee?" She shouts through from the other room

"That would be great thank you" I hear the tinkle of the shop bell I poke my head out the curtain, momentarily terrified this is it, I see the shop assistant walking over to the coffee truck in the middle of the arcade.

I try on the trousers as I think of my strategy. By now they will have officers patrolling the tubes and posted at stations, If I remember rightly the boats run up river as far as Hampton Court but I think that's only in the summer? If I can get a boat and go passed the scene of the trap I'll be on the right side of the city and away from the direction they know I fled in.

I leave on one pair of trousers, black of course and walk out into the shop, I pick up a roll neck jumper and a black faux leather jacket, Back in the changing room I pull off my top soaked with sweat from the exertion and excitement, I wipe my body and pull on the jumper, it clings to my curves, I put the jacket over the top, the door tinkles again as she returns with the coffee, I meet her as I step out of the changing rooms "Oh yes madam, excellent choices, very chic but do you think the jacket is right for an interview?" She says as she hands me the coffee.

"Sure it's a media company, they like a cool edge to these things, I don't want my hair to get blown around though, do you have any hats?"

"Your interview is today? You're cutting it a bit fine for outfit shopping if you don't mind me saying"

"I know, it's kind of an informal off the cuff sort of thing" I shrug.

"Ah I see well, we have some woolen hats that have just come in for autumn, would you like to try one of those?"

"Sure in black and do you have any leather boots? Size six"

"I have a gorgeous Chelsea boot in Burgundy that will set off your outfit beautifully, and I've got this fabulous belt to match that will just pull the whole thing together."

"Sounds great"

She gets the boots and I pull them on, if I have to run then new shoes are not going to be ideal, what I need right now is stealth. I pay for the items including a burgundy leather holdall to put my own items in, thank the shop assistant for all her help and head out back into the arcade and along the river to the London Bridge stop, the light up display tells me the 19:27 is due, it stops at Embankment and then Putney Bridge, that could not be more perfect luck is on my side.

I hang back keeping near to the buildings waiting for the last minute before boarding, I keep my eyes open, scanning in every direction but the plethora of lights combined with the darkness, make identifying shapes from a distance impossible, each new person in the distance potentially wanting to stop my progress.

19:25 I tap in with a different card and jog down the jetty, like a commuter running to catch the last bus. I take a seat on the futuristic looking catamaran, its sleek twinned hull pointing up stream with purpose. It's a risk as there is only one exit and entrance to the boat apart from the sealed emergency exits but I can't think of a better more direct route out of the city, right under their noses.

The Uber branded vessel leaves on time, the huge engines propelling it up river with ease, within seven minutes we are at Embankment, I sit pretending to read a discarded Metro my heart pounding all the time, convinced that everyone can feel the guilt pouring out of me. Glancing out of the window, my heart sinks, I see two uniformed officers standing at the top of the gantry leading up from the jetty to the riverside. I look around My only hope of escape is the emergency exit into the freezing river, the chances of survival in these powerful currents is minimal never mind the chance of escape. I try not to stare, concentrating hard on the paper, the doors open and the few passengers disembarking here get off and a trickle of passengers begin to get on-board. The police stand by the doors, are they waiting for me to give myself up?

Then I realise what is happening, they are only checking people getting on! I have to fold the paper my hands are visibly shaking and I sit on my hands so as not to give the game away, turning to look out of the window away from the police and towards the river, willing the doors to close.

The last of the passengers file in and I watch as one of the officers turns and walk down the jetty

towards us, I perch on the edge of my seat, ready
to sprint to the back of the boat and to fling open
the emergency exit, he reaches the half way point
and stops, looking up to where the helmsman
sits and gives him the thumbs up! He waves at
the boat and some of the passengers wave back
as to my relief the noise of the engines thunders
into life pulling us towards the stern as the boat
propels to the rear, the pilot switches the drive
and the bow points up river and I feel a wave of
relief as we pass under three bridges in quick
succession. I don't think I finally start breathing
again until we reach the millennium bridge
which is brightly lit with the London Eye rotating
slowly to the side of it on the left bank The glow
of Big Ben's clock face like a low lying moon off
to my right reminds me we are still in the heart
of the city but with no more scheduled stops I'll
know if anything is untoward. To my relief the
catamaran passes under the bridge and passed
the Houses of Parliament unhindered on our way
to Putney.

The journey is only 45 minutes long but it seems
like several lifetimes, I'm pretty sure I've aged at
least ten years on the way, I try to look calm but I
constantly scan the water for signs of police craft
and the roads and bridges for signs of police
vehicles. Every time I see a flashing blue light my
heart leaps and my stomach lurches, the vessel
pushes on, the hum of it's powerful engines
provides a comforting background to the
maelstrom in my head. by the time I reach

Putney I am exhausted and my nerves are shot. Thankfully nobody is waiting here to check off the passengers.

I walk the hour long journey back to my apartment, sticking mostly along the banks of the Thames, silently thanking her for carrying me to safety, I walk to clear my head and calm down, although I'm still angry with myself, I need to focus and analise my mistakes so I can learn and prevent them from happening again.

Chapter 11

Proper planning and preparation, prevents piss poor performance, one of my trainers used to say, if only I had remembered that advice yesterday I wouldn't have nearly fallen for their trap. As I soak in the bath I reflect on how stupid that had been, my first few kills I had researched extensively, this one I became arrogant, too cocky thinking I was untouchable, I won't make that mistake twice, research is always the answer if I had just dug a little deeper it would have been obvious.

It looks like the main dating sites are out of action now the police are clearly all over them. I'm not prepared to give up just yet I just need a change of tactics. If the police are going to play cat and mouse I'll have to be extremely careful, constantly swapping devices and checking data, I knew this might happen eventually and I figured they might get close at some point not through my own stupidity though, I just didn't think I would fall for that kind of thing. I doubt the story will make the press, they'll keep it under wraps in case they get a second attempt and there is no point panicking the public unnecessarily.

It might sound crazy but I think another kill in the capital is actually my best bet, having nearly caught me they will expect me to flee or go to ground but I have no plans to do that.

So what next? I still need two more to complete the chorus of jar of hearts, I could pick off a random but the risks are greater, not as great as getting caught by the police but still risky, this city, much like any other, is full of people trying to get laid and human nature is to believe it won't happen to you, especially when sex is on the table. I'm going to have to break my one week rule and stay here for a while but I can move quickly if I need to.

I was saving this next one to be the last kill, I have had him in mind for a while but I guess he's just been promoted. There are some sick bastards out there and this guy fits the bill perfectly.

His dating profile is that of a British Royal Marine, posted in Afghanistan. His type wasn't on my dating site list but probably should be, he is a 'romance scammer' or a 'catfish'. These people, and it's not always men, pick upon vulnerable people creating a fake online profile designed to lure you in. The person they use might be totally fictitious or they may take on the identity of a real person unbeknownst to them. This arsehole has gone one step further and is using the picture of a soldier who was killed in action in 2018.

These scammers express strong emotions towards their victims early on, pushing hard to establish a connection, often they will claim to be from Australia or another westernised country, but travelling in the military or as a medical professional. The goal is to lure the victim into believing their love is real and once they have hooked them in they then claim to be in trouble, reaching out to them either convince them to send money or sometimes using the victim to launder money from crimes.

He's using a Tor server so it's been hard to track him down but from his writing I could tell he was probably British. Often these scammers are Africa based and you can sometimes tell from the language style of the written English that not everything is as it should be. They rely on the victim being so overwhelmed that they look beyond what is right in front of them. Don't get me wrong, his grammar was still crap but it was more lazy British street patois than a lack of understanding.

These scammers will go to great lengths to gain your interest and trust, they have no remorse or feeling, you are simply a commodity to them and they prey on the most vulnerable. The recently bereaved are particularly susceptible to this type of scam. Part of the scheme is often to shower you with loving words, sharing intimate and personal information such as their family background and childhood. They'll have a very convincing back story, and some will even try sending you gifts.

That's what Greg (Real name Derrick Clark) did. He asked me for my address and sent me gifts, chocolate, some underwear and a cheap bracelet. Obviously I got them sent to a holding address but whilst I was smart, Derrick was not, he was having the gifts sent to him then mailing them out himself, stupidly he managed to leave the delivery slip stuck to the box of chocolates and just like that, I had his address! Dick head.

Derrick is 29, he lives in North West London,he has three children but a family man Derrick is not. Even though the three different mothers all live on the same estate, he does not live with any of them or the children. Unsurprisingly neither does he contribute to their upbringing financially. He does however manage to see one of his children every month for an hour supervised at his mums flat, the others he does not see at all unless in passing on the estate.

Once I had his address it was easy enough to track him, and judging by the transactions into his accounts he has taken at least £40,000 from unsuspecting women over the past twelve months. Luring them in via the dead Marine.

Harlesden is home to the notorious Stonebridge park estate, once a concrete jungle of high rise buildings, replaced in the late 2000s with new low rise flats and traditional housing in an attempt to regenerate the area, despite the efforts crime and drugs are still rife and the

NW10 postcode is considered by many to be a no go zone, certainly at night.

Derrick lives on this estate, it is hard not to look at his lifestyle choices without considering wider socioeconomic questions as to whether he is a product of a society that has marginalised black and ethnic communities by providing less opportunities for employment and lower quality of education. The long term unemployment, exacerbating absentee fathers and creating a void of responsibility and moral guidance. It is highly likely that Derrick is in many ways a victim of this system, with no positive male role models and limited opportunities young men turn to crime, gangs and violence. Be that as it may, it doesn't make him any less of an arsehole though now does it?

I guess I could just go round to Derricks flat, knock on his door and finish him off there and then, but where would be the sport in that? I can't resist playing him at his own game. Paul is stuck in my head and they say the best way to get over someone is to get under someone, so Derrick may have to put some work in before I dispatch him.

Once I knew who Derrick was it was easy enough to find him on Plenty of Fish, another of the free dating sites, his photos presented a polished image, he's good looking in a roguish way, slim but muscular and he clearly works out, his taste in clothes is deep into designer labels and bling territory, he describes himself as an entrepreneur which I guess isn't a lie.

Striking again now, especially in London is going to be a high risk strategy but keeping the date casual and on Derricks home turf might make it work, the chat has been off the dating sites for a while and on to KIK so the chances of the Police having picked this up are highly unlikely, Derrick is not going to be hard to pursued to take me home after a first date either. He's a player and a fuck boy.

On the chat he is actually charming, he is clearly not stupid and had his life taken a different path, he could have been successful at many things. Sadly for him his path is about to come to an end. A dead end.

To be honest I expected him to be all sex talk and picture requests but he has a love of music and we chat about this for hours. He thinks I'm an air stewardess so we chat about travel, he is interested or at least seems to be, in other countries and what they are like, not just visually but also socially, I guess somebody who preys on emotions is interested in how people's minds work.

We arrange to meet at Harlesden Station and Derrick has booked us a table at Rubio, a cool looking relaxed restaurant / cafe, I check out their website, apparently it's owned by one of the DJ's from the dance music act Shapeshifters so the music should be good at least.

Arriving in Harlesden on a Vespa scooter, good for the London streets and immediately forgettable, I park it and lock it on the Stonebridge estate in a residential blocks visitor space, fastening the helmet to the wheel with a second lock, It's far less likely to get nicked from here than it is on the street and nobody will question why it is parked there. I need it for later and I don't want to be taking the tube if I can help it, after last time I want at least a couple of escape options.

Derrick lives in one of the older blocks on Stonebridge Park, there are storage containers and building works still going on and these last few seven story blocks represent all that is left of the old estate, they look tired and out of place against the modern brick and brightly coloured houses and flats that now make up the area. The refurbished estate may look different but the veneer is a thin one, look closely and the buildings are sealed with thick steel doors a nod to the levels of crime once notorious in this area and I still wouldn't want to be a vulnerable person here at night on my own.

I walk the mile back to the tube station twenty minutes early to ensure I am there before Derrick. I keep my leather jacket on with Jeans going for the rock chick look, the jacket over an

ACDC t-shirt, blonde hair, jeans and biker boots, I look cool.

Derrick turns up on time, well groomed and looking smart, black loafers with no socks, black jeans, white t-shirt and a god awful Versace jacket in white and gold bling that looks like an accident in a ecclesiastical suppliers, yet he pulls it off with his confident swagger. He is good looking with a charming smile.

He takes my hand and kisses me on both cheeks, "Hey babe, you look great, love the outfit"

"Thanks so do you"

He does in-spite of the jacket.

"So shall we go and get a drink? I've not been to this place before but it's meant to be pretty cool"

"Yeah I checked it out online looks good actually, I was surprised I thought Harlesden was going to be a bit rough but it seems trendy"

"I guess it's like everywhere in London, if it's close enough in to the centre it gets gentrified eventually, it looks like it's Harlesdens turn, they've got their work cut out though" He chuckles.

We walk through the main streets, the conversation flows and is easy, every now and again he lets a bit of street patois slip into the conversation but he is careful to keep up the act of the perfect gentleman.

We have a table by the window, the food is relaxed and delicious the music and atmosphere on point. People are complex, yes Derrick is a scum bag who is praying on the vulnerable but he is also intelligent and charming, you might be wondering how I can chat with this guy and consider having sex with him, knowing what he is up to, but it's not as simple as that. Right now he is attractive to me, I'm in control and therefore I can get what I want from this. Even a murderer on a life sentence will have parts of their personality that are agreeable, I mean look at me? I'm not all bad right?

We flirt across the table as the evening goes on. "You look like that journalist that's in the paper you know?"

"I've heard that before, is that a good thing?"

"Yeah fam she's a milf!" He laughs at himself letting his accent slip again for a minute "Sorry I mean she's hot, a bit uptight and serious but yeah I think she's sexy, you're funnier though and prettier"

"Well you have to say that now though don't you Derrick"

"You know what I mean, anyway what about me, do you like what you see?"

"Well let's just say that when you went to the toilet a minute ago I was checking out your fine arse which looks impeccable in those jeans and since you took that jacket off, your arms look pretty damn sexy in that tight t-shirt"

"That jacket? Do I detect a little dislike for it?"

"It's a bit bling for my tastes but you just about pull it off" I smile at him.

"Fair enough, so what do you want to do next?"

"Well Derrick, I want you to pay the bill, order an Uber and take me back to yours to show me what's inside those jeans, if you fancy it of course?"

He turns to the counter, "Can we get the bill please?" He launches the Uber app on his phone and orders a cab.

"We might have to get out a little before mine and walk, sometimes the drivers won't go on the estate after dark"

"Why what's wrong with it?" I look concerned, doubtful.

"It's got a reputation, mostly out of date now, it used to be really rough but it's pretty much ok now, especially if you live there, I know everyone so you'll be safe with me"

"I hope so Derrick, I'm trusting you" He smiles, "don't worry I'm perfectly trustworthy, I'll make sure you are safe" Of course you will Derrick

The first sign of the real Derrick comes to the forefront, he makes a big show of checking his pockets and then tells me he has forgotten his wallet, he plays it perfectly, embarrassed, apologetic, "I'll pay you back when we get to mine" I know full well that he wouldn't ever remember to give me the money back, banking on me to be too cool to ask him. You will be paying though Derrick believe me.

The cab arrives and happily drops us right outside the block, the driver himself lives on the estate so is unfazed by the stigma.

Derrick, loses his braggadocio for a moment, "Yeah so sorry about the block, we're the last ones on the estate to get upgraded, they are slowly relocating everyone so this time next year I should be in one of the new flats. Single guys on their own are low on the priority list so I guess I have to wait, it's nice inside the flat though"

"Don't worry about it, it's fine, I'm not judging you on where you live"

"What are you judging me on then?" He winks and smiles, I look down at his crotch and smirk "I'll tell you in a bit"

His flat is like a page from the Ikea catalogue but he is right it is nice enough, clean and presentable, the hallways up to his flat were pungent with the sweet smell of weed but the flat smells fresh.

He pours us drinks and we sit on the sofa, leaning in for a kiss, his lips are soft and tender he sucks gently at my bottom lip, Derrick has potential. He stands up kicking off his loafers and pulls down his jeans, hopping around amusingly as he pulls off the skin tight fabric. He stands in front of me in his white boxers, I pull them down and look up at him, he seems pleased with himself and I pretend to be impressed "Oh wow you are a big boy" He's not particularly but nothing to complain about either. I take him into my mouth and he arches his back and throws his head back, one hand on my head, to my annoyance he starts to pull my head onto him, attempting to roughly fuck my mouth. I pull away "Gentle I don't like it so rough, not straight away anyway" He looks perplexed, perhaps having never been challenged on his sexual prowess before or thinking that this must be what women want based on the hours of porn he has watched.

I stand up to meet him, kissing him passionately I turn him around and sit him on the sofa, he masturbates as he watches me undress. No lack of confidence in this one. I kick off my boots, peel the t-shirt over my head and drop it seductively to the floor. I turn and pull my jeans down letting him see my panty clad arse and pussy. I turn back to face him, unclipping my bra and letting my breasts hang free. He nods approvingly "Girl you have got a fine body"

I drop to my knees, taking him in my mouth again, his hand is back on my head and he attempts to push me down on to him. "I pull away again. "Are you going to behave?"

"Sorry, sorry"

"I think I'm going to have to tie you up"

"Nah I'm not into that"

"Why not, don't you trust me?'

"It's not that, it's just I dunno, I've not done that before, I've tied up some girls but I'm normally in charge"

"Do you want me to suck your dick?" I ask him looking at him with a pout

"Yeah obviously babe"

"Do you want me to fuck you?" I suck my finger suggestively twiddling my hair with my other hand.

"Yeah of course I do, what's this all about tho?" He looks puzzled and almost annoyed, used to women being submissive to him.

"Then you better let me tie you up, come on it'll be fun, I'll make it so you can escape easily. Where's the bedroom?"

"I ain't sure about that you know, I ain't into girls bossing me about, I like to be the big man innit?" His accent fully dropped now as he tries to exert his authority, feeling bolstered by my vulnerability and used to getting what he wants.

"I thought you'd be a bit more adventurous Derrick, but if Vanilla is your thing...." I pout at him, looking disappointed.

"Ah ok fuck it, you win, but make sure I can get out yeah?"

Reluctantly he gets up, not sure about this but eager to carry on the fun. He leads me into the bedroom. We kiss again and I push him onto the bed. "Stay here, I've got a scarf in my bag we can use that, don't worry it'll be fun"

Getting the bag I walk back in and pull the scarf out, "See it's only soft, you can wriggle out of this no problem I'll leave it loose" His dick is still hard and he nods, looking at my body

"Turn over then put your hands behind your back" Reluctantly he rolls over. I run the scarf around his hands and then reach into my backpack, slipping the thick cable ties that are already looped together into makeshift handcuffs around his wrists and pulling them tight. "What the fuck? What are you doing?" As he violently thrashes around on the bed, his arms straining to break the cable ties I mount his back and wrap the scarf around his mouth.

"Shush now Derrick or is it Greg?" I roll him over his eyes look up at me a mixture of fear and anger. His dick is still hard but fading rapidly, I grip it with my hand, wanking him back to firmness "Don't let that go yet Derrick, I have plans for that" There is a full length mirror on one side of the room, I drag it to the end of the bed. I mount him reverse cow girl so I can watch myself in the mirror. I push his dick inside me, feeling the initial resistance and then welcoming the fullness. My hand reaches down to my clit and I start to rub in small circles, my hips join in the rhythm, not bouncing up and down on him but rocking in a riding motion, keeping him as deep in me as I can. Derrick is merely here as an accessory and I have no interest in what he wants right now. He yells and moans but the noise is muffled against the scarf, behind me his hips writhe from side to side as if trying to buck me off , but with his hands pressed underneath his back and my legs locked into his side he has no chance. I fire a hammer fist back into his ribs as a reminder of who's in charge though. "Stop wriggling or at least make it count" He grunts as the strike leaves him winded.

I focus on myself in the full length mirror , his legs hang over the bed from under, me his dark skin a sharp contrast to mine I watch as my fingers move quickly over my pussy, the sensation intensified by the power I hold over him, It doesn't take me long, I can feel an orgasm building quickly and I slow my hips, bearing my weight down on him to get his dick to maximum depth. I hold it there relishing the sensation as I work my clit, faster and faster, the orgasm building until I'm finally over the edge and the release comes, a small but powerful one, shuddering across my body, I grab my boobs as I cum, closing my eyes momentarily, enjoying the absolute power and control I have in this moment.

"Fuck that feels better Derrick, how was it for you? Not quite what you expected I guess?"

His eyes follow me around the room, his dick rapidly becoming flaccid now that the stimulation has been removed.

I take a chair from the corner and straddle it leaning my hands on the back, looking at him as he squirms on the bed, his attempts at escape futile against the thick plastic. I pull the dagger from my bag balancing the point against the back of the chair the hilt under my finger tip letting him see the blade. His eyes widen and he tries to shrink backwards pulling his knees up into a foetal position.

"Derrick it's time we had a little chat, you asked me earlier what I was judging you on, well Derrick I know all about your alter ego Greg and what you have been getting up to. I also happen to know that you still have most of the money you managed to steal from these people and certainly enough to make sure they all get back what they gave to you, so lucky for you there is a chance to repent for your bad behaviour.

Now let me tell you exactly what's going to happen, you are going to log on to your computer and share out what's left between your victims, if you're a good boy and do as you are told, I might just let you live"

I won't of course but as I've said before people tend to comply when they think there is a chance of survival. I stand up from the chair picking up the Versace jacket, I put it on and zip it. "This thing really is vulgar you know Derrick? but it'll keep the chill off. Now are you going to be a good boy and do as you are told?"

I reach over and pull the scarf away from his mouth, he takes a couple of gulps of breath and then says "Fuck you, you crazy bitch you can't fucking make me" and he spits at me, SPITS!

I punch him hard in the face.

"You fucking dirty boy Derrick, with this virus around you could make somebody very ill spitting like that"

 I hold his mouth open and let a dribble of spit fall into his mouth. "see not nice is it?"

He spits it out retching and I pull the scarf back around his face. He looks feral with anger now. I'm not too worried about noise. People on these estates tend to keep themselves to themselves for fear of reprisal. Strange noises behind closed doors in this type of environment are not uncommon.

"If I'm honest Derrick I was secretly hoping you wouldn't just do as you are told, I mean where's the fun in that? But I do need you to know that I am serious"

I take a set of wire cutters from the bag and continue to talk;

"I read somewhere that apparently cutting through a finger only takes about the same applied pressure as cutting through a carrot, I've always wondered if that was true."

His eyes focus on the wire cutters and he knows I am serious. He's probably figured out who I am by now and knows he's not going to live. He writhes violently fruitlessly lashing out at me with his feet. I take two more cable ties from the bag and throw my weight onto the bed pining his legs, I cable tie those together too.

"Now you have gone and made it all a bit awkward wiggling about and now your hands are behind your back, but that's OK Derrick, here I am sitting with your feet at such easy reach so I guess a toe will have to do"

I sit on his legs with my back to him using my wait to pin his legs to the bed, I place the cold steel of the wire cutter jaws on either side of his little toe and begin to squeeze. The toe resists in a few stages first the skin breaks, that bit is quite easy, I have to increase the pressure to get through the thin layer of soft tissues and finally a full strength squeeze as they cut he bone. He screams through the scarf as I remove his pinkie.

He roars in pain as I make the cut, the sound muffled and his breathing ragged against the scarf. The roar subsides to a whimper, his eyes streaming, no longer filled with hate and anger but now with fear and pleading. I hold up the bloodied stump in front of his watery eyes and start to speak; "Well that surprised me Derrick, that was definitely harder than a carrot and that was only the little one, I think the big toe is going to be really hard, of course you'll probably have complied long before I get to that one so perhaps I'll just skip to that one next. He shakes his head vigorously mumbling something against the fabric in his mouth. I pull the scarf down to his chin "I'll do it, no more, please no more" He begs, terror in his eyes, no longer looking at me just staring wide eyed at the wire cutters.

"So soon Derrick? Well that's spoiled my fun, sadly as you have proven that you can't be trusted, we are going to have to keep you tied up, you are going to give me the numbers one by one and just to be clear, if you try to give me bullshit information or it locks me out, I'll take all of your toes, do I make myself clear?"

He nods vigorously, his eyes still staring at the clippers. I open his laptop and he talks me through the screen log ins until we get to his bank accounts. He hesitates, even now unable to resist an attempt to talk himself out of the

313

situation. "I'll split the money with you, don't send it back to these people, they are fucking idiots, stupid enough to fall for a scam, they deserve everything they get, someone else will just take their money."

"Interesting Derrick and you wouldn't fall for such a scam? Yet here you are, naked, minus a toe with a woman who you thought was interested in you, it's quite easy to fall for something when you want to believe in it isn't it? Now I did say the big toe was next didn't I?"

It takes a huge effort to force the small wire cutters through the bone of the big toe, I really should have opted for some bolt croppers instead. Derrick passes out from the pain before I'm even half way through it. I need to keep him alive, at least until he has transferred the money so I use a pillow case to stem the flow of blood and fasten a cable tie around the middle of his foot tightening it as much as I can to create a makeshift tourniquet.

I walk through to the kitchen to get a glass for some water to throw on his face. As I walk into the kitchen, naked apart from the jacket, I let out a scream as I turn on the light.

Sitting at the kitchen table is a man, not just a man but a giant hulk of a man, dressed in a suit.

"Who the fuck are you?" I ask him trying to regain my composure.

I walk passed him trying to not look fazed as I poor a glass of water, turning my back on him and washing the blood off my hands as quickly as I can under the running tap.

"I could ask you the same thing sweetheart, I'm Big Terry, I'm surprised Derrick hasn't mentioned me, mind you he hasn't mentioned you either" He makes no effort to disguise the fact that he is looking at my arse, his eyes devouring me in a way that makes my skin crawl.

"We only met tonight" I tell him, he raises an eyebrow and nods. "Fair enough I didn't like to disturb you, sounded like you were having some right kinky sex in there, lucky bastard. Well when you get back in there tell the little fucker that we've got some business to discuss"

"Ok, will do, give us a minute to clean up"

"No rush, take your time, I'm not going anywhere" He smiles, making no effort to disguise that he is looking me up and down.

I walk from the kitchen back to the bedroom closing the door. Fuck! Who was this guy? I can't risk waking Derrick up and letting the cat out of the bag. I pick up my stuff and head into the living room, popping my head around the kitchen door first to say "I'm just going to grab my clothes and get dressed, Derrick says he'll be in, in a minute."

"Fair doos sweet heart, do you live on the estate? I've not seen you around before?"

"I shout back from the living room, no West London, we met on a dating site"

"Up west huh? You got a job sweetheart?"

"Yeah I'm an air stewardess, long haul"

"Ever thought about carrying stuff?" Clearly not one to miss an opportunity.

"What do you mean?"

"you know what I mean, narcotics"

Dressed, I walk back into the kitchen, "Not really my thing, they carry out thorough checks these days too"

"Smart girl, stay away from all that shit. Does no harm to ask."

"Tea?" I ask switching on the kettle and adding in "What do you do?"

"Yeah I'll have a brew, let's just say I'm an entrepreneur, Derrick and lots of others like him work for me, we have a number of different business interests, talking of which where is the lazy little fucker?" He moves as if to stand up, thankfully his bulk means I have time to get to the door before he is even out of the chair.

"I'll go and check, he's probably fallen back to sleep, I might have worn him out"

316

He leans back and laughs "You're a live one aren't you sweet heart, go on then and tell him to hurry the fuck up!

I leave the kettle boiling and walk into the bedroom, Derrick is thankfully still unconscious. I roll him off the bed onto the floor, hiding him from the view of the door, bundling the blood stained sheets into the bathroom and turning on the shower.

Walking back into the kitchen I look at him, "He's just getting in the shower, how do you take your tea?"

"White, three sugars"

"Three sugars?!" I reply in mock horror.

"I've got a reputation to uphold you know, I'm not called big Tel for nothing" He rolls his head back and laughs in a raucous deep huh huh huh and I laugh along with him.

With my back turned to him I pour the water into the cups both of which I have half filled with sugar, the boiling water slowly dissolving it into a hot sticky syrup as I stir with a spoon. With most of the sugar dissolved I pick up both cups and turn. Looking directly at Terry I smile "Here's your tea"

He holds out a hand to take the cup "Ta babe" As he reaches out I throw both of the cups of hot liquid into his face. He roars grabbing at his skin the boiling hot melted sugar sticking to his skin. He tries to stand up lumbering off the chair knocking the small kitchen table over as he does. He lurches towards me, his giant frame fills the tiny room, his large bulk bearing down on me.

I turn around grabbing the kettle, slamming the hot metal against his face holding it there as long as I can, the skin sizzles and sticks to the surface, some of it peels off as he pulls his head away from me. He throws a wild punch catching me in the side of the jaw, it drops me to the floor in a daze the rapidly cooling mess on the floor soaking into my jeans, it's still hot but the denim protects me and I scramble for the door, he thrashes around erratically but I manage to further avoid connecting with his giant fists.

Hauling myself up on the door frame I pull the dagger from my boot, He turns for the sink splashing the cold water onto his burning skin, still shouting, the words coming out of his mouth incoherent in his rage. With his back bent over the sink I plunge the dagger quickly in and out of his lower back aiming at the left kidney then the right, then up his back puncturing both lungs, four stabs in quick succession,inflicting maximum damage in the shortest time possible. With the air whistling out of his lungs through the freshly made holes in his back he slumps to his knees and crashes onto the kitchen floor.

I stand trembling, taking stock of what just happened. I put my ear to the front door, listening out. No sign of anyone coming, I chance a look through the spy hole. Big Terry may have somebody waiting for him so I need to get a move on before anyone else arrives, I could be here all night picking people off otherwise.

I have a decision to make. It's highly likely that Big Terry is a fucking scum bag, but I've got nothing to evidence that, do I set this up as a double murder and finish off the Queen of Hearts here and now?

I look in his jacket on the back of the chair. His driving licence tells me his name is Terrance Andrew Price. I head back into the bedroom with the licence. I pull Derrick into the shower, turning the water to cold letting it wake him up. He comes round and instantly begins to complain, confused about his whereabouts but instantly aware of the pain messages reaching his brain. I strip off my clothes again, no point making any more mess.

"Wakey wakey Derrick. Turns out you had a visitor whilst you were asleep. Big Terry came to see you but don't worry I made him a cup of tea"

"TERRY!!" Derrick shouts. A short punch to the nose silences him, the blood trickles onto his top lip"

"I killed him Derrick, he can't hear you. Now if you want to live you need to get busy with those digits or face losing the rest of yours"

He gives me no more challenges, apart from earache from the moaning noises as he mourns the loss of his toes. Finally he gives me the codes to log into his bank accounts, I take the money and transfer it to each of his victims in turn, making sure to return exactly the amounts Derrick took from them to the penny. I drain all of the accounts I can find, transferring the last few grand to the charity Refuge, for victims of domestic violence.

"You shouldn't have killed Terry, he runs this estate, he's a big time gangster, you'll have so many people after you now, you're going to get merked no doubt" Derrick offers.

"Well Derrick that's a valid point isn't it? The problem with that of course is it's only you knows that it was me!"

Without waiting for his answer I run the dagger across his throat, the precision of the cut better this time the blade severing the wind pipe and carotid artery in one movement, the blood hits the laptop screen and covers the keys. I use the Versace to wipe enough blood off so I can see what I am typing, tapping the keyboard with a pencil I stick Terry's name into Google.

A pillar of the community he is not, the list of convictions reads like a phone book, the list of overturned convictions is longer still, it looks like Terry has had a long and successful career in witness intimidation. The list includes drugs, extortion and varying degrees of violence including being implicated in several disappearances. The unexpected guest, far from being a hindrance has turned out to be top trumps for the Queen of Hearts.

Time to get to work sorting out the bodies, I'll arrange the big one first I think, seeing as he technically died first and after all Derrick was always my planned eighth kill so it seems fitting to do it that way round. It's going to be hard work to get through his bulk, I need some tools but nothing electric, the neighbours will turn a blind eye to most things but power tools at midnight are probably a step too far, they might not knock on the door but they might call the police.

I wander naked around the flat apart from a pair of Derricks slippers and some gloves, no need to leave foot prints in the sticky sugar or blood. Opening doors and cupboards, I'll know what I'm looking for when I find it, I dig around until I find something that looks promising, a samurai katana sword in the back of a cupboard. Upon close inspection it turns out to be a cheap replica and there appears to be signs of dried blood on the blade, I doubt the flimsy steel will be up to much. What I find in the shoe box underneath the sword is more interesting though, a 9mm handgun with a box of rounds, now this could be useful.

I check over the weapon, it's not been looked after and definitely needs a clean but it hasn't been decommissioned and is capable of firing. I consider taking it but firearms are something I prefer as a last resort, this weapon has probably been used in multiple crimes so I'll leave it for the police to find, my parting gift as the Queen of Hearts can be two scum bags and a chance to wipe a few crimes off the unsolved list.

Back in the kitchen drawers I find a meat cleaver, why is it that all the best parties end up in the kitchen? I drag Derricks body from the bedroom and lay him face up next to the big man. Systematically I use the cleaver to hack both of them open, getting to the hearts. I take a chunk of each and put them in to the same jar, sadly I didn't bring a spare.

I stand the table and chairs back up, positioning Derrick on one side and using all of my strength I manage to drag Terry onto the other one. I prop them up so they are sitting facing each other across the table, their chest cavities spread open.

On the kitchen wall above terry I write in blood:

'Don't come back for me'

and above Derrick

'Don't come back at all'

The chorus of the song is now complete but not quite yet my work as the Queen of Hearts, that moment will come soon though. I join their hands across the table and place the playing card between their entwined fingers, in Terry's other hand I place the handgun and in Derricks the sword, the scene looks like a Hieronymus Bosch painting, the floor barely recognisable under a sea of blood and entrails.

I walk into the bedroom and catch site of myself in the mirror. I look like I am the one who has been murdered, my naked body covered in blood and gore, I try not to think about how disgusting it feels as I head into the shower and wash off as much as I can, aware that I have been in the flat for a long time and a lot longer than I anticipated.

I still need to clean the scene and spread the other jar around, the police forensics are going to have a hard time with this one and I chuckle to myself shaking my head, even I'm surprised at the level of mess, bits of toe in one room, drag marks in different directions, burnt skin, swords, guns, where do you begin!?

I dress in the living room, the only room pretty much untouched by the violence, my jeans are still wet and sticky from the sugary water so I leave them off and take a pair of Derricks cinching the waste with a belt, stuffing the wet ones into my bag. I wipe down everything I may have touched before I put on the gloves, making three laps of the flat to ensure I am meticulous, the cloth dipped periodically into the jar of entrails, smearing it on every handle or surface.

By the time I leave the flat it is one in the morning. Friday the 13th far from being unlucky has been good to me, giving me two for the price of one. I walk down the stairs the aroma of piss mixes with the still present stench of weed. I reach the bottom of the unlit stairwell and crouch at the bottom to scan the car. I can see the faint glow and intermittent brightness of two cigarettes being smoked in a Silver Range Rover just a few metres away from the door, the outline of two figures barely perceptible in the darkness, Terry's cronies waiting for him no doubt. The longer the murders go undetected the easier it is for me to get away so ideally I need to keep them unawares, I wonder how long they will wait dutifully for their boss before going to look?

I'm exhausted after tonight's activities, my jaw still ringing from that heavyweight punch and I could do with a smooth journey home. The flats have a fire escape at the end of the corridor, I duck under the front door glass and head for the other, I slip out unnoticed the alarm long since vandalised or disconnected. Doubling back around the rear of the building I walk into the car park and calmly to the scooter, my breath makes clouds in the cooling autumnal air, lit by the yellow glow of the street lights.

With my head once again throbbing inside a motorbike helmet, I turn the key and the electric ignition fires first time in the cold night air. I twist the throttle slowly giving the bike just enough revs to pull forward, easing out of the parking space and onto the road, unnoticed by the goons in the Range Rover.

Chapter 12

I awake late the next morning, the previous nights activities having exhausted me, I make soft scrambled eggs and granary toast, pouring myself some mango juice and a coffee. Whilst I sit at the kitchen island and eat my breakfast, BBC news 24 plays on the counter top TV. The news team are discussing an item on Donald Trump but the information reel along the bottom of the screen let's me know my work has been discovered. 'Gruesome discovery in North West London, possible double murder'

Once the Trump story is finished the news anchor introduces my story and transfers live to a concerned looking reporter who stands under an umbrella outside the block, held back at a distance by the Police tape. Small groups of local residents stand around on the street opposite, with arms folded and necks craned trying to catch a glimpse of something gory, perhaps less sensitive than some to the shocking events having been hardened by life on the estate. Other news groups can be seen on the periphery trying to get their own scoop on what is going on.

Police forensics in white paper suits and masks, wander in and out of the building, the reporter tells us that the police have yet to comment and she speculates on what limited information they do have. The discovery of two bodies, found by people known to the victims, early hours of the morning, victims possibly known criminals according to local reports, several people suggesting a possible link to the Queen of Hearts murders but too early to comment at this stage

I turn off the TV, relieved that the killing part is over. I take time to reflect considering whether I should have any concerns about them linking me to this one. I run over the scenes in my head and think back to the Crimewatch programme; what clues did they have? Nothing substantial only circumstantial stuff: some CCTV footage of a woman in a face mask, eye witness descriptions and perhaps whatever Paul may have given them. They won't have anything new from last night to add either, despite the paranoia there is no way they can link any of this to me, There is no 'me' to link it to. Unless they physically catch me in the act they will not find a motive or anyone that fits that description and there were no witnesses to last nights activities.

I have been careful and where things have gone wrong I've adapted the plan. A wave of emotion washes over me and surprises me as I begin to cry, partly it's relief that it's over, partly the realisation that my plan is almost finished and a little part of me feels remorse for my victims, does anyone deserve to die without a chance to redeem themselves?

Just like Banrigh these people are just out for themselves, not caring who they damage along the way so why should I care?

Elizabeth Banrigh sits in her garden office tapping away furiously at her Mac, trying to find the file that she has been working on that seems to have frustratingly disappeared, the Hive doorbell announces a visitor and she clicks the app open on her screen. To her surprise and bemusement she can see a number of uniformed police officers, their faces distorted as they lean in to the wide angle lens making them look as if they are reflected In the back of a spoon. She speaks through the app. "Hello officers, can I help you?"

"Elizabeth Banrigh?"

"Yes"

"Miss Banrigh could you open the door please, we need to speak with you"

Puzzled as to why the police would be at her door she rolls back her chair and slides open the glass door to her office, making the short trip across the garden she notice her upstairs neighbour watching her from the window. "Nosey bitch" She mutters under her breath and gives her a cursory wave. She slides open the heavy folding doors and goes through into the main house.

She checks herself quickly in the mirror as she walks past, adjusting her hair behind one ear as she opens the door.

"Good afternoon....." Her speech is cut short by the lead officer.

"Elizabeth Banrigh. I am arresting you on suspicion of murder, *you do not have to say anything, but it may harm your defense if you do not mention when questioned something you later rely on in court. Anything you do say may be given in evidence.* I have a warrant to search these premises in relation to the suspected crimes"

"Murder? Who's murder?"

"Miss Banrigh everything will be explained once we get to the station" As the officer explains her rights, two of the more junior officers flank her, taking her hands and handcuffing her, Banrigh is so shocked that she complies without objection. As the officers lead her to the waiting car she notes the presence of several other police vehicles including several people she recognises as forensic officers exiting a scenes of crimes vehicle, covered head to toe in their white paper suits.

Over her shoulder she hears the lead police officer who had read her rights to her address the leader of the team in white suits "Tony it's over to you, we'll establish a garden perimeter, none of my officers have entered the property beyond the porch and the scene remains uncontaminated"

"Cheers Steve. Right my team! Firstly get the canopy up and over that door, nobody enters any room until a full photographic overview has been taken, establish a cordon at this door and nobody goes in or out without my say so, we don't know exactly what we are looking for and it is unlikely that this was a crime scene however go with open minds and check everything. I want all clothing bagged and labeled, any and all electronic communication devices, laptops etc, bagged and labeled. Team one; once Mike has photographed the main areas of lounge and kitchen area you are on that detail. Mike if you can photograph the master bedroom and en-suite next. Team two; you are on that detail as soon as Mike is done, do not go in there until it has been photographed, understood? Suzanne you are on the garden office room with Cat, take photographs first and be meticulous with any electronics you find. Whichever team is finished first will be deployed to the basement room. Be meticulous people, anything we find today could be significant and this is a high profile situation, lets make sure our work reflects our abilities. Any questions?"

As Banrigh is lead to the car a reporter and photographer seem to appear from nowhere, the cameras electronic shutter whirs repeatedly as the paparazzo takes a volley of shots, the light gun flashing rapidly in her face. The Journalist barks at her "What's going on Liz? Are you the murderer Liz? Why did you do it? Give us a comment Liz!" His voice rising as one of the officers positions himself in front blocking the view of Banrigh.

The uniformed officer closes the rear door of the car, cocooning her inside, the solid plastic seats and fittings that now replace the original interior are hard against her body, a stark change from the luxury of her home, she faces a Perspex screen that separates her from the driver, like a black taxi cab but with much less space and with only one destination. It feels claustrophobic and oppressive no doubt designed this way to scare its occupants into early confession.

Banrigh stares out of the window open mouthed watching the surreal scene happening in the house, her house. 'I need my lawyer' she says to nobody in particular.

Elizabeth Banrigh lives in a smart tree lined street in Ladbroke Grove West London, her garden flat converted from the ground floor of a Victorian town house sympathetically restored and modernised. The day before her arrest I sit outside her house in a white van. I watch the well-healed residents walking their pampered pooches and pushing their designer buggies off to the playgroup or school. I wear a light blue polo shirt under a navy fleece and gilet, teamed with safety boots and combat trousers. The photo ID badge with the logo of a well known parcel delivery company upon it and matching baseball cap completes the look. I sit in the van tapping away on a tablet as if organising my next delivery, nobody paying me a second glance.

I arrived this morning at ten, armed with the knowledge that on Thursday afternoons, she goes into the offices of the paper for a weekly briefing. According to her Strava records she also likes to take a morning run, I watched her leave just under an hour ago, dressed in her running gear, headphones on, taking off at a light jog towards Portobello Road.

I see her approaching; she is walking not running, carrying a small bag of Waitrose shopping in one hand, no doubt this morning's breakfast, talking into her phone with the other.

She makes her way up the pathway and fiddles around in the small zip pocket at the back of her leggings for her key fob, still chatting on her headphones, the phone strapped to her arm in a transparent strap designed for exercise.

As she approaches her door I step out of the van, The package in my hand correctly addressed to her neighbour who I know went to work earlier this morning, like he does every week day morning his career seemingly unaffected by the pandemic. She places the shopping bag on the floor to free up her extra hand and turns to look at me, the neighbouring gate lets out tired squeak as I enter, alerting her to my presence "Good morning" I say in a cheery voice, walking up the next door path, I turn my back to Banrigh ringing the doorbell as I lean on the waist high dividing wall. As she taps the fob against the door lock scanner in my bag lets out a barely audible beep as it picks up the frequency.

"You can leave that with me if they are not in" Banrigh announces, I turn to face her, my cap pulled down tight over my face and mask firmly in place.

"Thanks that's kind of you, I'll leave them a card to let them know you have it"

I reply looking down and fiddling with the pockets of my combats as if locating one.

"I know the neighbours, I'm out for most of the day but I'll get it to them later or tomorrow" She says nudging the door open with her elbow and placing the bag down ready to receive the parcel.

"Thanks very much, that saves me coming back"

She takes the parcel from my hands and wedges it under her arm, steps over the shopping bag and pushes the door the rest of the way open with her backside, I watch her as she places the parcel on a table in the entrance hall. She nods at me as she closes the door behind her. My heart races and I take slow deep breaths to calm myself down.

Hoping back into the van I drive around the next corner out of sight, I take the scanner and plug it into the laptop uploading the unique frequency and transferring into a key fob of my own.

The radio microphone in the parcel picks up the movement in her flat, I hear the distant sounds of radio four and breakfast being made, I take a sip of the cold coffee in the cup holder. the thought of food makes my stomach rumble.

After eating breakfast, taking a shower and blow drying her hair, I hear her leave at 12.15pm. I give it five more minutes to allow for the 'return for forgotten item' window that seems to plague us all, to pass. I prop a 'back in 5 minutes parcel delivery' sign on the dashboard and depress the red triangle, switching the hazard lights on. I'm not concerned about getting a ticket but it's important to preserve the integrity of the façade. Exiting the van I climb in through the back doors, taking off the delivery clothes. Changing my outfit for one that Banrigh herself might wear. I change the cap for a more stylish woolen hat, letting the blonde hair, so similar to hers, flow out of the bottom. Checking for any passers by and being careful not to be seen I exit the van and lock the door, the contents of the holdall clinking heavily on my shoulder.

It takes less than a minute to walk around the corner and down the street back to her house, letting myself in with the electronic key-fob that automatically disables the alarm. The package sits where she left it on the entrance hall table. The house is open plan the walls that once separated the rooms knocked through to create a large airy modern space, the back of the building removed and replaced with a large glass box that houses the kitchen and extends into the garden, I like it, very stylish Liz. I wander across the main living area, behind the luxurious l-shaped sofa that overlooks a large television. The couch dominates the front part of the space and acts as a divider between lounge and kitchen, I enter the white kitchen the dark granite worktop contrasting with the brightness of the cabinets and place the heavy holdall on to the central island that is surrounded by bar stools creating an informal dining area.

The rear and side of the glass box are made of sliding door panels that allow the room to be completely opened up to the garden. I twist the lock in the corner and open one of the doors enough to allow me to step out on to the deck and down on to the manicured lawn. At the far end is a designer 'shed' that she uses as her office and work room. I say shed, as a student I lived in smaller apartments than this thing. Another stylish wood and glass structure that mirrors the architecture of the extension and looks back over the garden and house.

Simply furnished with a small kitchen area for making drinks and snacks whilst working, an armchair in which to sit and read or reflect upon on whatever article she is working on perhaps and a large desk with a bank of three computer monitors. Another large TV screen sits on the wall above and behind the monitors. Her own television and radio awards are casually displayed on a set of shelves in the middle of the space, modestly positioned perhaps, but easily visible if you glance this way from the kitchen or indeed from any of the neighbouring houses into the back garden.

Switching on her computer, I wait for it to power up before inserting the memory stick I have brought with me, the software algorithm it contains makes light work of the her password.

I spend the next fifteen minutes working through her email and files selecting and deleting what I need. Once finished I take a minute to look around the room, taking in the awards on the shelf, trinkets and trophies that congratulate a career she has formed with the pretence of helping others but more often causing irreparable collateral damage in search of the story and with no real concern for those involved, just her own career aspirations.

When I'm finished I slide the office door shut and walk back along the path through the garden, looking around I see a neighbour wave from an upstairs window, I return the gesture, the mind sees what it wants to see, nothing out of the ordinary.

Back in the house, I take the stairs through the open the door to the basement, heading into an area that is almost as big as the footprint of the house itself, a cinema room fills one end of the space with a home gym at the other. The screen is a vast LCD television set into a false wall, a panel opens along one side of the screen and houses the electronics and wires for the TV and sound system. I reach inside and place the jars one by one into the small cavity between the structure and the building walls, along with a handful of playing cards.

Cautiously taking the lid from the one remaining jar I draw up some of the contents into a syringe, with the needle I inject the smallest amount of the blood and tissue under the carpet, not enough to soak up through the deep pile as a stain but enough to leave a trail. I repeat a few times on the way back up the stairs to the ground floor.

Off to one side of the living space is a hallway that leads into the bedrooms and bathroom. The master bedroom is huge with a window that looks onto the back garden, a super king size bed dominates the room, made up with white linen, monochrome scatter cushions line the bed with a single peacock blue central one adding the only splash of colour. Yet another large TV adorns the wall opposite the bed, I cross the room and into

Liz's walk in dressing room, carefully sliding open a drawer to take a photograph of the position of the contents before selecting a single item of clothing, a black bra. Using a small spray bottle I mist tiny blood droplets onto the fabric, using the photo to ensure I place it back exactly as I found it. Two pairs of panties next from the same drawer, once I've placed these back I move on to the lower drawer selecting some leggings and a few long sleeve tops.

Opening the wardrobe reveals a black leather jacket and a jumper that are suitable for my needs. I place them all carefully back where I found them, the droplets so small that they dry almost instantly in the air and remain nearly invisible to the naked eye.

The house is neat and tidy, ordered and organised, her dressing room is the only space in the house that demonstrates a different side to her. The dressing table displays an eclectic array of things, expensive bottles of perfume, piles of make up and beauty products, in amongst the chaos stands a large jewellery box. Inside the box I find a tangle of designer pieces, all seemingly piled in together, I look through them, woven into the expensive bling a cheap looking piece catches my eye, it's a heart on a thin chain, the sort that has half letters on each side so that when you spin the heart it spells out 'I love you'. I've seen her wear this once before. It's the sort of high street jewellery exchanged by young lovers, that costs so little but at the time means so much. I carefully untangle it from the rest of the items and put it into my pocket.

On the shoe rack, I use an artists paint brush to press some of the gloopy matter from the jar deep into the treads of a pair of boots and a pair of running shoes, spraying the top of the leather boots in the fine mist with the spray bottle.

Finally into the en-suite bathroom, more lotions and potions cover the surfaces but ordered and neat as if on display in a salon or boutique. I take the syringe and insert the tip of the needle between the seal and the metal ring of the shower drainage hole, I lift off the silver cover and using my gloved fingers I scoop a dollop of the rotting material from the last jar and push it down into the waste pipe. It'll probably all wash away but it will still leave DNA traces, I take the syringe again and position it in a gap between two tiles barely big enough for the thin needle to fit. I squeeze nothing bigger than a pin head drop into the crevice. I repeat the process a few more times, leaving tiny pockets in the grout and sealant between the shower and floor tiles.

When I'm finished I examine it carefully, ensuring not a single spot is visible.

I return the last jar to the basement, its contents almost gone, and place it alongside the others. I drop the tools into the now empty holdall and make my way back upstairs.

Suddenly I hear the front door above me open and close and then the soft pad of footsteps on the carpeted floor above. Fuck how can she be back?! I freeze in panic, thankfully I have the holdall with me but did I leave anything out? My mind races, the worktop? I don't think so. The bedroom? I was careful to put everything back. What should I do? I need to get out of here now. There is a small window at the back of the basement that leads to the garden, but even if I can get out of it, the garden is surrounded on all sides by buildings and walls, even if Banrigh doesn't spot me I would surely be seen by a neighbour scrambling over the fences. Shit, I need that parcel too.

Perhaps if I just wait it out she'll leave again or go back into her office but the cellar door is standing wide open at the top of the stairs and the lights are on which they weren't when she left, I can see the light switch looking at me mockingly from just inside the door at the top, frustratingly out of reach. I crouch back into the corner, putting on my mask and tucking my hair into the hat. If I'm going to have to confront her it needs to be quick, look like a break in of some sort. Fuck, fuck , fuck I hadn't planned for this!

Just then a voice calls out from the top of the stairs "Miss Banrigh, hello Miss Liz is that you?" A voice with an accent calls out. So if not Liz, then who?

"It's me Magdalena, I come to do cleaning, are you ok?"

"I'll be up in a minute!" I shout whilst covering my mouth with my hand as well as the mask in an attempt to sound like Banrigh.

I take the blonde hair back out from under the hat, my outfit, hair and mask should be enough to convince her, who else is she expecting to find in this house? and as I said before the mind sees what it wants to see, speed is of the essence here though and once I'm gone I can't come back. I double check I have everything, check the zips on the bag, the key fob. I peel off the gloves shoving them into the bag and throw it over my shoulder. Running up the stairs in twos as if in a real hurry, bursting into the bright winter sunlit kitchen, startling the cleaner as I do.

"Ah Miss Banrigh you gave me a fright"

The cleaning lady stands in front of me, a navy cleaning tabard stained with orange bleach marks covers her other clothes, a thin middle aged woman with dyed jet black hair pulled back into a pony tail. Her pale white skin in stark contrast, she does not wear a mask and her smile is more of a grimace in her gaunt angular face as she attempts to look pleased to see me.

I pant my words out as if out of breath trying my best to sound like Banrigh "Sorry I'm in a crazy rush, just forgot something, had to run back I've got to go but have a good day" without waiting for a reply I turn and head for the front door picking up the parcel as I do.

"Ok Miss Banrigh have a good day, I lock up when finished" The cleaner shouts behind me.

The van sits where I left it hazard lights still blinking and amazingly without a parking ticket, I climb into the driver's seat, chucking the parcel into the foot-well and pull away, my heart racing for the second time today.

An hour later I am back in Chiswick for the last time, at least for a while, I take a final walk along the river, the time has come to put the last part of my plan into action and put the Queen of Hearts to bed. As I walk along the bank I run through everything one last time in my head making sure that all the pieces are in place. I take a box from my bag removing the new mobile phone from its packaging to make the tip-off call to the police, the call will have more clout now that I can pretend to be a cleaning lady who has discovered something shocking in the house.

Is the call enough on its own to cause them to get a warrant? Maybe not but it will definitely be enough when added to the interest the police already have in her. After the Crimewatch debacle and the amount of times it has been suggested we look alike, they'll appreciate an excuse to investigate her even if it turns out to be a false alarm.

She must be on the police radar by now as a potential suspectt, and without any other leads to go on, they are going to take this one seriously.

I make one more call and then smash the phone on the riverside wall, pushing out the sim card and dropping the pieces into the Thames.

Chapter 13

It's a relief to finally be able to travel without having to change direction multiple times, the black Ducati Multistrada makes light work of the roads and I take my time enjoying the ride without having to constantly check over my shoulder. I haven't adjusted enough yet to stop my eyes occasionally flicking to the mirrors and assessing every car behind me with mild suspicion, healthy paranoia is never far away with this life and perhaps that's a good thing.

The journey from Chiswick down to the South coast and Portsmouth goes smoothly, I take the A and B roads avoiding the motorways, not for any other reason but for the pleasure of the ride. I reach the coast and journey onwards into the ferry terminal and onto a boat soon to depart for the Isle of Wight. The journey goes without a hitch and in less than two hours since leaving the apartment I'm sat on the deck of the Wightlink ferry feeling the sea breeze on my face. I watch the mainland fade into the distance in one direction and the autumnal sun breaking through the clouds over the island from the other. The sea is calm and the ferry is emptier than normal for this time of year, holidays canceled or postponed due to the pandemic.

A fellow passengers newspaper is emblazoned with the headline 'Killer Queen?' With a picture of the handcuffed Elizabeth Banrigh taking up the rest of the page.

I watch the breaking news unfold on one of the lounge TV's there is no sound but the ticker tape along the bottom shouts out the headlines and it's clear from the pictures what is going on. The reporters now form a swarm behind the police cordon that has now been extended to the end of road to keep the prying eyes of the press pack at bay.

The white police tent covering her front door is still visible from this angle, the forensic officers in the familiar white paper suits and masks, carrying black briefcases containing the tools of the their macabre trade, mill around the scene like white worker ants.

The screen flicks to a video of Banrigh being lead from her home, a reporter and photographer pushing a microphone at her seeming to demand answers to questions. The gutter press quickly responding to another anonymous tip off no doubt. I allow a smile to pass over my lips.

I ride off the ferry, the winter air is fresh and the light still good. The bike is a joy to ride and I'm not yet tired so I decide to take it along the coast to the Needles, putting all thoughts of Elizabeth Banrigh behind me for a while and reminiscing about childhood holidays spent here with mum, dad and Charlie. The light begins to fade as the low winter sun sets over the horizon and I smile to myself, contented that my plan is complete.

Later that day when I am settled down on the sofa in the Air B&B apartment in Ventnor I finally get to watch the news properly;

"Elizabeth Banrigh was arrested at 1:15pm today at her home in Ladbroke Grove London. It is believed that the journalist and television presenter has been detained in connection to the recent spate of murders, labeled the 'Queen of Hearts' serial killings. Police received information that resulted in a warrant being obtained to search her home and newspaper office.

Eye witnesses state that forensic officers have been seen removing several items from Ms Banrigh's home. No details have yet been released on what exactly has been discovered at the property.

Our team have been working hard to piece together the background story and it's over to Melissa Finch now for a special report"

"Thanks Steven, we have been looking at the time line of the murders and the movements of Elizabeth Banrigh, we have discovered some very disturbing information.

The First Murder of Jake Simmonds took place on Friday March the 6th in the Clifton area of Bristol between the hours of 9pm and 3am . Ms

Banrigh is believed to have been staying at the Berkeley Suites hotel just over a mile away from the crime scene. Having that day attended the Foyles bookshop where she was promoting her controversial and recently published book 'Bang to Rights'.

It is as yet unknown if she has been able to provide an alibi to police for her whereabouts at the time of the murder.

The Murder of Shaun McBride took place in the City of Brighton & Hove on the 10th of July in the Poets Corner area of Hove. Mr McBride was found dead in the living room of his rented apartment, Allegedly Banrigh was in the same area staying just three miles from the crime scene at the famous Grand Hotel. Again that day she had been attending a book signing at the Waterstone's store in the city centre. Police are yet to comment.

Kevin Gower the third victim was the first crime reported and attributed to the name 'Queen of Hearts' in an article written by Elizabeth Banrigh herself. Mr Gower was brutally murdered in his own home in the Leigh area of Greater Manchester on Friday July the 31st again late in the evening or the early hours of the following morning. It appears from hotel records that Ms Banrigh had stayed in near by Manchester for two consecutive nights attending book signings during the day and giving a talk at a university.

The murder of James 'Jim' Whittaker, took place on Thursday August the 13th in Walsgrave Coventry. Mr Whitakers body lay undiscovered for a number of days having been left in a derelict public house. His body was reported to have been impaled on the remains of a bar pump. Again Banrigh is reported as being less than 20 miles away at the time on her book tour.

The same applies to Murder number five of Julian Tyrell in Sheffield. It is a very unlikely coincidence to be close to all of the murder scenes completely innocently and it looks to be a potentially damming pattern of events.

Murder number six is where things take a particularly interesting turn; Banrigh was that evening presenting the Crimewatch TV programme discussing the very murders that it is alleged she has now been arrested in connection with, one of them having only been committed just a few days before. The programme was broadcast from the BBC studios in White City, in that very same evening Pavel Terzic was murdered less than a mile from the studio, is it possible that Banrigh presented the show knowing that not only was she the killer but that she planned to kill again that very evening?

The last two murders we believe are linked to the case involve two men in North West London just 10 miles from where Elizabeth Banrighs residence is based, this is the Banrigh property you see behind me and as you can see from our images there is heavy police activity with forensic officers in attendance. Elizabeth Banrigh was lead away from the property earlier today in handcuffs.

Police investigations are still on-going into the crime scene of the most recent two murders and it has not officially been connected to the case but sources close to the scene suggest it it bears all the hallmarks of the killer. At this time the Police are refusing to comment on the connected dates, we will continue to report on developments as they unfold. It's now back to Steven in the Studio"

"Thanks to Melissa Finch for that shocking report there, it is of course too early to confirm with the police the validity of any of the information in Melissa's report but it does raise some glaring questions. Is it possible that the prominent journalist is really a killer and if so how did it happen? Elizabeth Banrigh has always courted controversy, even before her journalistic career started; she came to prominence when she was caught in a sex act with the then Vice chancellor of her university, Banrigh claimed at the time that she was an innocent girl pursued by a predatory man, however it now draws questions as to the validity of her claims and one could speculate that she engineered the situation in order to gain eminence over her peers and to improve her chances of gaining a coveted graduate position.

Throughout her career Banrigh has continued to court controversy. To gather material for her recent book 'Bang to Rights' it was discovered she had posed as a victim of domestic violence and had used information gleaned from actual victims to expose their assailants. The police interviewed her at this time and expressed concern and disdain for the way she had conducted the investigation as well as the risk posed to the people she exposed.

Perhaps because of the controversy the book has been highly successful and the subsequent book tour has been well attended in-spite of social distancing.

Could it be that in her pursuit of fame and notoriety she has in fact orchestrated these murders to allow herself a platform to perform from?

Banrigh claimed to have received several letters from the assailant and was privy to information that other members of the press were not, could this be because Banrigh herself is the killer? If this is the case this will be a very embarrassing situation for the police who via the Crimewatch programme inadvertently gave Banrigh exactly the platform she craved.

If Banrigh really is the killer, what has driven her to kill?"

The story continues to unfold with the news anchors wildly speculating on her motives, damning her before any official police statement has yet been issued. The police comment at this stage is only to say 'Banrigh is helping them with their enquiries in relation to a number of crimes'

I am impressed and a little shocked at how quickly they have made the link between her book tour and the murder dates, however journalists are not that different from detectives when it comes to seeking out the truth and probably have more time and better resources.

When I found out about the tour, it was as if the plan was ready made for me. I got a list of the dates from her own articles in the paper, with over twenty book signings and appearances to choose from, it made finding murder locations easy. Knowing that I had plenty more opportunities coming up meant I could spread them out, pick and choose and not draw attention to Banrigh too soon, It should have meant I didn't have to panic.

Of course I hadn't planned for the Paul debacle and then the Crimewatch special fell into my lap which was too good to resist, risky to deviate from the plan but sometimes you have to adapt. I'm learning to control my emotions better but perhaps I still have some work to do.

Once I had the dates, I started to put together the next phase of my plan. It was all well and good framing Banrigh with the forensic evidence but a decent defence lawyer could cast doubt if she had multiple alibis. I needed to create enough confusion on her whereabouts at the time of the murders for a jury to find her guilty.

Whist not the most challenging part of the plan to deliver it was certainly the longest to research and put together, I looked at all twenty of the locations detailed for the book signings and tour and then trawled through police reports and records to find potential know paedophiles in any of the local areas.

My plan was to give Banrigh an irresistible trail of breadcrumbs that would ensure she would be out of her hotel following up leads around the times of the murders, leads she had unknowingly been supplied by me. These trips would give her gaps in her alibi that she would have no way of backing up especially with her computer records missing. With enough doubt and all the damning physical evidence and biased press coverage a jury would be sure to convict her.

I started the trail on the dark web, I made contact with the first paedophile that I had found in Bristol, posing as a man with similar interests I eventually got him to send me some pictures from his collection, these disgusting predators can't resist their urges and it wasn't long before I had started to create my own network of these vile creatures. I shared the images he sent me with another, getting him to send images back to me, that I then sent back to the first, building trust. then to the next, and the next. Over several months I was able to identify several in the cities I was targeting and I created a secret chat room for them to share their stories.

I shared bits of these stories with Banrigh, I told her I was a woman married to a paedophile, detailing how disgusted I was by his behaviour having discovered his group I wanted revenge on him but I also wanted to bring down the whole group. I told her I was too afraid to go to the police. I knew Banrigh would not be able to resist the potential of the story and would be inclined to research it. I gave her snippets of information each time, always within plenty of time for her going to a new location so as not to look to obvious or coincidental but knowing that she would take the opportunity of being near by to investigate and selecting only the cities where I planned to make a kill. That way with the only time she was out investigating being in the cities where murders were committed, her whole story would look weak.

I sent details of where some of them lived, knowing she would be inclined to check it out and knowing how she worked that she would not tell anyone where she was going, great for getting the scoop but not so good when you need to prove where you were.

I gave her enough to keep her interested and involved enough real people already with criminal records that it would appear entirely plausible. I pretended that I could only get bits of information from 'his' computer at a time in-case I got caught and blew the whole thing. She reveled in it, persistently probing me for more information, encouraging and coercing me to take risks to get more information, she kept saying'in the interests of the victims' but all she cared about was her story, she was happy for my pretend persona to take all the risks.

I told her the information had would also implicate police officers, teachers and even some prominent figures, and that's why I was scared to go to the police. I knew there was no way she would overlook the opportunity and no way she would reveal that evidence to the police, not until she knew who was involved at least. Yet that part of my story never really bore fruit, there was no ring other than the one I had created, a few small time paedophiles already known to the police.

The original file I had sent her was deleted when I left the evidence in her home. I cleared all of the work she has done in relation to the ring from her computer then I swapped out the hard drive, taking all of her research into the murders and left her instead with my own specially prepared hard drive; that contained lots of app conversations with men on dating sites of course including all of the dead ones. I also made sure it contained internet searches for the GPS locations of the crimes and other incriminating evidence.

Of course I protected it and hid it on her computer, I don't want her to appear stupid but the tech boys in the police will make light work of it.

The beauty of it is I don't need it to be perfect, just cast enough doubt with the stack of physical evidence it would be an easy case to bring for the CPS and a hard one to defend.

With these e-mails planted and all of her own defence deleted from her computer Ishe has nothing to corroborate her story, her alibi is non existent.

I stay on the Island for a few weeks, walking along the coastal cliffs and running on the beaches, the secluded property attracts little attention and with Banrigh in police custody the cautious untrusting glances have been replaced by the familiar friendliness of the island. My hair colour has changed and the style been shortened, I keep my face free of make up, making any similarities to her far less obvious.

Over the past few weeks the media have worked themselves into a frenzy, rather than protecting one of their own, the press turn on her with a vengeance reserved only for situations where one of your own has been caught, like a bent police or prison officer, colleagues do not take kindly to having the wool pulled over their eyes and their reputations tarnished by association. With Banrigh protesting her innocence they fall over themselves to present as many different angles and speculative reasons as to why she had been motivated to do it.

They focused heavily on her previous interviews and conversations with the police, highlighting that it had started at university with the vice principal, they dug further uncovering that she had also been interviewed into the death of a fellow student at the time, who had caught her in the act with the vice principal taking his own life shortly after.

They too focused on the more recent controversial events surrounding her book and took great pleasure pointing out that she had been arrested for posing as a battered wife and thus no stranger to pretending to be someone else, presenting her as someone who would stop at nothing to elevate her career.

As is known to happen in the British press, without counter argument or challenge, speculation soon becomes presented as more or less fact. Within weeks it was the generally accepted view that Banrigh had started the whole thing to give herself more attention, through her obvious hatred of men that she had demonstrated throughout her career had been the catalyst, her pursuit of fame had kept her going, driving her to write letters to herself to publish in the newspaper.

There have been a number of TV specials, populated by previous colleagues and friends, keen to comment on her and offer their own opinions as to why she may have done it. Perhaps afraid to lose favour with the public themselves, fearful that the contamination of association might infect them, not one of them had a good word to say about her. They painted a picture of a cold calculating ruthless woman who would let nothing get in the way of a good story, including murder it would seem.

They had even linked Cardiff to her, the Police information leaked, as invariably it does when the offer of a brown envelope becomes too tempting. The link showed that the police believe the unsolved case of a man attacked violently by a woman in a hotel room was most likely to have been her as the victim had apparently described his attacker as looking like Banrigh at the time.

When the incident with Paul happened I really thought that my plan might fall apart. Maybe they would make the link between his description of me looking like her especially with her being in the same city at the time. If that had happened the chance to plant evidence and opportunity to frame her would have been gone. With hindsight I guess that is the power of celebrity, nobody wants to believe that a well know press and television journalist would attack a man in a hotel.

Whatever they assumed had gone on I guess it just went into a database, and with no permanent damage to the victim and no suspect it was only when everything else came to the forefront that it became relevant again.

Paul was nowhere to be seen in any of the television interviews or press, staying well out of the limelight, the two security guards who had grappled with him have become minor celebrities in their own right, describing in great and highly inaccurate detail how they met the Queen of Hearts and lived to tell the tail.

With all this press attention a fair trial would be highly unlikely and public opinion is strongly against her, she is remanded in custody partly for her own protection and her psychological state of mind has been evaluated.

Once her trial is underway I'll tip off the police to one of the paedophiles and make sure they find all the chat room evidence on his computer, it won't lead to Banrigh in anyway and won't serve as an alibi for her, it'll just be the police getting a lucky break and cracking the case.

Epilogue

I paddle the kayak on the ocean, it feels great to be free, the boat glides effortlessly through the water, on the eerily calm sea, the autumnal morning sun sits low in the sky, casting a bright reflection, the water bouncing it back at me like a mirror. Thankfully the way I am heading I can angle the craft to keep the sun over my shoulder and the warmth of it's rays combined with the exertion of paddling are enough to keep the chill at bay. I have a small backpack in the waterproof hull compartment of the boat which contains the ashes of my brother.

Paddling east from Freshwater bay I alight on the beach at Watcombe bay, an isolated beach only accessible from the water and I have it to myself. After pulling the kayak onto the shore and dragging it up the beach to the high tide line, denoted by the washed up flotsam and jetsam, I sit on the beach, my bare feet feeling the course sand, still wet from the receding tide.

Looking out over the English channel, the sun now drying the perspiration on my face, I can taste the saltiness of the air upon my lips. I pull the water bottle from the bag and take a long drink, the contents still cold and refreshing. I remove the urn containing the ashes from my bag and place it between my feet

"You'll be safe here Charlie" I say to him
"Remember when we had that holiday with mum

and dad? We spent every day on the beach just a few miles from here, digging in the sand and splashing in the sea. It's how I think of mum when I see her in my head, sitting on the picnic blanket, handing out sandwiches and orange squash, fussing over us all with the sun cream.

I think we were about eight on that holiday, it was the summer before mum got sick, she was such a lovely person, caring and kind, I remember she always knew the right thing to say whenever we were hurt or struggling with something, she had such patience too, I can't honestly ever remember her losing her temper with us Charlie. I'm sure she must have, all mums do I guess, but my memories are all happy. She was dads rock , she was the thread that bound us all together. When she died I guess dad didn't know what to do.

I don't blame Dad, he did what he thought was for the best, working hard to provide for us financially, but we needed mum there too, she was the one that provided all the love and care. I guess that's why it all went wrong when we lost her.

When he died I put him into the same mental picture too, looking proud of his family, his chest puffed out, his tough manly hands picking us up and throwing us into the sea and helping us dig tunnels for the water to run into in the sand. I never felt as close to dad as I did to mum not in the same way anyway, I felt like I could tell her anything and she would know what to do, I missed the emotional connection, thinking back I think it was even worse for you. I always felt safe when he was around though, his big bear hugs, do you remember when he used to say 'squeezing the air out and the love in'? I don't blame him for Carol either, I guess he was just as lost without mum as we were. I don't really blame her either, she just wanted the man she had always desired and instead got two kids to look after and a house to run, I'm not really surprised she was bitter at the end, she got short changed too.

You're in that picture now too Charlie, I can feel you there next to me, your curly hair flopping onto your shoulders, dad constantly ribbing you to get it cut, 'they'll think you are twin sisters' he would pretend to be Edward scissor hands and chase you around do you remember? Mum always refused to let him chop it off, you would run to her pretending to hide from him, she would wrap her arms around you and mock scold dad, 'keep your snippety snips away from my boys lovely curls Mr Scissor hands'. I remember being jealous of those curls that day on the beach, my straight brown hair looking boring in contrast to yours, I got over it though when I watched your face as mum tried to comb the salt and sand out of it once back at the guest house.

I can see your smile, looking at me, you look contented and happy, still innocent and safe in the family bubble. The sand sticks to your sun-creamed legs, your toes squashing into the beach, making patterns, a ring of ice-cream around your mouth. You were always more sensitive than me, you would run and play with me but you were always glancing back, making sure mum was still there, that safety blanket to cling to. We played well together, sure we bickered but it never went too far, there was something always underlying between us Charlie, a calmness, an unbreakable bond, maybe it's because we were twins, somehow an extension of each other? I remember when we were young, not long after Mum had died and you said to me, 'I always feel safe when I'm with you Alys'. I wish I could have kept us both safe. It's all over now though Charlie, there's nobody left to hurt us anymore, I took care of Louis and I took care of Elizabeth for you too"

I read Charlie's letter one last time before I tear it into pieces and scatter it with his ashes into the sea.

Dear Alys,

Every time I try to love someone they are taken away from me. First Mum, then you and then dad. Now my heart has been wrenched from my chest a final time. The pain and humiliation are simply

363

too much to bear again. I am tired and weary, why is life so hard and people so cruel?

I always loved you and still do with all my being but know we could never be together, I realised long ago that you were telling the truth about Louis. I didn't understand why you would not have spoken up if it was true but I understand a little more now and see now how difficult it must have been. It broke my heart again knowing that I of all people rejected you and was not there to support you, I was jealous and hurt and I put myself first instead of you. Even If you could ever forgive me for how I behaved, society would not forgive us and allow us to be together, like everyone else in this life they would just hound us and destroy us.

You were always stronger than me, stay strong for both of us. I'm sorry I couldn't be.

I only realise now how painful that betrayal must have been for you by what Liz has done to me. She has been having an affair with the Vice Chancellor of the university behind my back, she made sure I caught them having sex, not because she wanted to be with him but because she wanted a witness, I don't think she ever cared about me, she just used me. I confronted her and she laughed in my face, saying I was a pathetic loser, always following her around, doing as I was told. I guess she is right. I wanted to love her so badly, I just wanted to please her so that she would love me back, so I could maybe feel what you and I had together, I thought maybe if I could love someone else it might make it easier to forget about you.

She humiliated me, and everyone at university knows we were a couple and that I found them together, I can't bear the mocking looks any longer. I felt like that when I found out about you and Louis and realise now that none of that was your fault and that you truly loved me.

When you came to visit me a few months ago and saw me with her, I wanted to try to explain to you what I had realised about us, I couldn't look you in the eye I was so ashamed. I had bought you a necklace, a silly thing just to say I loved you, Liz had found it in the car, I couldn't say it wasn't for her once she had opened it. I wanted to get away from her to talk to you the next day but you sent me that message and I knew I had ruined it for ever.

Don't let your life been ruined by these people Alys, I'm leaving everything to you so you can have a better life. Free yourself from the bullies and be the brave strong Alys that I know you are.

You will always be the queen of my heart.

Charlie

I let the ashes blow from their container onto the water, freeing his ashes from the box and us both from the bullies.

When Charlie sent me the letter I hadn't planned any of this, it wasn't until I accidentally killed Louis and it felt good, I knew I had a way to make peace with my brother. The police interviewed Elizabeth at the time of Charlies death but as it was suicide they had nothing to pin on her, I never showed them his letter, not that it would have changed things.

Sure I could have just killed her but I want her to suffer, to lose everything she loves like I did.

The fact that people think I look like her is no coincidence, I don't doubt that Charlie was drawn to her because of the similarities, you can't really change your appearance with surgery to look exactly like someone else but I underwent surgery for chin and cheek augmentation to get that little bit closer to her look, with the same make up and hair we share more than a passing resemblance.

The hair was easier to replicate, all the wigs have been burned and I've removed all other traces of her from my life. Seeing her taken down has been liberating and cathartic, freeing me from her also, like a butterfly emerging from a chrysalis.

Now that the chapter is closed I consider how my life has come to this, was this always in me, was I destined to become this person? Am I evil or a product of my circumstances? Many times I have considered suicide convinced the world would be better off without me, if anything exists beyond death then we would all be re-united as a family, if nothing exists then at least the pain will stop. I allow myself a few minutes to let the emotion pour out of me, the tears stream down my face drying into salty rivulets as the sea-breeze hits them.

I can do this, I mean what have I got to lose? If I die in the process so be it. The rage and anger drives me on, why should I die when horrible people like Liz and Louis get to exist, treating others like shit without a second thought, taking what they want and using them along the way.

I am this person now, there is no way back, block out the emotion, push it down, channel it into anger, there is work yet to be done.

I'll stay around here on the Island for just a few more days before heading home to pack, I have an appointment in Brazil to see a plastic surgeon, time for those cheek implants to be replaced, after all nobody wants to look like a serial killer.

Before I fly I have someone I want to say goodbye to.

Through the dappled sunshine coming into the woods I can see him, he looks well, muscular and toned, still svelte but powerful looking now. His scruffy coat a little shinier and healthier.

I couldn't leave without saying goodbye to him. I edge closer, keeping low, no sign of movement In the cottage, the builders seem to have gone too, the Land rover is outside the front, and a gentle trickle of smoke wafts from the chimney. The back door is open and Paul is probably in the cottage so I need to be stealthy, just a few moments with the dog before I go.

I move a little closer, keeping my centre of mass close to the base of the trees, no sudden movements just slow steady progress, my camouflage jacket making me harder to spot. I'm No more than twenty feet from the back of the house now, I crouch down and take a particularly smelly sausage from the plastic bag in my pocket. Just holding it out in front of me.

Charlie continues sniffing around then stops, his ears prick up as he catches the scent. Moving his head slowly from side to side as if using a metal detector he fixes on the aroma and begins to walk towards me, using his nose to seek out the source of the delicious smell rather than his eyes, as his nose reaches the sausage he visibly jumps as he finally spots me.

Thankfully he recognises me and doesn't bark, after wolfing down the sausage greedily he licks my face. "Hey Charlie, are you two looking after each other? I'm heading off for a while but I didn't want to leave without saying goodbye, it's all done now I've finished everything off, we did it" I kiss his head inhaling his delicious doggy smell and ruffling his ears as I give him the second sausage I have secreted in my pocket. He nudges me and I put my arms around him, hugging him close to me. He rests his head on my shoulder as if returning the affection.

"I've got to go now Charlie" I whisper to him, unwrapping my arms from around him, he really does look happy as I give him a gentle nudge back towards home.

I turn on my heels to leave and as I stand up from my crouching position, my heart stops.

Standing not ten feet behind me, a bundle of firewood in his arms is Paul.

Coming soon the second book in the Alys White series MOTHER NATURE

CHAPTER 1

9.45am Tuesday morning, the March light still contains a wintery hue, grey and pale over the London skyline outlining the buildings on the horizon. I can see from my 28th floor vantage point the top of St Pauls cathedral below me, it's hard to imagine a London where this was the tallest building for two hundred and fifty years. As I stand in the Shard I wonder if it too will stand for 250 years never mind hold the title of tallest building for that long? Things change so quickly now, often it is presented as progress but usually the change is driven by profit.

The shadow of the point of the building that extends above seems to loom over the dome of the cathedral threatening to pierce it, the floor to ceiling glass is unnerving, I'm not afraid of heights but looking down from here, makes my head swim a little with vertigo, so sit back at the desk and turn away.

The intercom in front of me on the expensive leather desktop buzzes, breaking me from my train of thought and dragging me back into the present.

"Sophie is everything set up for the conference call at ten?" The nasal, voice on the other end asks in a disdainful tone.

"Everything is ready sir"

"Good girl, connect my video screen once everyone else is in the meeting would you? Also keep them hanging on for a minute or two, let's remind them who the boss is shall we?" His penetrating high pitched tone is enough to make me wince as it pierces through the speaker. He clearly enjoys his position and revels in the power.

"Very good sir"

Sophie Whittaker is 28 years old and has been with the company for the past seven years, last year she was promoted to the role of Executive Assistant to the CEO, the same CEO that is the irritating pompous prick sat in the next room. Having beaten several of her colleagues and three external applicants to the role, she is viewed as a 'go getter' with a meticulous eye for detail and an ambitious attitude, despite beating many of them to the job, she is well liked and popular with her colleagues.

Poor Sophie is currently confined to bed in her tiny but expensive riverside apartment in Vauxhall. Her mouth is gagged with duct tape, the hoop of a solid' D' shaped bicycle lock anchors her neck to the metal bedhead, her hands are fastened behind her back with handcuffs. She is undoubtedly terrified and most probably very uncomfortable but she is not going to die. The voice on the other end of the intercom however is.

Sir Dudley Barnard is the CEO of Prolet Fuels, the fourth largest Petrochemical company on the planet. The call he is about to head is with the Moscow and Saudi Arabia offices to discuss supply and pricing ahead of next weeks AGM. Unbeknownst to Prolet, the call will also be beamed live to the YouTube channel of Syla Neal a seventeen year old environmental activist who currently has 1200 followers, that number is about to change.

This morning I knocked on the door of Sophie's apartment at 6.25am having followed the postman into the building. Sophie normally arises at around 5.45am where she has Earl Grey tea with milk and muesli with fruit, she then showers and spends the next hour getting ready before leaving for work at 7.30am. In the summer she sometimes walks to work along the river but usually she takes the Northern line from Vauxhall to London Bridge arriving at the office around 8am. This morning didn't go quiet to plan for Sophie;

As she opens the door, the flash from the Polaroid camera startles her, before her brain can register what is going on, the sharp and discombobulating pain of a short fast punch to her nose makes her brain momentarily freeze, stars explode inside her mind and her eyes immediately begin to water impairing her vision. The impact and subsequent confusions cause her to stumble backwards onto her backside in the tiny hallway. Before she has time to think or protest I have rolled her over and she is lay face down on the floor, the tape on her mouth already in place and a bag over her head. As I fasten on the handcuffs I bark the order; "On your feet"

Using the cuffs to pull her up to standing, causing her a little pain, to reinforce the threat. I lead her into the bedroom, pushing her down onto the unmade and recently vacated bed.

Sophie starts to hyperventilate as I fasten the lock around her neck, pressing her head and back against the cold metal bedstead, the fear and the restricted breathing are unsurprisingly causing her to panic. I feel a pang of guilt, Sophie is after all an innocent party in all this, however she'll be fine, perhaps a little traumatised and requiring therapy for the next few years but she'll be OK. In an attempt to calm her down and perhaps reassure her, I position myself close to her ear and talk in a quiet voice;

"Sophie, Calm down and listen to me, I am not going to hurt you unless you give me reason to do so. I am here because of your boss not you, I am going to take some of your clothes and your work security pass, whilst I am gone I will leave you secured to the bed. I will be a few hours and then I promise you will be released. If you co-operate, no harm will come to you. If you fail to co-operate I will have no hesitation in ending you. Is that clear?"

Her body quivers as she sobs but she manages to nod an affirmative. I turn my attention to the rest of the room.

Hanging on the wardrobe is the outfit she has selected for today, it's nice but not practical for what I need so I slide open the mirrored door to her wardrobe. She has an impressive selection of workwear, image just as important as the work you produce in the cut throat corporate world in which she has chosen to make her career. Browsing through the garments a Stella McCartney wide legged trouser suit in black catches my eye, honestly I can't wait to try it on. Sophie is thankfully a similar height and build to me, although with smaller breasts. The suit fits perfectly, the wide trousers brushing the floor allowing me to keep on my black Converse pumps and long socks. I have a wig that closely matches Sophie's chestnut brown hair. Sitting on the floor in front of the full length mirror as I imagine she does each morning, I apply her make up to my face, looking at the Polaroid wedged into the frame of the mirror to give me an idea of the colour palette and style she would use.

42 minutes later I walk into the Shard, smile a good morning at the security guard and tap my pass on top of the automatic barrier, he glances at the screen and up at me, satisfied that the

image matches the woman in front of him, he barely glances into my back pack, giving it a cursory wave with a detector. I take the lift up to the 28th floor.

Sir Dudley enters the office at 8.33am, he collects the letters I have opened and placed on the edge of the desk for him, nods a cursory greeting and says "Coffee please Sophie" I face the window as he enters, taking in that amazing view, marvelling at the juxtaposition of human intelligence and knowledge. We can create giant sky-scraping monoliths like this, a testament to our brilliance and ingenuity, all the time destroying the very world in which we live in order to create them.

I watch him in the reflection of the glass, not turning around until he is ensconced in his corner office.

At 10.03am I switch on the video call to his computer, also connecting the video link to the hacked Youtube account. As the video conferencing administrator begins the introductions, I wrap the trouser suit legs tight around me and tuck the fabric into the knee length socks, unzipping the bag I remove a long sleeve black top and a balaclava, a lunch box and a re-usable coffee cup. I put the bag back on, fastening the chest straps as I do.

Taking the roll of duct tape from inside the lunch box I fashion it into four large circles. His office sits in the corner of the building, the glass panels meeting I the corner and the disappearing to the floor above, creating a triangular shaped room. I pick up two umbrellas from the rack in the corner of the office, emblazoned with the company logo. He sits with his back to the door facing the screen that pops up out of his expansive desk, a few of the executives on the call notice my presence and start to gesture, their faces a picture of shock and horror. It's too late for Sir Dudley Bernard CEO to realise what is happening , I throw the bands of tape over his head and around the chair, twisting them tightly together using one of the umbrellas like a tourniquet to pull the hoops together as I fasten him to his leather throne.

As he struggles against the tight bands of tape he blusters "What is the meaning of this, what is going on?" I move around to the front of the chair and as he sees my ski mask clad face he stops talking, his eyes searching the room in panic and he struggles furiously against the tape but it is surprisingly strong and impossible to break like this. He shouts out, roaring for Sophie not yet connecting the dots, then "SECURITY". I have limited time to do what I am about to do. Whilst security will not hear his shouts from his glass cage, one or more of the executives will have alerted somebody by now. The lift up from the ground floor will only take two minutes so I need to be quick.

I tape his hands to the arms of his seat to stop him struggling and fasten his feet together, wrapping a final piece of tape around his mouth, silencing his protestations,ripping it off at the back before I turn to face the camera.

"For too long now you have been raping the worlds resources for profit, despite all the evidence that the planet is on its knees your organisation and others like it have continued to abuse our world without any consideration for the consequences.

The oil industry is one of the worst global polluters and yet you continue to produce an outdated fuel bribing and blackmail people and refusing to invest in new cleaner technologies, putting shareholder profits before the good of the human race.

Dudley Barnard, repeatedly you have been presented with evidence from Greenpeace that you and the rest of the oil industry are fuelling a climate emergency.

The bottom line, as you well know Dudley is that we already have too much oil and gas in production or under development to keep global emissions to where we need it to be.

You conducted a press conference about the Paris Climate Agreement The crux of which states that in order to stop our planet from becoming a *"hell-fire wasteland"* we need to stop the mining and burning of fossil fuels immediately . You personally pledged commitment from Prolet to reaching agreed levels by 2030. In-spite of this that you have continued to pay funds to at least 35 politicians and political influencers across the world to lobby their governments to allow drilling in the incredibly fragile Arctic region, as the world has just seen via your video call, you have explicitly instructed your employees to actively pursue this route and as you said two minutes ago 'keep it highly classified'

Even with the knowledge that you are killing the planet you will not stop putting short term profit before anything else. People like you will never learn, your greed has long since drowned any sense of morality you may have once had. No longer can we stand by and watch helplessly.

Sir Dudley Barnard our planet is burning and now so will you"

Unscrewing the lid from the coffee cup I pour the contents over his head, the pungent sweet smell of benzene immediately fills the room as the petrol seeps into his clothes, he struggles in his chair frantically trying to escape, the makeshift bounds hold him fast to the expensive leather, the faces on the screen look horrified, voices shout out and a woman screams, I flip the lid open on a zippo lighter, and spin the wheel with my thumb, the wick igniting first time.

His eyes unblinking stare only at the flame and he squirms and writhes against his bounds, his efforts useless against the strength of the tape.

I step forward and address the camera;

"POLLUTERS AND PLANET ABUSERS BEWARE, THE TIDE IS TURNING AND MOTHER NATURE IS FIGHTING BACK" with that I drop the lighter and stand back as Sir Dudley Barnard bursts into flames.

His scream is short but agonising as the heat and fumes engulf him, his lungs filling with the toxic gases as he attempts to breath, the Shard sprinkler system kicks in almost immediately, covering the office in circular jets of water, the one above the burning chair trickles as the pressure of the water fights against the tape that I applied to the nozzle earlier this morning. The second umbrella providing me protection from the deluge.

I walk calmly out of the room and towards the main floor of the offices removing the mask and dropping the umbrella as I do, I pull off the wig and put on a baseball cap and protective facemask. The sophisticated sprinklers run only in the room where the alarm detects the fire and the rest of the building remains dry, the shrill sound of the fire alarm claxon compels the workers from their desks and towards the lifts and stairs.

I join the throng of people heading out of the main office, nobody questions my presence, some others wear masks, the fear of COVID still fresh in people's minds , my own therefore not drawing any attention. Everybody is far to busy concentrating on their own needs to worry about who is around them. Some are wearing high-vis vests to denote them as fire marshals, the conversations between the workers seeming to lean towards a fire drill or false alarm, some annoyed by the disruption others eager to get away from the desk for a while, some try to hide their concern at being on the 28th floor of a potentially burning building.

The Shard is a 'vertical city' and unlike most other buildings the lifts keep on working during a fire alarm. With so many people in the building to evacuate and from a number of different areas getting them out quickly is of paramount importance. With this in mind the lift system continuously sends lifts back up from the 28th floor to the 70th as soon as they empty. The lift returns all the way to the top and will only stop at requested floors on the way back down to ensure the people at the top can get out. I step into one of the skyward bound lifts as the people form the upper floors empty out crossing the lobby to join the lifts that run down from the 28th floor to the ground. The lift pauses detecting my weight but I hit the 70th floor button to override it. The chrome box speeds up the floors at six metres a second, the journey to the highest possible point taking less than a minute.

The doors open at the 70th floor, this area contains the public viewing areas, a central staircase dominates the area that is made up of two floors. Banks of telescopes line the edges giving views across London in all directions, the area also contains and exhibition that takes viewers on an interactive tour of the landmarks and the history of the building and the city below. Once on the second floor, another internal staircase leads up to the 72nd floor and to the open air viewing platform. The area is already deserted the tourists, quickly escorted to the lifts as soon as the first alarms soundded. I scan the open area through the doors, making sure the coast is clear and checking my exit route. The wind is stronger than I would like up here but nothing I can do about it now.

I open the door and step out into the blustery air, it's a few degrees colder up here and it makes me shiver momentarily, adding to the slight trembling in my hands from the adrenalin surging through my body, a feeling I've grown accustomed to and learned to control over time.

The sides of the Shard glass extend up, protecting me from most of the wind, the corners are left open and some of the 'shards' reach their apex here, The framework of steel holding them in place. It's through one of these gaps that I'll make my exit. I walk across the Astro-turfed surface, laid to create a garden in the sky effect, the table and chairs, unaligned, no doubt left hastily by the patrons of the viewing platform. I reach the corner, the glass wall eight feet high in front of me provides a view immediately down over the undulating roof of London Bridge train station and onto the Thames. I jump up, my hands gripping the lip of one of the structural steels, hooking a heel over the edge, I pull myself up, rolling my body onto the top of the beam. Tentatively I stand, edging closer to the end of the steel and to the 72 floor drop below. The wind buffets against the fabric of the jump suit, chilling me further, I hold onto the edge of the glass with one hand, reaching around into my back pack with the other. I locate my landing spot on the other side of the river, take three steps back and run forwards launching myself into the abyss.

The rate of free fall is approximately 200 feet per second, the 72nd floor is 801ft off the ground, if my parachute does not open I will be dead in exactly four seconds. I point my head forward and pull the chord, hoping there is enough room between me and the building to stop me from slamming hard into the side as the chute inflates. My body is jerked as the opening canopy fills with air slowing my descent with a g-force of four, so rapidly that it feels as if you are going upwards. I pull the toggle hard right forcing the edge of the canopy to dip and drop towards the right pulling me away from the building just before I make contact with the corner! Hard pull on the left toggle I swoop down and away from the building correcting with the right keeping myself parallel to the river.

I can see flashing blue lights coming from several directions and hear the cacophony of sirens bouncing up off the building. Paranoia says that are coming for me, logic says they are responding to the fire alarm or a call from security. Nobody is going to be looking for a parachute and the grey canopy should make me less conspicuous against the building and the sky. My descent has now slowed to thirty feet per second with my forward speed at seventeen miles per hour, I have approximately ten seconds to get the chute to my landing point. I make a few more pulls on both toggles to slow my descent, making eye contact with a stunned bus driver who sees me coming in from above on his right. He manages to slam on the breaks of his red Routemaster just before Southwark bridge as I pull the two toggles hard to stall my decent I swoop in front of the bus, my body inches from the windscreen, two Japanese tourists stare open mouthed from the front seats of the top deck. I land with both feet on the ground and break into a run bundling the parachute up as I go.

Printed in Great Britain
by Amazon